Songs Without
WORDS

Robbi McCoy

Bella
BOOKS
2010

Bella Books, Inc.
P.O. Box 10543
Tallahassee, FL 32302

Printed in the United States of America on acid-free paper
First Edition

Editor: Medora MacDougall
Cover Designer: Linda Callaghan

ISBN 10: 1-59493-166-6
ISBN 13:978-1-59493-166-6

Dedication

To Jan, who remains a mystery best left unsolved.

Acknowledgments

I am grateful to my life partner Dot for her continuing interest in my work and her cherished presence in my life. If I have ever come near that elusive concept of happiness, then it would have to be because of her. Many thanks to Maureen McDonald for her helpful suggestions regarding music and musicianship. I am also indebted to Marianne Garver for the hours she has devoted to reading, critiquing and listening to me wailing over this book. A woman of such patience.

Thank you to Gladys, who introduced me to classical music, without which my world would be considerably less. Much appreciation to the several selfless lovers of fiction who gave their time and talent to offer advice: Cherie, Jeanne and Marcia. Without you, this book would have emerged into the world from a void filled with only my own ego and, thankfully, we will never know what form it would have taken in that case.

Finally, I remain awestruck by the intense, meticulous contribution of my editor, Medora MacDougall. Indefatigable! Or, perhaps, tireless. Or maybe...unflagging? What do you think, Medora?

Chapter 1

JUNE 4

Sometimes it seemed to Harper that the only time her life took place was in the summer.

At least, the most interesting parts took place in the summer, the parts that, if a person's life had an editor, would remain after the cuts. So of course she was excited. It was the last day of school. Summer stretched before her like a promise.

Before she could redeem that promise, though, she had to finish putting her office in order. When she returned in the fall she wanted an uncluttered fresh start. One of the many rewards of having summers off was the feeling, whether it was valid or not, of getting a new beginning each fall.

A stack of books in hand, Harper ventured out of her office and into the main floor of the library, past the cluster of computers and the audio/visual desk, past shelves of DVDs and books on tape. She stopped at the reference section and slipped her books

1

one by one back where they belonged.

At some point this library, like so many others, had quit being a repository of books. It had undergone an insidious transformation, starting with the videotape shelves outgrowing their allotted space at the back of the first floor, spreading like a relentless lava flow, eventually engulfing the card catalogue and the numerous volumes of the periodical guide. Banks of computers and printers had sprung up, multiplying rapidly, giving rise to self-service checkout kiosks and sprawling collections of digitized music and movies. The shelf space devoted to those quaint old printed books, by comparison, was shrinking, even disappearing.

The forward march of the digital revolution had proven too much for some librarians, overwhelming their skill level and sabotaging their entire philosophy of life. They continued to believe in the sanctity of books and in their role of protectors against vandals and censors and loud-talking revelers. The library was their church. It was a place of worship. They had thought it was sacred.

That had been true for Harper too, once. Veneration for books was one of the reasons that she had become a librarian. But as the years passed, she had found that her particular talents, her precision, patience and artistic bent, had meshed well with the requirements of the digital age. She had not merely adapted. She had thrived. That might have surprised her if she had simply observed the end result. But she had lived it every day, adapting to the changes in an unhurried, comfortable manner—much as a slow river takes its turns, flowing this way, then that, as the course dictated. She had eventually found herself in a position that hadn't even existed when she was a graduate student, Director of Digital Library Systems. She liked that about herself, that she was capable of reinventing herself.

As the last book slid into place, a student approached. "Do you work here?"

For a brief, delicious moment Harper contemplated saying no. It was, after all, the last hour of the last day before summer

2

vacation began. She glanced at the reference desk, confirming that the reference librarian had already left for the day, then said, "Yes. Can I help you?"

"I'm trying to look something up on that computer over there," the girl said, pointing to a cluster of workstations. "I think it's broken."

Harper strode over to the unoccupied station, where she found a blank screen and an unresponsive machine. After going through the usual routine of key clicking, button pushing and cable wiggling, she stepped over to the reference desk and called the IT department.

"No, I didn't reboot it," Harper said into the phone. "I told you, it's dead. The monitor has power, but the rest, nothing. No fan, no light, nothing."

"Is the CPU plugged in?" asked the tech.

Harper balked. "Did you really just ask me that? Look, send somebody over, okay? I think the power supply's gone."

"Can't send anybody today. It's Friday, after five."

"All right. I'll put a sign on it until Monday." Harper hung up, then turned to see that the student was still waiting expectantly for help. "Try one of the other machines."

"They're all being used." The girl gave her a helpless look. "This is for a paper that's due tomorrow. It's my final, my Saturday class."

"Come to my office," Harper said. "We can look it up there."

As she led the girl down the row of staff offices, all dark except for her own, she thought briefly of the old card catalogue with its sturdy wooden cabinetry and typed three-by-five cards. Though inferior to a database in a myriad of ways, it had never "gone down" and had never needed rebooting. This student had probably never used a card catalogue in her life, Harper mused, or one of those stubby little pencils they had kept on hand to write down call numbers.

Harper slid into her desk chair and tapped the space bar to dissolve the screen saver, an alluring beach scene with the caption

3

"Happy Summer, Everyone!" courtesy of the IT department. "What are you looking for?" she asked.

"Sophie Janssen, the sculptor. It's for my art class."

Harper looked at the student more closely, surprised to hear the name of someone she had interviewed for one of her video biographies. "Really?" she said. "What's the assignment?"

"Just to write a paper about an artist you admire and explain why, what you like about her."

"And you picked Sophie Janssen?"

"Well, sort of. The teacher gave us a list. We could pick one of our own or one off the list."

"Oh. So why did you pick her, then?"

The girl shrugged. "Nobody else had picked her yet. And the teacher seemed to like her."

Harper was disappointed. For a moment, she had considered loaning the girl her video. Hearing the apathy in the girl's voice, she changed her mind.

"I'm sure you'll find her fascinating." Harper said. She wasn't sure of that, actually. It was hard to know what a nineteen-year-old would find fascinating. She pulled up a list of related books and articles, printed it out and handed it to the girl, who thanked her and left.

Harper walked over to her DVD shelf and pulled out the case with Sophie Janssen's name neatly labeled on the spine. She hadn't looked at this since finishing it last summer. It was the fourth in the series. She took the others off the shelf as well: Mary Tillotson, the one that had gotten her started, followed by Catherine Gardiner, the fiery-tempered poet, and then Wilona Freeman, the photographer and Harper's friend. She put the DVDs in her backpack to take home to re-watch. She had a new subject this summer, Carmen Silva, a weaver, and she was impatient to get started.

Summers, when you have them off work, present a sort of dare, thought Harper, a challenge to spend the time wisely. You could nibble away at them with the odds and ends of ordinary life like organizing your sock drawer. You could get a summer job or do some volunteer work. You could travel, of course, and that was what the majority of the staff did. You could visit family and friends that you didn't see much during the school year. You could have a summer romance if you were single and, for some, even if you weren't.

Harper had done all of these things with her summers off. It was a perk she didn't take for granted, even though she had always had summers free, all through school and then for the sixteen years of her career at Morrison University. Morrison, a school located near, but not competing with, U.C. Berkeley, appealed to women more than to men and even more narrowly to the type of young woman who wanted something approaching a classical education. Which was not to say that the school was stuck in the past. They did have their computer science department and that fancy new electron microscopy lab. But this was a place where the English and history professors might have just a little more cachet than the math and science professors. Harper found that endlessly satisfying, a sort of ironic coup for her, considering that her father was a physics professor. She loved and respected her father, but after a childhood spent feeling inferior because she wasn't very good at science, she had celebrated a private victory in finding a school like this.

Returning to where she had left off with her office organizing, Harper discarded everything that was still pinned to her bulletin board—Dilbert cartoons, quotations from famous authors—until, finally, only one item remained, a tarot card pinned in the lower left corner. The card depicted a colorfully dressed entertainer carrying a lute—The Fool, also known as The Wandering Minstrel. She had adopted this image as her talisman a few years ago. The Fool was the voice of reason, wit and wisdom, but Harper kept in mind the paradox that he might just as well be a genuine simpleton. She left the card where it was. It was one of the few things that survived the seasonal purging each year. She stared at the card for a moment, remembering Chelsea's Shakespearean response to it: "Better a witty fool, than a foolish wit."

So, she wondered, *how long did I manage to go this time without a thought of Chelsea? Fifteen minutes? Maybe twenty?*

Two years later, and there she still was, always on the edge of Harper's consciousness, the summer romance that had transformed her life. Even though it had ended badly, she couldn't regret the affair with Chelsea, because it had given her a wonderful gift—self-knowledge. She only regretted that she seemed unable to get past it.

How long, she wondered, *will monarch butterflies conjure up Chelsea's smile, or the taste of a nectarine evoke her sweet mouth?* There had been butterflies and nectarines before, but somehow all of those earlier memories had been displaced by that one summer. In Harper's mind, Chelsea was nearly the personification of the summer sun, all brilliance and warmth, shimmering like a Greek goddess with the flush of youth and a golden glow like the sun's rays. If Harper had turned her into some kind of supernatural being in her mind, it was simply because she had become unattainable.

This was the summer she would move on, Harper vowed to herself. She would cast off Chelsea's hold for good. She didn't like living with longing or regret. She was definitely ready for something new. And at thirty-eight, she really didn't have time to waste, especially now that she understood what it was she wanted.

She wrote "Out of Order" on a sheet of paper using a thick black marker, then walked back out to tape it to the dead computer. Hearing her stomach growl, Harper detoured to the break room. Stephanie, one of the younger staff members, was there cleaning up.

"Hey, Harper, are you still here?" Stephanie asked.

"Hopefully not much longer. If I don't get going, though, I'm going to miss the summer completely."

She joined Stephanie in throwing away paper plates and plastic utensils from the afternoon farewell party. "Are any of those cupcakes left?" she asked.

"A few. They're in the refrigerator."

Harper opened the refrigerator and removed a red velvet cupcake from under a sheet of plastic wrap, placing it on a napkin.

"That's not going to be your dinner, is it?" Stephanie asked.

"You know what, you're right. I'll just take it with me and have it later tonight."

"Well, I think I'm done here," Stephanie said. "Enjoy your summer, Harper. Just don't gloat."

"I wouldn't dream of it."

Stephanie worked the audio/visual desk and, like the rest of the classified employees, worked year-round. Summer school was probably the best part of the year for them, Harper imagined. Not so busy. No bigwigs around. As a computer science major, she possessed skills perfectly suited to working in a modern college library. *She's probably never used one of those stubby pencils to write down a call number either*, Harper thought.

Why am I so stuck on those stubby pencils today? she wondered, taking her cupcake back to her office. Nostalgia? There was really nothing about those three-inch, eraserless pencils to make a person nostalgic. It wasn't like the old checkout cards, for instance, where you could see the names and dates of all of the people who had checked out a book before you. Whenever Harper had selected a library book, she had taken a moment to read through the names, written in various colors of ink by the people checking out the book, the due date stamped beside it to chronicle the book's journey. Some of them spanned decades. Some of them had only one or two names, which seemed a little sad, especially if it was a good book. That list of names had made her feel like she had shared something with someone else, that reading the book wasn't an isolated experience. The whole system had a sort of charm about it, despite how primitive it now seemed. Now that, she thought, was a special bit of library obsolescence to be nostalgic about.

Harper had hoped to get out by five, and it was now almost six. She set the cupcake on her desk, licking a bit of cream cheese frosting from her index finger. Then, deciding she didn't want to wait, she peeled off the paper and took a bite. She then prepared an Out-of-Office message for her e-mail account, explaining that it was summer break, in case anyone could have missed that, and that she would return on Monday, August 29.

Harper finished her cupcake, savoring that last bite a little longer than the others, then returned to an earlier thought.

Yes, she was capable of reinventing herself and not just professionally, but also personally. The fact that it had taken her so long to actually do it, though, disappointed her. Not because she thought she had wasted her life, but because she had always tried so hard to know herself. She had thought that she was more self-aware than the average person. That was why it was so ironic that she'd taken so long to understand the most fundamental fact about her own heart, that it sought its home in the heart of another woman.

Thinking back, she could see that if she had proceeded in a straight line, she'd have gotten there ages ago. But the course she had taken was, simply, her own unique and wonderful path, however indirect it had been. No point in second-guessing all of that.

Harper turned her focus to her last task and hurried through the unread e-mails in her inbox, noticing one from Lynn, sent around noon. She clicked on it, remembering their date two weeks ago, a pleasant dinner cruise on the Delta, then the rush to Lynn's townhouse, groping of breasts and buttocks, straining toward an impersonal climax. It had been their second date, their first time in bed. And their last, Harper had decided, even before morning had arrived.

There was nothing really wrong with Lynn. She was an attractive, interesting woman. But she wasn't Chelsea. After Chelsea, Harper had naïvely thought that she could replicate those feelings with any interesting woman. She had thought that the unique and wonderful flavor of their passion was that it was female, *simply* that it was female. But now she understood that it was more than that.

"Want to get together this weekend?" Lynn asked.

8

Harper studied the note. She didn't get the impression that Lynn cared for her particularly. She was probably just bored or lonely or both and wanted company.

Harper dashed off a reply. "Sorry, I really can't manage it. Very busy weekend. Final symphony performance tomorrow, et. al. Just out the door here. Hooray, it's summer!" Before she hit send, she added a happy face emoticon, reasoning that it might lighten the impact of her negative reply. Then, when it was too late, she regretted the happy face because it might look like she was being flippant. *Oh, well*, she thought, *I have to get the message across somehow. Why is it so much harder to turn down a woman than a man?*

Harper left the library a few minutes later, a load of folders under her arm and a crammed backpack slung over her shoulder. As she skipped up the steps to the Administration Building, the door swung open and Mary Tillotson stepped out, sunglasses in hand. They both stopped short. As Harper worked to get her folders under control again, she saw the unhappily startled look on Mary's face give way to carefully constructed indifference.

Wow, Harper thought, *this sucks*.

"Harper," Mary said, stiffly, sliding her sunglasses into place.

"Hi, Mary," Harper said, trying to sound nonchalant. "Turning in your grades?"

"No. I didn't teach this semester. I had a committee meeting."

"Oh."

Though they were able to be civil to one another, Mary's distaste for this exchange was palpable. Years ago, before Harper had any inkling that she could be Chelsea's lover, she had hoped for a real friendship with Mary. Now, obviously, that was never going to happen.

It was always anybody's guess what they'd say to one another whenever they met. The answer this time, apparently, was practically nothing.

"Well, have a nice summer," Harper said, moving past her into the building.

That was awkward, Harper thought. Thankfully, it didn't happen very often. Mary never seemed to come to the library anymore, which wasn't too surprising under the circumstances. Still, she was bound to be on campus now and then. And even when she wasn't there incarnate like today, it was hard to avoid other reminders such as the Volkswagen-sized Tillotson in the lobby of the Administration Building. Harper stopped in front of the painting, an impressionistic portrait of a woman in blues and golds. It was typical of her work, bold, beautiful and suggestive, but not explicit. Harper sighed, then swung by the mailboxes for one last check. Peering through the glass door of her box, she saw that it was empty.

She headed across campus toward the parking lot, enjoying the warm spring evening. Preston Carlisle, a foreign language professor, was suddenly walking beside her. "Hey, Harper," he said, "congratulations on another school year."

"Oh, Preston, hi. You too. Any exciting travel destination for you this summer?"

"Oxford," Preston enthused. "I can't wait for a chance to work in the Bodleian Library, in those great halls of classical learning."

He was sincere. And passionate. Sincerely passionate. Harper was moved by his passion. She could easily imagine him opening the dusty cover of an obscure book with the ecstasy of a young man unveiling for the first time the breasts of a lover. Here was a man lamenting the obsolescence of books. He probably assumed she shared his admiration for this most prestigious of libraries. She was a librarian, after all. Unlike most bibliophiles she knew, though, she valued the wisdom imparted by books, but the medium didn't really matter to her. A library of the future, she imagined, would be a phenomenally rich electronic database of texts encompassing all of written history, from Sumerian hieroglyphics to the latest Spiderman comic book, where no one would preside over the value or ranking of the information. It would be freely available to everyone via some miniature device held in the hand or implanted in the brain. Libraries, in the sense of a building a person visited, would no longer exist. This process was already well underway. To Harper, these were cheerful concepts.

"How about you?" Preston asked as they stood at the fork in the cobbled path where they would separate.

"House maintenance I've been putting off," she told him. "Visiting the folks in Cape Cod, as usual. And there's a video series that I've been working on for several years. I'm hoping to spend some time on that."

"You know," he said, "I saw your video of Mary Tillotson. Someone told me about it and I checked it out of the library. I thought it was excellent."

Mary again, Harper thought dejectedly. No escaping her around here. Well, she was a campus celebrity. That was the reason Harper had chosen her for the project, after all. Harper's film biography of Mary had earned her not only an "A" in Lerner's class, but also two cable TV broadcasts. Lerner, she remembered, had been impressed with the way she had captured the "artist's inner spark." Harper had been thrilled with the success of that attempt, contributing it in large part to Mary herself—dynamic, voluble and photogenic, not to mention exacting. It was Mary's insistence on excellence, after all, that had motivated Harper to work so hard on perfecting every detail. The fact that the video had turned out so well had convinced Harper to continue the hobby. It fit perfectly with her lifelong admiration for women in the arts.

"Thank you," she said to Preston. "That was my first one. It started as a class assignment."

"Oh, well, then, even more impressive," Preston said. "It managed to isolate her particular, distinguishing style, which seems to me essentially feminine, like Georgia O'Keeffe's, not derived from the male tradition at all. And that's what makes her interesting."

Harper, hearing his description, thought that he was exactly right and was impressed with his assessment. That wasn't the sort of summation that Harper could ever make herself.

"Yes," she said, "you're right. That *is* what makes her interesting. I guess that's what appeals to me about all of these artists, the feminine perspective."

"That's an extremely valid criteria, Harper. It's such a shame, isn't it, all of the talent lost to history over the centuries because of the suppression or neglect of female artists. So anything we can do to promote that talent, or to rediscover those earlier talents, is important. Like that piece the symphony did last season by Mendelssohn's sister, a piece of music to rival anything her brother wrote. What was her name?"

"Fanny," Harper said. "Fanny Mendelssohn Hensel."

"That's the sort of thing I mean. If we can find them, let's flush out these extraordinary women and let them have their day in the sun."

"Preston, what a feminist you are!"

"My wife and daughters insist on it."

She laughed. "Good for them!"

"See you in September," Preston said, turning down his path.

Harper, turning the other way toward her car, recognized the title from an old song. She hummed the tune to herself as she walked through the parking lot. The song's suggestion of a summer love prompted her to walk just a little faster. The summer had begun and there wasn't a moment to waste.

Chapter 2

SUMMER, EIGHT YEARS AGO

Harper tucked a bulging folder of sheet music into her backpack and slung it over one shoulder, then locked her office. Summer school was in session, so the campus was only sparsely populated and the library was quiet, occupied by a few well-behaved students and a skeleton staff. As she crossed the main floor on her way out, she noticed Mary Tillotson at one of the computers, squinting at the monitor and looking frustrated. Pleased to see her, Harper detoured to the computer corral for a chat.

Mary, a literature professor and successful artist, was older than Harper, around fifty, she guessed. Her brown hair was just beginning to lighten with the first hint of gray. She was attractive, aging well, with a willowy figure and a thin face that frequently held an expression of delight, as if she found everything going on around her pleasantly interesting. Her light eyes sparkled with intelligence and intensity. Mary was the real thing, a successful artist living an artist's life. She used to be a teacher at Morrison and did still teach from time to time, not out of financial necessity, Harper assumed, although even artists who had "made it" didn't always make it that way. Harper regarded her as she did all artists, with awe and a touch of envy.

"Can I help you find something, Mary?" she asked.

Mary turned to her with a startled expression. Her expressive gray eyes focused. "Oh, Harper, thank God! Why did you have to remove the card catalogue? Couldn't it have peacefully coexisted with the computer database? I'm lost without those cards."

Harper smiled. "Too difficult to maintain both systems."

"What a bother! By the way, what are you doing here? You have summers off, don't you?"

"Yes. I just stopped by to pick up some sheet music."

"That reminds me," Mary said, "I heard that you've joined the symphony orchestra. Is that right?"

Harper nodded. "I'm very excited about it."

"Well, congratulations. I didn't realize you were a musician. What do you play?"

"Cello."

"Oh, I love the cello!" Mary exclaimed. "I'll be there, you know. I've subscribed to the symphony for ages. It's one of the few things that I always look forward to. Modern life fragments a person so. For those couple of hours a month, I'm doing nothing but listening to music. So relaxing."

"Then I guess I'll see you there this fall." Harper glanced at the computer screen. "So what are you looking for anyway?"

"Elsa Gidlow's autobiography," Mary answered. "I want to recommend it to a student. So I was checking to see if there's a copy here in our library. This computer thinks I want to check the entire universe. Why would I care to do that? Why would anyone care to do that? If there's a copy on Neptune, how is that of any value to me?"

Mary had an air of melodrama about her, a sort of childlike petulance that Harper found entertaining. Although she was scowling, she also seemed amused. One of Mary's most common expressions, in fact, was a peculiar frown-smile. It was only in her eyes that you could discern which reaction was relevant to the situation. Harper had learned, however, that they both were often appropriate because, even when Mary was unhappy with the situation around her, most of the time she was also highly entertained by her own response to it.

"We do have a copy," Harper said. "Two, actually. I keep one in my office."

"Well, then," Mary said, rising from the little plastic chair, "that's okay, then. What a coincidence."

What did it mean, if anything, Harper wondered, that Mary was recommending the autobiography of a pioneering lesbian poet to a student? Mary was a lesbian herself, she was fairly certain, though they had never spoken about their personal lives. There were occasional, malicious stories about Mary and this or that female student. Such stories were inevitable, Harper thought, in the case of a woman who had achieved success without the help of a man. She had no way of knowing if any of the rumors were true.

Mary looked purposefully into Harper's eyes for a moment. "Is Gidlow of some particular interest to you?" she asked.

"I'm always interested in revolutionary female artists," Harper said.

"Yes, so I've noticed."

"She was a remarkable poet, don't you think?"

"Yes, of course. A fearless bushwhacker." Mary hooted as she recognized her own unintended pun. Harper got the joke a second later and laughed as well.

"My favorite," Harper said, recalling one of Gidlow's poems, "is that one about the garden."

Mary's eyes sparkled with recognition. "You mean, 'For the Goddess Too Well Known.' Yes, that's one of my favorites too." Mary eyed Harper with one raised eyebrow.

Harper felt herself flush with embarrassment as she realized that the poem in question was about two women making love.

Shit, she thought, *I'm discussing a poem about lesbian sex with a lesbian!*

"Now, that," Mary said, with an exaggerated sigh, "is a poem! If any of my students ever write a poem like that, I will count myself among the immortals."

"Your student, the one you want the book for, is she a poet?"

"She aspires to be. She has the heart of a poet, a fresh, unsullied poet, all tenderness and deep feeling. She's taking my summer workshop—My Mother, My Muse. Intense, artistic young women flock to that sort of thing."

"A poetry class?" Harper asked.

"No. More generalized. It doesn't matter what medium they use. It can be paint, yarn, ceramic, words. Excrement, if they so choose, which I sincerely hope they do not!" Mary laughed. "The point is to channel the soul of your mother, or your matriarchal lineage anyway, into art, to allow that ancestral creative energy to express itself through you. It's sort of a gimmick to get the creative juices flowing."

Harper thought of her own mother, of how she might be an artistic muse. Her imagination fell short. "Ancestral creative energy," she repeated. "Sounds interesting."

"Well, it can be, given the right mix of students. Most of them are so-so. But this one, she's a standout. Very good. Needs a little guidance, of course. But she's talented. She's a reader. The best part is, she even knows how to spell and punctuate. Most of them consider those skills irrelevant to poetry. They think *free verse* means that you're free to do whatever you damn well please with no regard for pleasing the ear or...oh, well, you know what I mean, Harper, because it's the same as in music. What's music without tempo, harmony, meter?"

"Noise," Harper suggested.

"Exactly! They're so self-congratulatory, these students. Before I can teach them anything, I have to disabuse them of the notion, drummed into them by their parents, that they're gifted and interesting." Mary was worked up, gesturing flamboyantly.

16

"Look at e. e. cummings, they say. Crazy grammatical structure and not a punctuation mark anywhere and he's famous. Well, yes, he's famous! That's an excellent point. And when you're famous, I tell them, you're free to make your own rules."

Harper laughed. "What's your student's name?"

"Chelsea Nichols. She's full-time here. Do you know her?"

Harper shook her head. The name wasn't familiar.

"She's really exceptional, full of potential. And only twenty-one. I love to get hold of these promising young minds with all of that enthusiasm and optimism. They're just sponges. They can't get enough." Mary's eyes flashed excitedly. "And she isn't all full of herself either, which is refreshing. She actually thinks I can teach her something. It makes it all worth it when you get a student like that."

"I'm sure," Harper agreed.

"You'll probably see her around," Mary said brightly. "I suspect she spends a lot of time in the library."

"Come on back to the office and I'll get that book for you."

As Harper led Mary to the staff area, she thought about how an intense young woman of an artistic temperament would thrive under her tutelage. Even if none of the scandalous rumors were true, Mary must inspire a tremendous amount of adoration among her students, including the occasional case of adolescent love. Harper had no difficulty imagining such a thing.

Chapter 3

JUNE 5

The din of the patrons as they moved throughout the music hall created an air of excitement for the musicians backstage. Harper stood in the wings with the others, tense and invigorated as she always was before a performance. The crowd, all in motion in the rows and aisles, was growing and becoming louder. As Harper turned away from the audience, she saw Roxie coming toward her. At five foot ten, she was hard to miss.

"Hi, Harper," Roxie said, sounding a little breathless, then hugged her with one arm, holding her violin case in the other hand. Roxie, a high school music teacher and Harper's closest friend, was second violin. They had their usual jokes about second fiddle, but she was unquestionably a first-rate musician. Roxie swept her straight brown hair off her forehead, then pulled at the back of her black slacks with a grimace.

"Full house tonight?" Roxie asked.

"That's what I heard. Lots of excitement about our guest soloist."

"People love classical guitar."

Harper nodded, thinking back to rehearsal and the young woman who had played Rodrigo with a smooth, unforced style and unbelievable confidence. The woman had achieved success at an early age and looked like she thought she deserved it. Which she did. Her talent was immense.

"I ran into Joyce yesterday," Harper said. "We were wondering if you'd be up to the Renaissance Faire this year."

"Oh, yeah, sure. I'm looking forward to it."

"Good. It's no fun without you."

Roxie had missed one year when one of her sons was sick, and the experience just wasn't the same. Harper had been prepared to cancel this year, thinking Roxie might not feel up to this kind of frivolity yet. Her husband Dave had died of a heart attack in March, quite unexpectedly, and she and her children, David and Kevin, were understandably struggling. Harper had taken the boys to the Monterey Aquarium in early May. It had been okay. They had forgotten for a while, watching jellyfish float, that they were fatherless.

"Let's get together weekend after next, then," Harper suggested. "Choose our songs."

"Okay. I can probably manage that. I'll check my schedule and give you a call." Roxie smiled reassuringly.

Dave had been Harper's age, far too young to die. It had been a shock to everyone, including Harper, who was forced to think about the fact that she too could die before she ever hit forty and that whatever she was going to accomplish in her life might be nearly finished. She didn't feel that she had accomplished much so far and nothing of lasting value. She knew that most people's lives were like that. Not everyone could be Mother Teresa or Emily Dickinson. She didn't aspire to those heights, but she would like to do something that she could be proud of before she died.

Chelsea had said something very like that last summer when

she explained her decision to become a teacher. What she had done so far felt self-indulgent, she said. Living for yourself, just for yourself, could only sustain you for so long.

Harper had done her share of volunteer work for charitable causes, but these were fillers, often summer fillers, and weren't what her life was essentially about. This was partly why she felt restless. She had always felt a little like that, like there was something she needed to do, but she couldn't figure out what it was. The feeling was stronger now, as if her time were growing short, which, of course, it was. Shorter, anyway, with each passing year.

It had always seemed to Harper that everybody else just knew what to do, as if they saw road signs along the course of their lives—turn left here, go straight at the next intersection. Her friend Peggy, for instance, declared in high school that she was going to be an engineer, and that's exactly what she did. How did she know that? Harper wondered. How did she know she should be an engineer instead of a biologist, for instance? Did she have some kind of dream or vision of herself in the future with an engineering degree in her hand?

Even if it was chance that had led Harper to become a librarian, she wasn't unhappy with her career. She was unhappy with the rest of her life, the part where her drive and deeper needs resided. She wanted to be fully absorbed in something, like Sophie with her sculpture or this guitarist who seemed to have known what she would be from the age of four. Harper longed for such a passion to seize and possess her like a demon.

The feeling that there was something missing had grown gradually, almost imperceptibly, like the insistent strains of Ravel's *Bolero*, eventually breaking into her consciousness with such force that it had finally led to her breakup with Eliot two years ago. Well, that, and the recognition that she preferred girls, of course.

Harper's relationship with Eliot, her long-term, part-time boyfriend, had always been unconventional. They had lived together for a year during college, then split after graduation to pursue their careers. After a brief period of complete separation, they had gotten together again, but never really together, since they had taken jobs almost a thousand miles apart. Eliot was a math professor at Washington State, a pragmatist who appealed, she supposed, to her occasional need for an anchor. Or a father figure.

Each year, for three, four or five weeks, he would arrive with the summer sun and they would be a couple again. He would repair leaky faucets, clean the rain gutters and change the recording on her voice mail, briefly assuming the role of head of household. Harper could stomach this male posturing without much difficulty because Eliot was always about to go back to his own life.

She wondered why she had kept the relationship up so long. Because it was comfortable and undemanding, she supposed. Harper had allowed him a harbor because she always had. As long as they had clung to one another, there was always an excuse to reach back through time rather than forward.

Now, she wanted to move forward. Two years ago, moving forward had meant leaving Eliot. Now it meant exorcising the ghost of Chelsea.

Some of the musicians were now making their way on stage. Harper lingered behind with Roxie.

"Why were you late?" she asked.

"Kevin decided to get sick right before I left. He threw up on my shoes."

"Flu?"

"No, I don't think so. Whenever I leave the house now he has these anxiety attacks."

"Poor guy."

"That's one reason I've decided not to play the summer series this year. I want to spend as much time at home with the boys as I can. What about you? You're not doing it either, right?"

"Right. Not this year."

"So what are you going to do with your summer, Harper?"

Without hesitation, Harper replied, "I'm going to fall in love."

Roxie laughed. "Oh, really? Who with?"

"I don't know yet."

"I thought you were seeing someone."

"Lynn, yes. Not anymore. She just didn't do anything for me."

"In that case," said Roxie, lowering her voice, "how about that guitarist over there? She's pretty cute."

Harper smiled. Roxie wasn't taking her seriously. That was okay. She wasn't sure herself how serious she was. They went onstage to take their places. Falling in love wasn't out of the question, though, she thought. Not at all.

She took her chair and placed her music on the stand as the cacophony of warm-up filled the space around her. Despite herself, she glanced at the seventh row—to Mary and Chelsea's usual seats. They had season tickets, had been going to the symphony for years. Harper had memorized the location without intending to, and she could never stop herself from searching them out. They hadn't arrived yet. She knew what to expect when they did. She had watched them many times, even before that incredible summer two years ago, when they were just acquaintances, interesting people she knew, and not two people who had conspired to break her heart. *No*, she thought, *"conspired" was too harsh. None of it had been planned.*

Mary, who was on the kind side of sixty, would be wearing something conservative, slacks with a blouse, a scarf, a stylish jacket. Chelsea, however, who was twenty-nine, would be arrayed in elegance, a radical departure from the knit tops and blue jeans she usually wore. She never looked more beautiful than when she came to the music hall. Her smart, close-fitting dresses, cut several inches above her knees, showed off her smooth, lean legs and sometimes revealed the barest hint of cleavage, just enough to tantalize.

She wore her hair up, usually, with a sparkly clip in it that reflected the bright ceiling lamplight, like a princess in a glittering tiara. When she walked in on her three-inch heels, men would watch her and fantasize about sweeping her into their arms and bending her backward, low and close to the floor, and then scooping her up again. All of those old men with their youthful dreams! But Harper's fantasies were the same as theirs. When that radiant young woman entered the room, there was no way she could keep her head from turning.

On the rare occasion that their eyes met, Chelsea usually offered no response, no acknowledgment other than an obvious averting of her gaze. Only once had she given any indication that she even saw Harper. Three months ago, seconds before the conductor finished his introduction to the third movement of Brahms' *Third Symphony*, Harper had looked up to find Chelsea gazing directly at her, her eyes humorless, even sad, her face stark and world-weary, the expression of a much older woman. When she saw Harper looking back at her, one side of her mouth turned up in a self-conscious half-smile before she lowered her gaze. Then the lights went down over the audience.

Harper had been so distracted that she nearly missed her first notes. That would have been disastrous, since the opening of the piece highlighted the cellos and the cello section occupied the outer edge of the stage, easily seen by the audience. When the lights had come on at intermission, Harper had looked toward the seventh row, hoping to catch Chelsea's eye again, but she was already out of her seat and walking up the aisle.

As she tuned, Harper prepared for Chelsea's entrance. A few minutes before performance time, she saw Mary coming down the aisle. Chelsea wasn't with her. Instead, there was a young woman with a broad smile and large round eyes. She was in her twenties, petite and pretty. *Perhaps Chelsea's sick*, Harper thought. *Or perhaps she just can't bear Rimsky-Korsakov.*

She watched with unease and disappointment as Mary and the stranger settled into their seats. She hadn't realized until that moment how much she looked forward to this fleeting encounter each month. Since this was the last performance of the season, she probably wouldn't see Chelsea, wouldn't experience even this meager crumb of her, for at least three more months.

But even if she never saw Chelsea in the flesh, Harper's

vibrant memories of those butterflies and nectarines were enough to bring her vividly to life as summer approached. Harper was like a sleeping toad buried in mud. All she needed was a certain angle of the sun's rays to rouse her instincts, to draw her toward wakefulness. The sun had moved into its summer realm now, wrenching the most poignant of sensations from her mind and body.

As the concert began, Harper tried to lose herself in the music. That shouldn't have been hard to do, considering how brilliantly their guest soloist made her instrument laugh and cry. The guitarist and guitar seemed to fuse together in an ecstatic embrace during the slow movements, then to thrash about in violent combat during the fast ones, tightly coupled in a passionate struggle to the last exultant pluck of the strings. As the piece ended, the guitarist, spent but euphoric, opened her eyes and, lifting her head to the audience, let her right hand fall limp to her side.

As much as Harper wanted to be free of longing, she knew how truly difficult that was going to be. Two years later, she still vibrated from Chelsea's touch like the note now lingering on the soloist's guitar.

Chapter 4

SUMMER, NINETEEN YEARS AGO

Almost too stoned or drunk to play a recognizable tune anymore, Harper went into the house, leaving what was left of the party out by the pool. Stepping carefully over the guy passed out on the floor in the living room, she leaned her guitar against the wall by the front door, where she'd be sure to see it on her way out. Now she just had to find a comfortable place to sleep it off. Home, a dorm room on the U.C. Santa Cruz campus, was an hour away. There was no chance of getting back there tonight.

"Hey, Harper," called Peggy from the kitchen doorway. Harper turned slowly to see her friend standing there, looking like Harper felt, eyes lazy and half shut, her usually wavy auburn hair stringy from swimming and drying uncombed. She was still in her bathing suit, a yellow terrycloth wrap hanging loosely from her shoulders. "Looking for a place to crash?"

Harper nodded. Peggy approached her and took hold of her

hand. "Come on. You can bunk with me. Nate's got his parents' bedroom, and he's put Eliot on the foldout couch. We've got the guest room."

Eliot was a friend of Nate's, a congenial physics major that Harper knew only slightly, and Nate was Peggy's ex-boyfriend. She had broken up with him months ago after an amiable few weeks of dating. They had remained friends, which Harper thought was cool and Peggy had mysteriously explained with, "We have an understanding." Peggy hadn't had a boyfriend since. She'd gotten deadly serious about academics instead. Harper thought that she should probably do the same, but she hadn't yet managed to put that plan into action. Peggy, who was going to be an engineer, was the class brainiac all through high school, a girl who stayed in the background socially but could always be counted on to excel at every academic challenge. Harper, by contrast, got good grades but wasn't driven to the level of performance that Peggy was. She had still not even declared a major. She was waiting for something to "click."

A counselor had suggested library science to her because, when questioned about her interests, she said that she would be happy to spend her entire life locked in a library reading. It happened that she had just discovered Aphra Behn, the seventeenth-century playwright, spy, and bisexual *bon vivant* and was, in fact, spending huge chunks of her life in the library reading her plays and several biographies. This included a biography by Vita Sackville-West, another fascinating writer who was now on Harper's must-read list. Behn described her own life as "dedicated to pleasure and poetry," and that philosophy resonated deeply with Harper. She was enjoying the biographies more than the plays, for it was Behn's lifestyle that intrigued her most. Behn satisfied Harper's ideal of what an artist should be. A true artist should live her life as if she were creating an interesting character. Her life, as much as her work, should be her art.

The idea of library science as a major was working on Harper, but she was uncommitted so far. She loved libraries and felt at home in them, but had never given any thought to making her career in them. She needed a little time to absorb the idea and make it her own.

"You know I love that song," Peggy said, rummaging through a dresser in the bedroom. "The one you just played, 'Baby Can I Hold You.'"

"Duh," Harper said, kicking off her sandals. "Why do you think I played it? I learned it just for you, of course."

"Thanks. That was sweet." Peggy pulled a big blue T-shirt out of the dresser drawer. "Try this," she said, tossing the shirt to Harper. "It's Nate's. Ought to make a good nightshirt."

Harper fumbled the shirt, dropping it to the floor. She picked it up as Peggy started humming the Tracy Chapman song and pulled a similar shirt out of the dresser drawer for herself. She peeled off her damp bathing suit and slipped into the shirt, flashing her round rump briefly at Harper.

Harper unbuttoned her blouse, tossed it into a corner, then unhooked her bra and threw that into the corner as well while Peggy sat on the bed, staring dispassionately at her. *She's stoned*, Harper decided, observing her friend's unfocused eyes. Peggy's humming trailed off to silence. Harper quickly slipped out of her shorts and threw them into the corner with her bra, then pulled on Nate's shirt, which fell to mid-thigh, covering her underpants completely.

"I wish I had a body like yours," Peggy said as Harper hopped into bed beside her. Peggy was much rounder than Harper, more feminine with well-defined curves. Of course, Harper envied that and would have preferred it. "You're so strong, so athletic. Your boobs don't get in the way of everything."

"I'll trade boobs with you any day," Harper said, glancing at the soft curve of Peggy's breast under her shirt. "That's why the boys like you."

Harper was convinced that Peggy's pronounced bustline, not her personality or her lovely clear skin and dimples, was the reason boys hovered around her. She was never flirtatious, nor did she go out on many dates. She was admirably selective.

"Boys, what do they know?" Peggy said, dismissively. She

27

reached out to Harper's chest, cupping her left breast loosely, as if weighing it. "Your tits look very...winsome to me," she said, her eyes glazed. "Winsome, that's the word I'll use for them. They are tantalizingly winsome."

Harper laughed nervously, knocking Peggy's hand away. "Shut up!"

Peggy's eyes were trained on Harper's chest, avoiding her eyes. "Winsome," Peggy said again, taking both of Harper's breasts in her hands, caressing her through the shirt, her thumbs finding and bringing the nipples to attention.

Stop her, Harper told herself, but it felt really nice, the friction of the cotton against her skin, and so she waited. She would tell Peggy to stop in a minute. Peggy was just teasing her anyway, just playing around, trying to make her feel better about her body. She would stop herself.

But she didn't stop. Instead, she leaned closer, slipping a hand under the shirt and kneading a bare breast with her fingers and then pushing Harper flat on the bed with her body. She lifted the shirt up, exposing Harper's chest to the pale light from the bedroom window. She then replaced her hand with her mouth, sucking the nipples, each in turn. That felt even better, and Harper let her continue, telling herself that it was just innocent petting, that it was okay because they were both drunk. Her priest and her mother had warned her frequently about sex, about boys and their insinuating penises, but nobody had ever told her not to let a girl suck her boobs. So this wasn't sex. This wasn't what they were talking about. And Harper had already rationalized that anything short of a penis inside her was okay anyway, because this wasn't the first time someone had touched her this way. It was, however, the first time a girl had.

As Peggy fondled and sucked her breasts, Harper became more and more excited. Peggy reached one hand down across her stomach and between her legs, feeling her through the fabric of her panties. No one had ever touched her there before. Not that they hadn't tried, but she had always deflected them at this point. She didn't deflect Peggy and didn't really think about why. The sensation was divine. Harper heard herself moan softly, and her body moved under the rhythm of Peggy's touch, fingers stroking lightly through nylon.

Peggy rested her head on Harper's shoulder. "I've wanted to touch you like this for so long," she whispered.

This was a surprise. Her best friend since the age of sixteen, Peggy had never done anything before to alert Harper to this possibility.

As Peggy slipped her hand under the elastic encircling her hips, Harper made a little cry of alarm. She twisted sideways in an unsuccessful attempt to free herself, an automatic response to such an intimate move. In a brief scramble of arms and legs, Peggy grabbed hold of her, one arm firmly around her waist, holding her fast from behind. Harper quit struggling, feeling the roundness of Peggy's breasts against her back. She liked the way it felt, she decided, liked the feeling of being held so commandingly.

"I love you, Harper," Peggy said urgently, and again she slid her hand under the elastic. Harper didn't resist this time. What Peggy was doing to her felt delightful. She felt like she would go crazy with delirious pleasure. She let her body move without restraint. She held back the cries trying to burst from her throat, however, because she knew that the boy sleeping on the other side of the wall might be a light sleeper or even still awake.

As Harper's body strained harder, Peggy's grip around her waist got tighter. She climaxed almost silently. Peggy relaxed the arm around Harper's waist and slipped her other hand away, then kissed the back of her neck tenderly.

Harper felt her body slowly cool as Peggy fell asleep beside her.

In the morning, she woke to find herself alone, an already hot sun shining through the bedroom window. Her mouth was dry and, predictably, her head felt like it was going to split open. She gradually remembered the previous evening, the swimming, the drinking, the music—and the sexual encounter with her best friend. She lay in bed for a while thinking about that. She could

29

hear movement in the house, the clatter of dishes and sonorous male laughter.

Will Peggy remember? she wondered. *Maybe not.* What should she do? Keep quiet about it? Pretend she didn't remember either? Or just dismiss it as a silly side effect of too much drinking? There were a lot of ways to sweep this under the rug.

She dressed and arrived in the kitchen barely in time for breakfast. Nate was cooking. Peggy was putting dishes in the dishwasher. She was a sort of mystery now, Harper thought. Her best friend, that sweet, funny girl she adored, was someone she didn't really know. In high school they had been inseparable. When Peggy, intent on getting as far away from her family as possible, announced that she was applying to colleges in California, Harper had been distraught. Peggy told her she had to come along, insisted that they had to stay together. "Can you imagine us being four thousand miles apart?" Peggy had asked.

Harper couldn't. She had never been to California, had never even considered going there, but she had applied to all the same schools Peggy had. When they both managed to get accepted at Santa Cruz, that settled it.

"Good morning," Peggy said, holding her hand briefly. The affectionate smile on her face told Harper that she hadn't forgotten. "Nate, give our troubadour a couple of those flapjacks."

Peggy gave Harper a glass of orange juice and set a place at the kitchen table. Through the sliding glass door, Harper could see the backyard. Eliot was out there, sitting on the edge of the pool, his feet in the water, his bare back to the house. Peggy put a plate of pancakes in front of her.

"Okay," Nate said with finality, putting his pan in the sink. "Kitchen's closed."

Peggy sat beside Harper at the table while Nate joined Eliot by the pool. Harper cut a bite-sized triangle out of a pancake and put it in her mouth.

"Do you remember what we did last night?" Peggy asked quietly.

Harper nodded and swallowed, wondering why Peggy was

30

talking about it. That was the absolute wrong thing to do.

"Well," Peggy persisted, "what do you think?" Her expression was hopeful.

"What do you mean?"

"I mean, did you like it? Do you think we could do it again?"

"I don't think we should do it again," Harper said. "We wouldn't have done it at all if we hadn't been drunk."

Peggy looked disappointed. "It wasn't because I was drunk."

Harper remembered that Peggy had said she'd wanted to do it for a long time. She had even mentioned love. So she was serious. She had these kinds of feelings for Harper.

"Well, that's why I did it," Harper said. "And I don't want to do it again."

She was uncomfortable, even frightened. "I never want to do it again," she said more firmly. "And you shouldn't either."

Peggy sat back in her chair and lowered her gaze, staring at her hands in her lap. Harper ate her pancakes without tasting them, feeling the awkward silence in the room. She knew she'd hurt Peggy's feelings, but she didn't see any alternative. If only Peggy had been quiet about it, if only she had acted like nothing had happened, then they could have gone on like before.

Eventually, Harper said, "You know, that Eliot is sort of cute." Through the glass door, she saw Eliot shove Nate into the pool. "I think I might like him."

Chapter 5

JUNE 11

Harper put her black symphony slacks on a hanger and hung them in the closet beside a black blouse, one of three such outfits she used as performance costumes. She had one jacket, also black, with a velvet collar, velvet cuffs and velvet placket down the front. They were all cleaned, pressed and ready to go in the fall. Likewise, she filed away her sheet music and programs and notes from the last season. The small bedroom she used as a music room was tidy, occupied by her guitar, cello, instrument cases, music chair and music stands.

As she put the last of the programs in a drawer, the yellow cover of a slim photo album caught her eye. She lifted the cover without removing the album from the drawer, not really wanting to see the photos but unable not to look. There was no need to, though, because she had looked at them so often over the last two years that she had memorized everything about them. On the inside cover of the album she had written "Chelsea" and nothing more. The picture on the first page was one of Harper's favorites, taken the day they were hiking near Pacific Grove and monarch butterflies had swarmed around them in a cloud of orange. One had lighted on Chelsea's hair. That's when Harper had snapped the photo.

Chelsea looked surprised and delighted with that butterfly perched on her head. So happy. She'd been looking at Harper, of course, taking the photo. *It wasn't just the butterfly that gave her such a joyful expression, was it?*

She closed the album and shut the drawer. She didn't want to look at those today. It was a kind of self-torture anyway, and she was done torturing herself with memories of Chelsea.

Harper felt restless. Chelsea had symbolized a huge turning point in her life, she had thought. Yes, she had broken off permanently with Eliot, but nothing else had really changed, not even the house. Her environment had remained static, like a museum display. She lived among relics.

That was going to change, though. Her intended summer projects included some serious redecorating, starting with the front room. She would repaint and get new furniture, replacing the worn brown sofa and the leather recliner that she and Eliot had picked out the summer she bought this house.

She observed the one bookcase in the room. It wasn't used for books, of course. She saw no reason to have books in her house; she worked in a library. She brought home one book at a time, whatever she was reading. She kept a dictionary and a couple of volumes of poetry on hand, but very little else. Instead the shelves displayed photos, family pictures and a few memorable vacation scenes. Among these was the photo Wilona had taken of her wielding a hammer on that Habitat for Humanity house ten years ago. Dressed in khaki shorts and a paint-stained T-shirt, she looked like she knew how to swing a hammer. Of course, Wilona had taken at least a dozen shots. It was possible that she didn't look quite so competent in any of the others.

At the very least, she thought, she should update the photos of her niece and nephews. The images were now four years out of date, freezing the children in time at ages twelve, five and one. Beside them were mementos from Harper's travels, global and spiritual, including the netsuke Hotei, Buddhist god of happiness, rendered in ivory-colored polymer. *I should get rid of that*, she thought, smiling at the laughing fat man who didn't look so much happy as dyspeptic.

The walls of Harper's house were mostly bare, decorated with only a handful of framed prints, a couple of which she had decided to replace this summer. She didn't like putting art on the walls just for the sake of covering up the space. She didn't mind a bare wall here and there, especially since the house was so small. Too many things would merely create clutter. In addition to the prints, though, the walls in the front room were home to her medieval musical instruments. On the wall across from the sofa hung a lute and a lyre. Above the sofa was a mandolin. She wouldn't change those. They were permanent fixtures. The latest addition to this collection of instruments, a handsome maple psaltery, hung in the bedroom. It had been a gift from Chelsea, presented with a quotation from Chaucer, pronouns altered:

She kiste her sweete and taketh her sawtrie,
And pleyeth faste, and maketh melodie.

Harper remembered playing the psaltery, or trying to anyway, on the occasion of that gift, her birthday two years ago. Though the attempt had been awkward, Chelsea had been delighted with a reasonably recognizable rendition of "Greensleeves." They had sat here in Harper's living room while she played and sang that beautiful old song. And now, like so many things, that song had taken on a new, bittersweet edge through its association with Chelsea. Harper could now only sing it with a wistfulness just marginally removed from sadness.

Greensleeves, now farewell, adieu
To God I pray to prosper thee

For I am still thy lover true,
Come once again and love me.

If she had known how everything was going to turn out, she would have chosen a song that day that she liked a little less. "My heart remains in captivity," she sang in her head, realizing with dismay how utterly true that was. But it wouldn't be true for long. She was determined to leave Chelsea behind, just as she had done with Eliot. Her summer plans were already rapidly coalescing, the days filling with activities that had nothing to do with Chelsea.

On one wall of the pantry, on a wide bulletin board, Harper had hung three pages of a wall calendar—June, July and August. She liked to be able to see the summer at a glance like that, writing in all her appointments, trips, anticipated visits and visitors. The more days with scribbled notes, the better, she reasoned. She wrote in her dates for her annual trip back East, working it around music festivals, Shakespeare in the park, the Renaissance Faire.

With dismay, she noticed that she had gotten "Greensleeves" stuck in her head. She turned on the radio to NPR. It was the jazz hour and they were playing Abbey Lincoln singing "The Music is the Magic." "Greensleeves" couldn't possibly stand up to that.

Somewhere in this summer lineup, Harper thought, looking over her calendars, *I need to find time to meet a fascinating woman and fall in love.* Just for the fun of it, she taped a fortune cookie fortune on June 29. She had gotten it just two days earlier, and it had seemed so portentous that she had hung onto it. "Do not shut the door to your heart when true love comes knocking." June 29 was an arbitrary date, but, looking at it, she felt chills, as though she had just imbued it with some marvelous significance.

Fantasizing meeting the woman of her dreams on June 29, she tried to imagine what she would look like. The list of women for whom she had felt physical desire was short, too short to draw conclusions about her tastes. Would she be blond and blue-eyed like Chelsea or dark-haired and lithe like Astral? Or perhaps curvy and round-faced like Peggy? Looking back, with her current perspective, she had to admit that she had shared Peggy's feelings, at least a little, all those years ago, but it had been too much for her nineteen-year-old mind to comprehend, hit with it as unexpectedly as she'd been.

Whenever Harper imagined a female object of desire these days, she invariably invoked the form of Chelsea. That was probably why she had gone out with Lynn in the first place, because of her blond hair and blue eyes. Harper hadn't expected Lynn to be like Chelsea based on a couple of similar physical traits, but it had made it easier for her to imagine making love with her. Ultimately, they were nothing alike. Harper was disappointed with herself, in how she kept comparing everyone to Chelsea.

Astral had in no way resembled Chelsea, but, of course, that had been nothing to do with love. They had met last spring at the Northern California Women's Music Festival in Laytonville, the only such event Harper had ever attended. It was a liberating experience and, with all of that female artistic energy present, it was a natural for Harper.

Astral, which was almost certainly not her real name, had been dark-skinned, dark-haired and dark-eyed. She was extremely confident about her desirability, and once her sights had landed on Harper, the rest was easily foretold.

The resort was packed with women, many walking about fully or partially nude, displaying a dazzling range of body types. Sitting on the grass, Harper stripped to the waist in the shade of pine trees to listen to a band playing traditional African instruments. When a rock singer with a guitar took the stage, she slipped her shirt back on and went over to browse the craft tent. After that, she wandered into a Middle Eastern dance class. Although she would have enjoyed the event more if she had been with someone, she was having a good time talking to people, listening to the different types of music, soaking in the lesbian culture. The vibe here was not like anything she'd been around before, and she always relished an adventure.

After the dancing, she stopped to listen to a woman playing a long-necked stringed instrument that she thought at first to be a strange type of lute. The musician was dressed in orange silk pants and wore nothing else other than several colorful bracelets and necklaces. Her upper body was decorated with black markings, tribal designs that circled her breasts and belly button. Similar designs looped around her upper arms. Her body was exotic, a match for her music.

Looking through the CDs the woman was selling, Harper learned that the instrument was a tanbur and the music was Turkish folk tunes. She lingered as the woman strummed her instrument, watching Harper with increasing interest. When her song ended, Astral sold Harper a couple of CDs and gave her a business card. They talked for a while about folk music and about traditional instruments, their obvious common ground. As they spoke, Harper's gaze followed the spirals around Astral's breasts, around and around, ending at dark, erect nipples.

Astral handed over her instrument, and Harper awkwardly attempted a tune.

"You could play this," Astral said, delighted with Harper's musical attempt. "You just need a few lessons."

"Do you play any other instruments?"

"Bouzouki," Astral said and, then, shrugging, as though she were reluctantly unveiling herself, "and guitar."

"Me too," Harper said. "The guitar. Not the bouzouki. But I've always wanted to try it."

"I've brought one with me," Astral said. "If you want, you can come play with me this evening." Astral grinned, her long lashes briefly obscuring her eyes.

After a light dinner, Astral led Harper to her home for the weekend, a cramped nineteen-foot-long Airstream travel trailer. They sat in front of the gleaming silver trailer in two lawn chairs and played folk songs on the tanbur and bouzouki while drinking cold beer from the trailer's refrigerator. Astral had put on a shirt, which helped Harper focus on playing the notes. They sang softly into the cool evening as the last pinks of the sunset gloomed into midnight blue and purple.

"Oh, Shenandoah, I love your daughter." Astral's voice was sweet, her harmonizing delightful, and the tune was slow and thick.

Harper felt relaxed, as she normally did when playing music. There was no conversation between them other than Astral's occasional instruction on the playing. She was the choreographer of this night's duet, and Harper was content with her role.

When the beer was gone, Astral put the instruments away and asked Harper inside. Harper squeezed past her in the Airstream, making her way to the back where a low bed occupied the entire width of the trailer. As soon as Astral had closed the door and shut off the main light, Harper found herself being rapidly undressed. She hadn't had a lover since Chelsea and was nervous, but also excited. She knew it would be different, that she and Astral were just two women satisfying their lust, and she was happy with that. She was, in fact, anxious for the anonymous encounter, as if Astral would somehow rescue her body from Chelsea's grasp and free her. She had no illusions about her place in Astral's plans and didn't care to know her real name.

Astral had obviously not been intending to spend the night alone. She had equipment—a box of potions and toys and precautionary devices. Harper learned a great deal that night about the ways women could enjoy one another's bodies. She hadn't kept Astral's card, but she did still have the CDs, and whenever she played the strange Turkish music, she remembered keenly the torrid night in that stuffy trailer.

Having settled on the dates for her visit back East, Harper telephoned her mother, noting, as she lifted the receiver, the beeping that indicated a voice mail message.

"You can put me down tentatively for July twenty-sixth," she told her mother. "Let me know how that works for everybody."

"Okay. That's about when we expected. I'll check with Neil to be sure."

"How is Neil these days?" Harper asked.

"Apparently Sarah is giving them some problems this year."

"Sarah? Sweet, studious Sarah?" Harper glanced at the photo of the innocent-looking twelve-year-old on her shelf, thinking again that she should update her pictures. The last time she had seen Sarah was at her Sweet Sixteen party last July. Sarah had been remarkably well-behaved despite the yard full of exuberant teenage girls. She had seemed, even then, child-like, but with an underlying air of deep insight that had intensified Harper's growing appreciation of her.

"I told them to expect it," Alice said, "to prepare for the rebellion. It's inevitable. Girls are so difficult."

"What form is the rebellion taking?" Harper asked, ignoring the implied complaint her mother was making about daughters.

"Oh, you know. General disobedience. Just last weekend, they told her she couldn't go on an overnight beach party. She went anyway. Came back totally defiant. No apology, no remorse."

"And still a virgin?" Harper asked.

"I don't think Neil is privy to that information. She really doesn't tell them much. Oh, and she got a tattoo."

"Where?"

"Lower back."

"Uh-oh." Harper said. "Not a virgin."

"I suppose they will all survive, but Neil and Kathy are banging their heads on the wall, wondering what they did wrong. I think they've grounded her for the next five years."

Harper laughed. "And how is Danny?"

"He's out of work. He's moved in with us again."

"Oh? Tough luck."

"Well, it's not so bad," Alice said. "He's a good boy."

"Mom, he's thirty-five years old! How does Dad feel about having him back home?"

"He doesn't mind. Danny's a help around the place."

There was nothing surprising about this. Danny was like the space shuttle, launching into orbit briefly with the best of intentions and then returning to base to sit idle in the hangar until the next time he felt compelled to earn his keep. Harper and Danny were close, but their lives had taken widely divergent paths. Danny had gone to seminary and become a priest, which was a great joy to their mother before he changed his mind a few years later. He loved theology, the scholarly pursuit of it, but he didn't see how to integrate that into the everyday practice of Catholicism. Since leaving the priesthood ten years earlier, Danny had drifted, mainly in and out of his parents' home.

Unlike Danny, Harper had rejected the Catholic faith of their childhood almost as soon as she could consider that as a possibility. She'd become a Buddhist for a while, then a Taoist and then a naturist for a summer. That had been interesting! She had tried various other philosophies and ideologies and had ended up absorbing little bits of them all without ever finding one that worked for her. None of them ever made her feel like the search was over. None of them stemmed the restlessness that was always with her. Sometimes she thought that maybe the search was all there was, that the answers, like the systems of belief created to answer them, were mythologies too.

For a while Harper had thought that she had found the answer in Chelsea's arms. She had never felt such a complete physical and spiritual connection with anyone before. She had loved the way her body rose up to meet Chelsea's touch without engaging her brain at all. Maybe she finally did know the answer to life's great mystery, but she was no closer to finding it, or finding it again anyway. She wasn't even sure you were allowed to find it twice in one lifetime. *Allowed by whom?* she asked herself, amused at this lingering remnant of belief in the supernatural.

Harper's mother, still a practicing Catholic, held out hope that Danny would return to the priesthood. Harper had no idea what her mother's hopes were for her. Her father, on the other hand, had always been very clear about his goals for his children. John Sheridan had no tolerance for mediocrity in his offspring. At the very least, he always said, they should all be college graduates. "You've got all the advantages," he would tell them. "You have no excuse for not succeeding, at least academically. I don't expect Danny to ever be good at sports, for instance, but I do expect academic excellence from all of you."

Harper had never thought this was logical. Just because he had a brilliant mind didn't mean his children would. For one thing, Harper knew that she took after her mother, who wasn't an intellectual by anyone's standards. This wasn't an argument that her father would accept. "Half of your genes are mine," he would say, "so, at the very least, you should be half as bright as I am."

That was his joke. But she couldn't find it amusing, because, when it came down to it, the B's and occasional C's she got in her math and science classes might as well have been F's. They were like blows upon her father's back, delivered by her own hand. At least that was her guilty impression. It didn't help that Neil, going a few years before her, had followed in their father's footsteps and was also accomplished at math and science.

Harper's subjects were art, music and literature, lying well to the other end of the spectrum from her father's expertise. He appreciated these, but he didn't live them.

"Well, math is a kind of art too," he said, when they had discussed these things, "at the higher levels. It has symmetry and grace and fluidity that you might not expect. It even has fiction, if you want, with its imaginary numbers. In fact, at the more complex levels, most sciences become akin to art. Even physics loses its certainty in the arena of the theoretical. There are molecules in two places at once and contradictions like wave-particle duality. What chaos! Well, not so much chaos as a sort of beautiful but enigmatic ballet in which we glimpse the hand of God."

By "hand of God," he really meant the mystery of the undiscovered truths, for Harper's father was an unwavering atheist. He thought it amusing and ironic to use terms like that. Most of his students, though, didn't get it. Harper got it, for she had lived it, sandwiched between the atheist father and the devout Catholic mother. Maybe that was why Danny had become a priest. Maybe it was his way of rebelling against their father. And maybe that was why Harper had been able to question her faith from an early age, to view it critically and then to reject it.

Her father seemed pleased with her accomplishments, but it was impossible for her to be reassured when their two disciplines of endeavor were so far removed from one another. He did sometimes say things that she thought were designed to bolster her confidence. "Art and science go hand in hand," he had told her, "as the forerunners of human culture. Neither can flourish without the other. Both Einstein and Bach are equally relevant in the shaping of human evolution." She had always felt that he was just being kind and keeping his deep disappointment hidden from her. Whatever else he said, the message she had gotten as a child was that if she couldn't do calculus, she was mentally deficient.

She thought it was odd the way her father was spending his retirement. After a career filled with intense mental stimulation, he now did almost nothing other than go fishing. He went almost every day, and he spent long hours at it. He had given up science and all types of study completely. His only explanation, when someone tried to engage him in a math problem or a discussion of quantum mechanics, was, "I've put in my time. Leave me be."

As was customary when her father was nearby during these phone conversations, he popped on the line briefly to say hello. He wasn't much of a phone person, so he was on and off without ceremony. "Hey, Harper," he said, dropping the first "r" in her name as usual. To his children, especially Neil, John Sheridan's Boston version of her name had sounded like "Hopper" and had encouraged his kung-fu crazy son to nickname her "Grasshopper." During the Seventies, Neil had often teased her with the condescending remark, "You still have much to learn, Grasshopper." And, of course, when Danny was old enough, he picked up on the nickname too, even though he wasn't familiar with the television series that had inspired it.

"Hi, Dad," she said, "how are you?"

"Good, good," he said. "How's my little girl?"

In a moment, after a few words about how glad she was to be on summer vacation, he was gone and Harper's mother was back on the line.

"Oh, I've been trying to remember to tell you something," Alice said. "Peggy Drummond has moved back here."

"Peggy?" Harper was alert at the mention of her childhood friend.

"Yes. Her mother has really gone downhill lately. Kate's sort of senile, you know. She can't live alone anymore."

"So Peggy's moved in with her mother?"

"Yes. Quite a surprise, isn't it? I don't think she's even been here to visit once since her father died about, oh, four years ago now. And I don't blame her, considering how Kate behaved at the funeral. You know, it was always Peggy's mother who disapproved. It wasn't her father at all. It was such a shame, I always thought, that Peggy and her father should be kept apart by Kate's small-mindedness."

"How long has she been back?"

"I believe they moved here in March."

"They?" Harper asked. "You mean Peggy's partner is there too?"

"Uh-huh. Do you think the sky is gonna fall? The three of them are living together, happy as clams. Peggy's still looking for a job. Considering that she was a pricey engineer in California, that could take a while, unless she's willing to take a significant pay cut. But her partner, I think her name is Christine or Kristin or something like that, she's a registered nurse, so she's already gotten on at the hospital. And that's perfect, of course, for the situation. A live-in nurse when you're old and sickly, well, what could be better?"

"So have you seen her? Have you talked to her?"

"Yes. I talked to her a couple of weeks ago. I told her you were coming this summer, as usual."

"What did she say?"

"She seemed happy to hear it. She'd like to see you if you have time. I told her of course you'd have time for an old friend."

"Mom," Harper said, "you didn't tell her anything about..." Harper hesitated, groping for the words.

"Your sex life?" her mother guessed. "Oh, sure, Harper, we discussed it at length. For hours and hours. And then she told me all about hers. We stayed up until three in the morning drinking Lemon Drops and talking about lesbian sex."

"Mom, I just meant did you tell her I was gay."

"No, I didn't. You can tell her yourself when you see her this summer."

Harper thought about how interesting and strange it would be to see Peggy after all of these years. It sounded like Peggy was looking forward to it, which was encouraging. Harper had never been sure, after how they ended their friendship. It didn't have to be a big deal, of course. Everyone has unrequited longings from their youth, but Harper had harbored some substantial guilt over the years for how she turned away from Peggy so abruptly and completely.

Her trips back to the Cape each summer were rejuvenating. They weren't just about visiting her family, although that was the primary reason, of course. They were also a chance to reconnect with her childhood, her simpler self. There was nothing more evocative of that for Harper than the sea.

She now lived within easy reach of the Pacific Ocean, which she treasured, but the East Coast and West Coast had entirely different personalities. You couldn't experience Cape Cod by going to Santa Barbara, for instance. You could experience a little of it, though, by going to Mendocino, so she was drawn there regularly. Mendocino had a flavor of those old Atlantic fishing villages about it—cold mists, the plaintive groan of lighthouses. The farther north you traveled along the California coastline, the more it felt like the "real" sea, the sea that had been imprinted on her as a child.

When she had told Chelsea of her love for Mendocino, she mentioned that her brother had a vacation home there, rarely used. They had discussed going there together, a happy prospect that would never be realized. At the time, Harper couldn't have imagined anything better than playing house with Chelsea by the sea. Or playing house anywhere with her, really.

There had been so much promise in those three months, so briefly savored. It had been like sitting down to a plentiful feast and tasting one heavenly morsel and then having the entire table snatched away, leaving nothing but the aroma. She had felt famished ever since.

After saying goodbye to her mother, Harper remembered the voice mail indicator. She dialed in and listened to the message. Her heart lost a beat as she recognized the hesitant voice. Emotion coursed through her body like a flash flood through a desert wash.

"Hi, Harper. This is Chelsea. Sorry I missed you. Could you call me...please? My cell phone number has changed. It's 609-4362. Anyway, I'd really like to talk to you. I hope you feel the same." There was a momentary hesitation, during which Harper realized she was holding her breath. She let it out as Chelsea repeated herself in an earnest near-whisper. "Please call."

Chapter 6

SUMMER, FOUR YEARS AGO

As usual, Harper was eating too much. Her mother seemed to have no idea how to entertain her adult children other than by feeding them. Their father commented frequently on the explosions of food that came out of the kitchen, so different from their usual bowl of Cheerios for breakfast or balogna sandwich for lunch. It was obvious to Harper that when her parents were alone, their lives were much more spartan. They were the sort of couple who enjoyed one another's presence amid persistent stretches of silent accord. Even with a house full of visitors, her father might go for hours without uttering more than a "yup."

Since Harper and Danny had timed their visits to coincide, the house dynamic for these two July weeks was much as it had been after Neil had left home. This morning Alice was cooking breakfast for her children even before they were out of bed, so they had no chance but to graciously accept. Her thick steel-gray hair was clipped back from her face with one pink and one blue clip. The older she got, the more wiry and contrary her hair became.

"You remember Peggy Drummond, of course," Alice said, putting a plate of two sunny-side up eggs in front of Harper at the dining room table.

Danny already had his and was sopping up egg yolk with his toast. He sat across the table, hunched over his plate, his wire-framed glasses riding the tip of his nose. A bright yellow drip of yolk clung to his new goatee.

"Peggy?" Harper said. "Yes, of course."

"Her father died earlier this year." Alice put a piece of buttered toast on Harper's plate.

"Oh, no! I hadn't heard that. Poor Peggy."

"I didn't think you'd heard. I know you haven't kept in touch with her."

"That's so sad. I didn't even know he was sick. I loved Mr. Drummond. He was so funny and kind."

"Peggy was here for the funeral. It was the first time I'd seen her in such a long time. Unlike you, Harper, she doesn't come back for visits. Understandable, I suppose. She brought her partner along. Her mother was not at all happy about that. She thought it was inconsiderate, an act of defiance or hostility. She thought it was disrespectful."

Harper cut the whites off of her eggs mechanically, leaving the yolk intact, saving it. "Oh?" she asked, glancing across the table at Danny, who had cleaned his plate and was now opening a newspaper. "That seems unreasonable."

"Yes," Alice said, "absolutely unreasonable. The poor woman lost her father. Why wouldn't she want to have her partner at her side at a time like that? Kate has never been able to reconcile herself to Peggy's lifestyle. She basically just pretends it doesn't exist. She's in complete denial. It's such a shame. I mean, she's all alone now in that big house. She's estranged from her only child, narrow-minded old biddy."

Alice wiped her hands on a dishtowel, then smiled approvingly at her children. "I know I would be overjoyed to welcome my daughter's lesbian lover into my family if I were in Kate's shoes."

Harper and Danny looked at each other across the table, their expressions communicating shared bewilderment. Alice sighed deeply and went into the kitchen. It wasn't at all unusual for her to make that sort of bizarre comment. She seemed to be perpetually trying to prove that she was open-minded and progressive when it came to gays and lesbians, as if someone were accusing her of being otherwise. But no one was. Harper had known for a long time that her parents supported gay rights as if they had a personal stake in those issues, and she was proud of them for that, especially her mother, because of her religious affiliation.

"Sometimes I think she wishes she had a gay child," Harper remarked to her brother.

He shrugged, saying, "Our parents are refreshingly liberal."

She reached across the table with a napkin and wiped the egg yolk out of his beard. "As are their children. Eliot and I just took part in our third peace rally since the war started."

"On your home turf?"

"San Francisco. It was fun and a little different because this time there were so many gay men there. There were as many rainbow flags being waved as there were 'End the War Now' signs."

"Are you sure you didn't get swept up in the pride parade?" Danny grinned, widening his already wide, thin mouth.

"Yes, I'm sure. Because I went to that *last* month."

"Did Eliot go with you to that too?"

"No. I went with my friend Roxie. She left the kids home with her husband, and we had a great day in the City. The pride parade in San Francisco is a pretty good party, as you might imagine."

Danny nodded. "Maybe you can take Mom next year. She can march with the PFLAG contingent with a sign that says 'I wish I had a gay son or lesbian daughter.'"

48

Harper laughed as Danny returned to his newspaper. Carefully lifting her egg yolk to place it unbroken on top of her toast, she recalled the pride parade and how Roxie had practically begged her to go because she didn't want to go alone.

"It'll be a blast," she insisted.

Harper had never been to the parade and decided it might be interesting, so she skipped her *t'ai chi* class and went into the City instead.

Roxie, who was never a wallflower, was more than usually cranked up that day. She was jumping up and down, hollering, whistling her impressive two-fingered whistle and waving madly, her necklaces of colored beads in constant motion. This was especially true when the peace officers came by. She did everything she could to get their attention, succeeding, finally, when one of the women in uniform waved to her and doffed her hat. Roxie had turned to look at Harper, beaming like a lighthouse beacon, and then turned her attention back to the cop and blew her a kiss. Harper didn't quite know what to make of it all.

"Do you know her?" Harper asked.

"She's one of ours. I mean, she's on our local force. I met her a few months ago. She gave me a ticket for running a stop sign." Roxie laughed ironically, as though this was much funnier than it seemed.

"So now you're flirting with her?"

Roxie turned to face Harper more calmly. "Oh," she said breathlessly, "I'm just getting caught up in the atmosphere, you know? Like that sign we saw, 'Everybody's gay for the day!'"

Harper could definitely understand that. She herself had made note of a particular leggy brunette riding a horse, wearing a black leather vest and black chaps, a black cowboy hat tilted up high on her forehead. The vest was open about three inches, revealing that she had nothing on underneath. The cowgirl had ridden fairly close to the crowd, close enough that Harper could feel the hot breath of her horse as they passed by. The woman in the saddle had glanced directly at her and winked, her mouth

49

curled into a seductive smile. She had felt her knees go a little weak at that.

Alice reappeared in the doorway as Harper stabbed the yolk of her egg with her fork and smeared it evenly over her toast. "What are your plans for today?" she asked.

"We're going out with Dad," Danny said. "He's putting the gear in the boat right now. Wanna come?"

"No, thanks. I have to get ready for Neil and Kathy. Besides, I'll appreciate the peace and quiet. When Neil arrives with that little baby of his, all hell's gonna break loose. That child never stops crying. And I might even be able to fit in an hour or so on the thimbles while you're gone. I'll pack you a lunch, then. Be home by five. Tell your father. I want you here for a nice family dinner."

Alice scooped up Danny's dishes and headed back to the kitchen.

"Don't forget the wine for our lunch," Harper called after her.

"No alcohol on the boat. You can have Kool-Aid."

Alice left the dining room again. Harper and Danny looked at each other, wrinkling their noses at the notion of Kool-Aid, then burst out laughing.

"What does she mean by thimbles?" Harper asked.

"She paints them. Paints scenes and pictures on them. It absorbs a lot of her time. There's one right here." He retrieved a thimble from a curio shelf, handing it to Harper.

She examined it, seeing a miniature scene with a girl, a dog, sun shining, a couple of trees and a kite. "Cute," she said, handing it back to Danny.

"At least it's a better hobby than those paint-by-numbers she used to do, years ago. Remember those?"

"Oh, God! I'd forgotten. Thankfully."

Danny stuck a finger in his mouth and gagged.

After clearing the breakfast table, Harper waited for everyone to be ready to launch, vaguely looking at familiar family photographs in the hallway. There were pictures of all of them—baby pictures, school pictures, family group pictures and photos of ancient relatives she had never known.

Her mother's cardboard-and-felt family tree also hung here, peppered all over with tiny photographs of people's faces with names pasted under them. Heading it up was a dour-looking couple—shadowy Irish ancestors. Then the branches spread, a widening pattern of names, a tangle of relationships, leading sometimes nowhere, but eventually to her own grandparents, parents and siblings, people connected to her with red yarn. Her great-grandparents, the Harpers of Connecticut, had immigrated as adults, but her grandparents were American-born. The Harpers were destitute farmers in Ireland, but prosperous farmers in New England. Their life had not been too difficult, not unreasonably so, and their children were well-off and had moved away from toiling in the dirt. Strife had not appreciably touched the family since they had arrived in the New World.

Positioned under these Connecticut Harpers were Alice Caitlin Harper and her Boston-born husband, John William Sheridan. Their three offspring were lined up on a lower tier. Beside Neil, his wife Kathy. Under them, three children. Under Harper, dead space. *There is something wrong with a perspective that implies that your only contribution can be children*, thought Harper. The space under her name suggested more than death of a lineage. It suggested failure, incompetence and disappointment. She had never liked this cardboard monstrosity, and today she liked it even less.

It might be a tremendous disappointment to her mother, she realized, that she didn't have children. She didn't see herself as the maternal type. It wasn't really a choice she had made, not consciously. But then, she didn't think that Alice Caitlin Harper had chosen her spot in this scheme either. Like so many women of her generation, Alice had had her role thrust upon her by circumstances. She had passively accepted what she stumbled into. Alice was a doggedly sensible woman with native intelligence, unhoned and unembellished. If she had made a plan for her life,

Harper didn't know about it, and it had obviously been set aside at age eighteen when she married John Sheridan.

This chart, then, which looked like there was a consciousness behind it because of all of the orderly connections, was ultimately designed by chance, she decided, like the lives of all of its individual members. There was only an illusion of control—strings of red yarn.

People talk about making plans, Harper thought, but, in the end, most of the decisions they make are made within the context of countless arbitrary movements of particles through space.

Her mother wouldn't subscribe to this point of view, she knew. She believed that there was a master plan, God's master plan, regardless of how convoluted and directionless it appeared. Harper had believed in the master plan long ago, but, because of her father, had modified it to fall in line with the laws of physics, as if God and physics were one and the same thing. To her father, they were, of course. All of the mysteries, all of the unknowns were just experiments waiting to be conducted by scientists. Harper embraced the mysteries too. She just had no inclination to solve them. She was open to the answers, and she was willing to accept explanations other than physics and other than God, even though she couldn't guess what else might offer up such explanations.

At last the men were ready. The three of them loaded into the boat and pushed off onto the lake. Harper sat astern, wearing dark glasses and a wide sun hat. Under a loose beach coat, she wore a one-piece bathing suit. Her father took the steering wheel. Danny started the motor. Soon they were gliding across the water, just as they had done twenty years before as children. The back of her father's head had changed, though. Wisps of gray hair now blew in the wind while the sunlight glistened on his shiny bald head. But everything else was the same. The shoreline of the lake was familiar, and its couple of small islands reminded Harper of many happy days of youthful play.

Speeding across the lake with her father at the helm and her brother sitting opposite, it took no great leap of imagination for

Harper to think of herself as eleven years old again. It was all here, complete and comfortable. Mom was home fussing in the kitchen. When they returned, she would greet them with food.

"How's this?" her father asked, cutting the engine.

The boat drifted offshore from a grass-covered island. "Great," Danny said, leaning over to get his fishing pole. "I remember once catching a black bass right here that was almost as tall as me."

"You were a mighty short kid, it's true," their father said, smiling affectionately.

For the next couple of hours, they cast out in three different directions and tended their silent poles. While waiting for a strike, Harper read *Sor Juana* by Octavio Paz, a book she'd gotten from the local library the day after her arrival. She had wanted to read it for a long time and was thoroughly engrossed in the story.

She always had a book going, sometimes more than one, frequently biographies or some nonfiction tale about someone like this, an artist, a revolutionary of some kind, a hero who would appeal to a modern woman. She did not read fiction, except on occasion when a novel was recommended by someone she admired.

"What's the book about?" Danny asked.

"Juana Inés de la Cruz, a seventeenth-century Mexican nun who became a self-taught scholar and important feminist writer. She was bold and astonishing, especially for the time."

"Really?" he replied. "You're reading a book about a nun?"

"I'm surprised you haven't heard about her. What did you study at that seminary anyway?"

"Christian theology," announced Danny, sticking his nose in the air. "That is the study of hypocrisy, misogyny and jingoism at work throughout the *Anno Domini* part of the history of mankind, and I emphasize *man*-kind."

"That place really turned you against the Church, didn't it?"

He nodded. "The whole system is just so archaic. The Church is its own worst enemy. Your nun there was probably held back from serving the church in her full capacity in the same way women are today. Or gay men. Or men who want to have sex, for Christ's sake!"

"Stop right there," their father said firmly. "I will not have you debating the ordination of women and gay men in my boat. This boat is not a forum for religious discussion. This boat is a safe zone."

Harper and Danny both stared at their father.

"No religion, no politics," he continued. "Talk about the weather."

"Weather, huh?" Danny said, looking mischievous. "Well, the climate at the Vatican—"

The look of warning he got from his father made him stop short and keep his thought to himself.

"Geez," Harper whispered to Danny, "he really takes retirement seriously."

She returned to her book and read silently until lunch. Afterward, she drowsed, her hat over her face and beach coat discarded, reclining against a foam cushion. The voices of her father and brother came in snatches—talk of fishing strategies, Danny's half-hearted job hunting, local characters that Harper didn't know. Her father's Boston accent was a soothing lullaby, mingling with the soft patter of water lapping against the sides of the boat.

When she got too warm, she dove into the water to cool off.

"You're scaring the fish," Danny complained as she resurfaced.

"For the last three hours I haven't been scaring them," she called. "I can't see it makes much difference."

She swam over to the island and crawled out of the water and up the grassy slope to the highest point. She'd been here before. She'd dubbed this rock Mount Olympus years ago and had considered it her own personal promontory. The grass-covered island was no more than fifty feet across and about twice that distance away from a larger island. Sitting at its pinnacle, she looked out across the lake, seeing only one other boat in the distance. The breeze was light and warm today. The water shimmered under the summer sun. A day like this must have been the happiest of her childhood, she decided, a day when she could feel the sun on her bare skin and lose all sense of time. She lay on the grass, closing her eyes. The breeze on her wet suit chilled her slightly, but soon her skin grew warm again.

She used to imagine herself as Zeus, throwing down thunderbolts from this rock. The Greek myths had entertained her through a good many years of her childhood. She loved the stories, all those jealous gods and their meddlesome schemes. They were so much more captivating than the Bible stories she had been expected to know. Mary and Joseph were incredibly dull compared to Hera and Zeus. Harper's father had given her a huge book titled *The Greek Myths*, an exhaustive collection with richly colored drawings. Even now when she recalled one of the myths, she often saw in her mind the illustration from that book, like the tender, wan face of Narcissus looking lovingly up at himself from a watery reflection.

Athena was her favorite of the gods. She was the goddess of wisdom, the virgin warrior. The idea that Athena had no lovers had appealed to Harper when she was young. She had resolved at an early age herself to have no lovers because that was how she knew she could be an independent woman. In fact, she had spent many hours in fantasies in which she sat upon plush cushions in a flowing white robe, entertained by a eunuch with a golden lyre, greeting handsome suitors with the phrase, "I shall take no lover, despite your pretty face."

If she had been born in an earlier time, she might have had to stick to that resolution, Harper realized. She might have had to become a nun. She had been born at the height of the sexual revolution, however, and the women's liberation movement. She had inherited the right to be independent and to have lovers, as many as she liked, and none of them could subdue her wanderlust unless she wished it.

So far, she didn't wish it. Harper didn't think it was a coincidence that in myth and legend so many women of achievement were either virgins or extremely promiscuous,

55

taking lovers as it pleased them, to touch their bodies, but never their hearts.

Eliot, the one lover who had managed to carve out a long-term spot for himself in her life, was getting harder to deter, pressuring her with his continuing hints that they should "settle down" together. She didn't like it. *I shall have to turn him into a boar*, she mused, casting herself again in the role of Olympian. *He really is such a boor.*

Chapter 7

SUMMER, THIRTEEN YEARS AGO

Sister Josephina, wearing a gray skirt, white blouse and milky-colored stockings, was running the length of the soccer field, kicking a ball ahead of her toward the goal. The sight of her tall, lanky frame speeding down the field in that inappropriate costume was hilarious. The children, most of whom were half her height, were running after her and laughing hysterically at the same time.

Harper was supervising the unloading of a truck piled high with bags of cement mix and two-by-fours. From her vantage point at the side of the school building, she had a first-rate view of the soccer field. Across the dusty street, in front of a small house, four-year-old Mia sat on a stool while her mother cut her hair. Periodically, Mia would let out a horrible cry of pain, as if her mother were cutting off her ears.

Harper showed the truck driver and his helper where to stack the cement bags, then turned her attention back to the soccer game. Sister Jo gave the ball a powerful kick toward the goalie, then lost her balance and fell backwards, landing on her rear end. The kids gathered around and helped her to her feet. Harper, seeing that Sister Jo was laughing and apparently unharmed, burst into laughter herself.

Sister Jo came trotting over to Harper, leaving the children to carry on without her. She was out of breath and flushed. As usual, her whole face was smiling—ruddy cheeks, thick-lashed brown eyes and of course her mouth, which was stretched across the width of her face.

In the two months that Harper had been in La Serena, she had become dear friends with Sister Josephina, working at her side, infected with her sense of purpose. Sister Jo was originally from Arizona. An American-born child of Mexican immigrants, she left her family's home after high school and went directly into a religious order. She graduated from college while still in the U.S. and eventually took an assignment in Oaxaca. She had served there for almost twenty years, battling poverty and disease in the small villages along the western coast of southern Mexico. The Catholic church in La Serena, presided over by Father Gabriel, had been her home for over ten years. At the present, there were no other sisters there, but there had been others from time to time.

La Serena, a village of a few hundred people, had been nearly destroyed by a hurricane the previous fall. Harper had learned of this through her brother Danny, whose church had been collecting donations of blankets, clothes and other supplies to send to the affected area. When she had expressed an interest in helping, Danny had asked if she wanted to donate money.

"Is there something else I could do?" she had asked him. "Something more personal?"

"Well, we are sending teams down there to work, to rebuild. Would you want to do something like that? Really dig right into the muck?"

"I would love to do that," she said.

So she had called Eliot to persuade him to change their summer plans, a camping trip with his parents.

"What are you talking about, Harper?" he asked. "We're going camping."

"Yes, I know, but we can go camping any time. Come on, Eliot. It will be fun."

"Oh, I don't know. This sounds like one of those cockamamie ideas that—"

"Eliot, please. I really want to do this."

"Why, Harper? Why do you really want to do it?"

"Because it would be something useful. It would help people. All those people, they don't have homes or enough to eat or anything. So we give up a few weeks of our summer. It would be for such a good cause."

After a hesitation and a deep sigh, Eliot said, "Okay."

And so they had traveled to La Serena for a three-week tour of duty, during which they mixed cement in wheelbarrows and hammered together walls and roofs, helping to rebuild a community. The schoolhouse, beside which she now stood, had come up from nothing but a concrete slab during her stay here. She felt a particularly personal sense of accomplishment in this simple whitewashed building. It wasn't finished yet, but it would be, in just a few weeks. She imagined with satisfaction the day that they would ring the school bell for the first day of class and, after a disruption of almost a year, the village children would resume their educations.

"Oh, my!" Sister Jo said, stopping beside Harper. "I've had enough of that for one day."

"It's too hot to be out there running around," Harper said. "Especially in that outfit."

"I've got to admit that you do look a lot more comfortable."

Harper was wearing shorts and a T-shirt. She handed her water bottle to Sister Jo, who sucked it dry without a shred of decorum.

Little Mia let out another scream, whereupon Sister Jo glanced over and waved at her.

"I'm going to run over to the church to get some money for these guys," Harper said, nodding toward the truck driver. "Can you tell them I'll just be a minute?"

Sister Jo stepped over to the delivery truck and began speaking in Spanish to the driver while Harper ran across a dirt road to the small Catholic church that served as headquarters for pretty much everything in this village. She unlocked the cash drawer in the office and counted out the exact number of pesos on the bill of sale, then added a few extra for the driver and his helper.

After the rest of the volunteers had gone back home, she had begun to take on more of an administrative role here, helping Sister Jo and Father Gabriel run the construction projects, keep the books and distribute clothing and food to the villagers. She was also helping to stock and organize a small lending library, a project she had initiated.

Remembering Eliot's departure, Harper felt a momentary twinge of guilt. It hadn't been easy to explain to him why she was staying.

"I love it here," she had told him. "I feel so alive. There's so much to do."

"Well, I can't stay. My parents are having a big anniversary party. I have to be there."

"That's okay. You don't have to stay. I'll stay alone."

"Harper, are you sure? This is so impulsive. I don't understand what you're drawn to here."

As always, it was hard for her to put into words what she simply felt. But Eliot deserved some sort of explanation. "When I look at Sister Jo, I see a woman who embodies what I want out of life. She really inspires me. I want to be like her."

"You want to be a nun? Last I heard you didn't even want to be Catholic."

"No, no, you aren't even trying to understand."

Eliot never did understand. The following day he left with the others to return to the U.S. Two weeks later, he posted a package to her with clothes, some CDs and a few photos he had collected from her house as she had requested.

After paying the deliverymen, Harper and Sister Jo walked together back to the church.

"You know you're filthy," Harper said, following the dusty skirt through the church door.

"Nothing a little soap and water won't take care of." Passing a stack of cardboard boxes, Sister Jo said, "So, what's this, then?"

"More books. I got them from a library in Los Angeles. They just arrived."

"Wonderful." Sister Jo turned to Harper and took hold of her hand, squeezing it. "You're a godsend. So much energy. Such a help."

Harper held tightly to Sister Jo's hand as they continued through the hallway to the back of the church where the living quarters were located. They parted when Sister Jo went to her room to clean up and Harper went to the kitchen to heat up a pot of beans. She put two bowls on the little wooden table, along with a stack of tortillas.

As she added a cup of water to the pot, the church pet, a gorgeous green parrot named Sailor, sat on his perch in a cage with an open door, muttering to himself. Named for his penchant for cursing, Sailor had a vocabulary that was meager but colorful. By most people's standards, his curses would be considered mild, but since he was the church pet, they were startling, if not downright shocking. Sister Jo had told Harper that nobody knew how Sailor learned his curse words. Harper was fairly sure that Josephina herself was teaching him. She thought Father Gabriel probably knew that too.

Harper stirred the beans, which they had been eating for three days now. The food wasn't usually very interesting, but she had no complaints. They were eating the same thing that most of the villagers ate. They supplemented their beans and rice diet with canned goods from the donations that came in from the U.S. and the Red Cross. There were a few fresh vegetables as well from the small garden in the churchyard that Sister Jo planted and tended each year. There wasn't much left of that, though. The summer heat was too much for all but the hardiest crops.

Sister Jo was an incredibly creative cook herself. When she spent the day in the kitchen, you knew there would be a feast. That usually happened on Sundays after Mass when they had a big meal in front of the church and Jo's kitchen produced fish and chicken and tomatoes and green beans. People brought dishes to share at this huge party each week. Harper loved it.

Though she had removed herself from the practice of Catholicism after she went away to college, she had started going to Mass here in La Serena after Eliot had gone home. It wasn't that her faith had been reignited. It was more a case of sharing the culture, traditions and daily life of the locals. She wanted to immerse herself in the authentic life of the village.

It had also made Sister Josephina happy to see her in church on Sunday mornings, and she was finding herself going out of her way to do whatever she could to make Sister Jo happy. That wasn't hard to do. Sister Jo was a joyful woman, full of love and goodwill. She was the embodiment of what Harper thought a woman of God should be. She lived every day of her life with a passionate zeal for doing good. Sister Jo was a woman in complete harmony with her life.

Harper was ladling beans into the bowls when Sister Jo entered the kitchen looking fresh and cheerful. She was wearing a pair of khaki pants and a blouse, looking much more comfortable than she had earlier. A simple silver cross hung from a chain around her neck. Her short, dark brown hair was damp from her shower.

"Buenas noches, Sailor," she said to the bird in a loud, cheerful voice.

"Stuff it, Sister," Sailor responded.

Sister Jo scrunched up her shoulders and grinned with delight, then turned to Harper and said, "So what did you cook for us tonight?" She peered into her bowl, then up at Harper and wrinkled her nose in a comical fashion.

"Poop!" Sailor interjected.

"Don't worry," Harper said. "This is the end of this pot. Tomorrow we'll have the empanadas that Yolanda made for us."

Sister Jo sat at the table. "Good. Let's make sure we finish these tonight, then."

Harper bowed her head as Sister Jo said a prayer of thanks for the meal. Despite her rejection of Catholicism, there was something oddly comforting about starting a meal with a nun saying a prayer. She had always liked the rituals that surrounded this religion—kneeling in prayer, taking the sacrament, making the sign of the cross. Out here in the Mexican countryside, they were far removed from the framework of the Church, far removed from the ideological controversies and the politics. She liked that too. This really did seem like God's work, helping the poor with the simple necessities of life—food, shelter and clean water. They were too busy with the fundamentals of living here to be worried about the Pope's official position on the use of condoms or what duties were appropriate for women in the Church. That may have been the reason that Sister Josephina liked being here so much. She didn't seem particularly bound by rules in general and her attitudes were refreshingly open-minded.

Harper hadn't seen it herself, but she had heard tell of Sister Josephina taking a glass of mescal now and then. And she danced when she felt like it, at festivals, in a peculiar manner that reminded Harper of a Scottish reel. She had seen that herself the night they had the going-away party for the rest of the American relief team. It was very funny, but Sister Jo didn't mind being laughed at. She didn't care why they were laughing, she said. She just liked the sound of laughter.

"Where's our padre?" Sister Jo asked as she took up her spoon.

"La Crucecita. He'll be back Saturday."

"I'll bet you're really looking forward to some fancy California food about now," Sister Jo said, sopping up bean juice with a tortilla. "Maybe a nice thick sirloin steak, huh?"

"Salad is more like what I'm missing about now."

"Oh, right. Well, it won't be long, will it? Summer's almost over. I'll be sorry to see you go. You've been such a help. And so easy to get along with too. If all of the American volunteers were as undemanding...well, I shouldn't complain. They do help. But they complain too, about the dirt, about the heat, about the plumbing. Not all of them, of course. But, you, I don't think I've heard a single complaint out of you since you arrived."

"I like living like the locals. Eat what the locals eat. I've never been a picky eater anyway."

"I'll say so! The night you ate those chapulines, I thought to myself, oh, Lord, this girl is a spunky one! Or else she's really hungry."

"Lord!" Sailor squawked, "Jesus, Mary and Joseph!"

Sister Jo cast a furtive glance at Sailor, suppressing a grin. The roasted grasshoppers, the chapulines, were a local delicacy, but one which few of the volunteers would try.

"If you were eating them," Harper said, "I figured I could. After all, you're an American raised on mac 'n' cheese too."

Sister Jo nodded appreciatively. "True. It's been a long time, though, for me."

She stood, picking up Harper's empty bowl and nesting it under her own. Before taking them away, she put one arm around Harper and squeezed her tight. "You're a treasure," she said, then put the bowls in the sink.

After the other volunteers left, Harper had moved into the church. She had been given a small room across the hall from Sister Jo's. Her host family, after all, had not signed on for more than three weeks. They might have been agreeable to an extension, but Sister Jo had been so enthusiastic about this new arrangement that Harper hadn't even asked. Since most of her duties were centered around the church, the move made sense. It seemed to suit everyone.

There was no television here. There was a radio, but it only got Spanish-speaking stations, so Harper's options for evening entertainment were either music on her CD player or reading, and both of those suited her just fine. It hadn't taken long for the two of them to develop some evening routines. With all of the books coming in for the library, they were well stocked with reading material, so they read to one another. They usually spent the evenings outside on a narrow balcony to escape the stuffy heat of the building. This is where Sister Jo revealed her penchant for a good cigar. Harper had never smoked cigars before and couldn't say she relished it as much as Sister Jo did, but the practice of sitting side-by-side amid a fragrant haze had become a ritual she treasured.

Harper's room at the church was small and spare, but she felt that she had everything she needed. She could live like this for much longer than a summer, she thought, and be perfectly happy. As the days flowed on, she felt that more and more strongly.

When her time was almost up, inflamed with a new sense of purpose, she asked Father Gabriel for a chat. He met her in the church office where they sat on either side of an old wooden desk.

"What can I do for you, Harper?" he asked, cupping one hand within the other on top of the desk.

"Father," she began, "I've really enjoyed my time here."

"We've enjoyed having you. I've especially enjoyed your piano playing. I know that old piano isn't what you're used to, but believe me, it sounds so much better than when Sister Josephina plays it. She tries, poor dear, but, oh, well, it's been good enough for us all these years, so it will serve very well for many more after this." He smiled benignly. "Sorry, what is it you wanted to tell me?"

"I've given this a lot of thought, Father. I think I'd like to stay, permanently. I think this is what I'm meant to do."

He gazed at her for a moment, tapping one finger on the desktop. "Hmmm. Stay and do what?"

"I could teach at the school. I can teach English or music or both. I'm sure I could learn to speak Spanish in no time if I applied myself."

He smiled thinly. "I've no doubt you could. But this is such a big step. You have a life in California, a job, friends. Why do you want to stay, Harper?"

"I like the people. I like the way they live and how happy and friendly they are. They live barely above subsistence level, but they're so joyful. And, of course, I like the feeling of doing something useful, something where the reward of your efforts is so immediately apparent."

Father Gabriel scratched his head through thinning white hair. "Well, I don't know. The problem is that this is a tiny village. The school isn't going to be able to support much of a staff, not enough to have specialized teachers like you're suggesting. Sister Josephina is pretty much it."

"Well, I don't have to teach then. I can do anything. There must be something I can do. I wouldn't need to make much money. Just enough to live on."

"There's a school near Linares that is much larger. Maybe you could teach there. I think you would be a tremendous asset to them. I know the priest there. I can speak to him about it. I would be willing to recommend you to him."

"Linares? But that's hundreds of miles from here."

"Yes, but the people there are just as they are here. I'm sure you would be able to be just as useful there."

Harper shifted in her chair, trying to think how to explain to Father Gabriel that she wanted to stay where she was.

"Is there something else that holds you here?" he asked.

"Well, to be honest, Sister Josephina and I have become very good friends. I like working with her. I think we make a great team. She said so herself."

He nodded sympathetically, then stood and looked out the window for a moment. When he turned back to face her, his expression was serious. "Sister Josephina is very fond of you too. Anyone can see that. And that's why I think it's time for you to go home."

Confused, Harper said, "What? I don't understand."

Father Gabriel sighed. "Harper, I've known Sister Josephina for a long time. She came here as a young girl, younger than you are now. I didn't want to tell you this, but I think it's best that you understand what kind of problem your presence causes us."

"Problem?"

"Yes. Sister Josephina was sent away from her community

in the United States to separate her from one of the novices, a young woman she had become...attached to. That was her choice. I'm sure she would say that she made the right choice. Do you understand what I'm saying?"

Harper stared, grasping his meaning. "But, Father, it isn't like that. We're just friends. There's been nothing—"

He waved a hand in her direction. "No, no, I'm not suggesting that anything has happened between you. It's what *could* happen that I'm concerned about. Sister Jo has a good life here and I think she's been happy. But it's a lonely life sometimes. Like I said, I've known her for a long time. I've seen how attached she's become to you and it frightens me. If you stay here, I believe she could lose her battle with her personal demons. I want you to consider that, how destructive your presence could be."

Harper sat silently watching Father Gabriel's humorless eyes and thinking about the joy she always saw on Sister Jo's face, a joy she had assumed was present for everyone.

"I had no idea," she said quietly.

"I can't make you go, but I hope you will. The sooner, the better."

Harper returned to her work with a heavy heart. She had thought she'd found something she could build a life around. Or maybe what she'd found was someone, after all. If Sister Josephina were removed from this picture, she had to wonder, would she still want to be here? Since, as she'd told Father Gabriel, she didn't want to work in Linares, the answer to that was apparently no.

When summer concluded, she took her leave of Oaxaca with a warm hug of gratitude from Father Gabriel and several tearful kisses from Sister Josephina. They vowed to one another that they would keep in touch. Seeing the tears streaming down Sister Jo's face as her ride rolled away from the village square, Harper hoped that she had not stayed too long after all. She watched Sister Jo growing smaller as the distance between them grew wider, until she could no longer see her at all.

Chapter 8

JUNE 17

Since Roxie wanted to go to the Renaissance Faire as usual, Harper called Joyce, the third member of their trio, to arrange a meeting to plan their program.

"This Saturday, then, my house," Harper told her. "Bring your tambourine."

She had become friends with Joyce at the university, where Joyce worked in administration and frequented the library in search of novels to fill in the gaps between the paperback romances she routinely devoured. She didn't play an instrument, but she sang beautifully.

"How's Roxie doing?" Joyce asked.

"Okay, I think. I worry about the boys, though. They're so young to lose their father."

"Yes, it's still such a shock."

"Well, this outing should cheer her up," Harper said. "It's always so much fun."

"I'll see you Saturday, then."

As soon as Harper hung up, her phone rang. It was her mother.

"Hi, Mom. How are you?"

"We're having a family crisis here."

"Oh? What's up?"

"Sarah has run away from home."

"Oh, no! When?"

"Yesterday." Harper listened as her mother recounted the events of the last twenty-four hours, during which Sarah and her parents had fought about her latest transgression, a nose piercing. Sarah had filled her backpack with clothes and stormed out. They'd checked the places they knew to check. They'd asked her friends for help. And now they had called in the police.

Listening to these details, Harper had trouble relating them to her niece who was, in her mind, a smart, innocent little girl with fanciful dreams and a powerful thirst for knowledge. Two years ago when Sarah was fourteen, Harper had promised her a visit to California, a prospect that had thrilled the girl, whipping her into a frenzy of fantasy. The visit had never actually come to pass. Sarah had reminded Harper a couple of times, and Harper had intended to follow through, but she hadn't. She felt a little guilty about that.

"I just pray that she's safe," Alice said, "and hasn't been picked up by some lunatic."

"Don't worry, Mom," Harper said. "She'll be fine. She'll come back in a couple of days. She's got a hideout, probably. Some friend is hiding her."

"I hope so," Alice replied, then laughed. "Remember the day you ran away, Harper? You got as far as the doghouse. You moved in with the dog."

"Yes, I remember," Harper said, recalling an afternoon spent cramped inside the wooden doghouse waiting for someone to notice that she'd disappeared, her dog Corky lying in front of the doorway because there was only room inside for one of them. After three hours, she'd given up and wandered back into the house, demanding to know why nobody had noticed her absence. She could have been murdered, hacked to pieces and buried already.

"But you were a lot younger than Sarah," Alice said, serious again. "Running away at her age isn't a joke."

Although Harper was worried too, she didn't want to amplify her mother's fears, so she said, simply, "Call me when she turns up."

After saying goodbye to her mother, Harper called Wilona to discuss their plans for next week's trip.

"I finally managed to get a message to Carmen Silva," Harper said, "telling her that we'd be there on Tuesday. She has no telephone. I get the impression that she lives very simply."

"This is where again?" Wilona asked.

"Somewhere up by Downieville, fairly remote. It's about a hundred miles from your place."

"So two hours to get there. I'll pack us some snacks. When can I expect you?"

"Monday around four or five."

The last time Harper had seen Wilona was nearly two years ago, over Christmas break, when she had filmed her for her third documentary. The one they were about to film of Carmen Silva would be the fifth, but it was the first one for which Harper would have a professional photographer. Six was the right number to build a series around, she thought. She had earlier considered doing nine because of her private idea that these artists were her muses, but six would be better. At Chelsea's suggestion, Harper had her eye out for a musician to round out the sextet. She could already imagine how the series would start, with square portrait-like stills of the artists tumbling across the screen in apparently random order while some lively music played, something like a Chopin violin concerto.

As she made her calls, her eyes returned often to the yellow sticky note beside the phone, the one on which she'd written

Chelsea's number six days ago. Since then, she had hovered near it on several occasions, trying to decide what to do.

It was hard not to want to see Chelsea, even if it hurt. The last time they'd talked, last summer, Chelsea had told her that they couldn't see one another again. *What happened to change her mind?* Harper wondered. Then she recalled the stranger who had occupied Chelsea's seat at the symphony.

If Chelsea and Mary had broken up again, if Chelsea wanted to resume their romance, if Harper could consent, how long would they have before Mary called Chelsea back? And how could Harper bear to lose her a second time? Chelsea hadn't even debated it two years ago. It was a foregone conclusion—if Mary wanted her back, she would go.

Another summer in Chelsea's arms could be worth a great deal, if Harper's heart could take it. But she had resolved to move on. And so she had orbited around that yellow note for a week, pondering it but doing nothing. Today, again, she turned away from it and moved on.

Sorting through the mail, Harper was happy to see a letter from her old friend Sister Josephina from Oaxaca. She and Sister Jo had corresponded sporadically, about twice a year, for the last thirteen years. She settled into her living room chair to read. The letter was long and satisfying, bringing to life the daily world of the small village and its inhabitants. Sister Jo described the activities of the school in fine detail, knowing how interested Harper was in it. She reported too on locals that Harper had met and would remember, like Jose Mendez, the crazy pig farmer, and Dr. Cuevas, and of course, Father Gabriel. She turned the final page over as Sister Jo continued the news of Father Gabriel.

He's not been feeling too well. I don't think he will ever retire, but the good Lord is going to take him anyway one of these days. He has a bit of the shaking palsy. It's not called that now, I know, but that's all I can think of. I have to say that my own brain isn't as reliable as it once was. But that doesn't slow me down much. I'm still doing the same as always. Lots of work just to keep up the church and the garden, but I have no complaints. I get along okay. I got a new box of really fine cigars from Colombia the other day and so of course I smoked one right away on the eastern balcony just like we did when you were here. So, you see, things haven't changed that much for us. You would still recognize the place, that's for sure!

Poor Sailor has finally given up the ghost. The last thing that old bird said was "Jesus, Mary and Joseph!" And then he was gone. Never be another one like him. It's a lot quieter without him around.

We received the books and music you sent. Much appreciated, as always. If you are moved to do the same again in the future, I have a couple of requests for Dean Martin. Okay, I admit it. That's for me. When I was a child, my mother used to play Dean Martin records hour after hour. For several years after I left home, I couldn't stand the sound of him, but things have a way of getting under your skin and into your heart. It's a small, forgivable indulgence, don't you think? God bless you, Harper, you've been a good friend to us all these years. I hope you'll come visit us again some day. I know this is no resort, but you seemed to like it here.

Love and peace to you always,
Sister Jo

Harper folded the pages back into the envelope and smiled, picturing Sister Josephina with her feet propped up on the railing of the balcony, blowing cigar smoke into the still evening air. She should go back to visit some day. It would be nice to see the place back on its feet.

For the rest of the day, she worked at the tedium of life—balancing her checkbook, tossing junk mail, making, eating and cleaning up after dinner, taking out the trash—all with a persistent unease. The calendar on the pantry wall revealed a rush of appointments for the end of June. A full calendar. A full life?

She noted the fortune cookie fortune she had taped on June 29. "Do not shut the door to your heart when true love comes knocking." The only person knocking on her heart right now was Chelsea. She dialed her voice mail and listened to the week-old message again. Chelsea sounded unsure of herself, unsure of how Harper would respond to her request. Understandable.

Her voice brought to mind her face. Her face brought to mind her mouth. Harper felt herself caving in.

Chapter 9

SUMMER, SIXTEEN YEARS AGO

Harper's twenty-third birthday party was shared with Neil's baby daughter Sarah, who was turning one. The party was held on the day between the two official birth dates. Harper spent her actual birthday fishing with her father, just the two of them, a peaceful, satisfying day. The next day, Neil and family descended on the household, bringing ice cream, toys and laughter into it. Sarah was a darling, happy child who, understandably, stole the day, her big shining eyes moving rapidly from cake to grandparents to the presents that they lavished on her.

Harper was content because she had secured the approval of her father by successfully completing her master's degree. That's the milestone she was celebrating.

"Excellent work," he told her. "We never had any doubt, of course. Any idea where you go from here, then?"

"Yes," she told him. "I've got a job at Morrison University, starting in September. It's a small liberal arts college."

"In California?"

"Yes. Not far from where I am now. It's a good job. Full-time position in the university library."

He nodded approvingly and squeezed her tight. "That's my girl. Although we thought you might come back here after college. You know we'd love to have you back. I could put a word in for you. I don't see why you couldn't get on here."

"Morrison is a good school," she said.

He looked at her for a moment, smiling calmly. "Well, then, congratulations," he said. "I'm proud of you, Harper, I hope you know that. Doing it all on your own like you did, that's impressive. It wasn't necessary, but it is impressive."

This sentiment was more important to Harper than practically anything else she could have wished for. The pressure was finally off. She might not have garnered the accolades of her older brother, but she had done okay, good enough. And now it was finished. She was done with studying and ready to get on with her life, with her real life. To travel and have adventures. To make herself into a colorful, enigmatic character, someone who might surprise you at any moment with her derring-do. To lead a life so full of interesting activities that she would never be bored, nor would anyone around her. She wasn't sure, however, how to obtain that kind of life.

It was for that reason that Harper borrowed her mother's car the day after the birthday celebration and took off for Connecticut and a scheduled appointment with Hilda Perry. The postcard she'd received a month ago was on the seat next to her, its contents memorized.

"I'll be happy to meet with you, Harper," Hilda had written. "We can have tea."

The invitation was the result of a long, flattering letter to Hilda and a follow-up phone call which, Harper assumed, was to find out if she was a lunatic or just a harmless admirer. On the passenger seat beside her sat a canvas bag stuffed with books that she hoped to have autographed.

For the last twenty years, Hilda Perry had lived in a small cottage on the Atlantic Coast, giving almost no interviews and producing no new material. She was eighty-one now, a celebrated author who could afford to rest on her laurels.

Harper found the cottage without difficulty and parked in front of it. As she stepped out of the car and shouldered her bag of books, she felt that she was touching down on hallowed ground. Hilda Perry was legendary. Harper had read every one of her books, as well as several biographies. The woman's life was as entertaining and inspirational as her writing, a splendid example of how to live like an artist, creatively and passionately.

She rang the bell, noticing a faint smell of the sea. The ocean was out of sight, still a couple of miles away. When the door opened, she recognized, from decades-old photos in the books, the features of a younger Hilda Perry in the tiny, stooped old woman standing there. Her hair was pure white, wispy and boldly disarrayed. Blue veins displayed themselves in the pale, thin skin of her arms and temples. She narrowed her eyes, peering intently at her visitor.

"Hello," Harper said, holding out her hand. "I'm Harper Sheridan."

"Come in," Hilda said, taking her hand briefly. Her skin was dry and papery. "I've made us tea and scones. I thought you'd like that."

Harper pulled the door shut behind her and followed, noticing how the delicate pink of the old woman's scalp showed through the sparse field of her hair. The cottage was dark, musty and extremely cluttered with books, magazines and newspapers, stacks of them in and around bookcases that had long ago reached their capacity and, judging by the dust, hadn't been touched in decades. *She could donate these books to some library*, Harper thought, realizing almost immediately that they weren't really there for reading. They were companions, reminders of journeys of the mind and perhaps, in some cases, journeys of the body as well.

Books were like that to people who really love them, she thought. A book that you read once becomes a part of you. The physical entity on the shelf becomes a symbol of how it has lived in your mind, given itself to you and merged with your story like an ex-lover, as part of your experience for the rest of your life. The book may go on to have other adventures, to caress the imaginations of other readers, but what it means to you remains yours alone.

Harper sidled past a stack of books capped by a hardcover edition of *Canterbury Tales*. It was much better, she decided, for an old woman to surround herself with beloved books than with cats.

Hilda's laboring gait took them through the main room, through the kitchen and into a small, sunny nook with two overstuffed chairs and a coffee table. It occurred to Harper that Hilda probably lived mainly here and in the kitchen, that the dark, cluttered main rooms of her house had become nothing more than storerooms.

"Let's sit in here," Hilda suggested. She poured the tea and offered Harper milk and sugar and then a blueberry scone.

"So," said Hilda, letting herself drop into her chair, "tell me why you've come."

"Well, as I told you, I'm a big fan of yours. I just wanted to meet you in person. Your books have been so inspirational to me."

"Really? In what way?"

Harper didn't know how to answer that. She hesitated. "Just as the voice of wisdom, you know? The things you say, they're just so true. There's a revelation on every page."

"Oh, my dear!" Hilda laughed. "What an exaggeration."

"No, really, that's how it feels for me. I'm sure others have told you that."

"Yes, I suppose. Other young women like you. Nobody comes around much anymore, though. My life here has gotten narrower and narrower."

"You don't write anymore?"

"I've tried to write but can't really. Between the bad eyesight and the deteriorating mental state, it's about all I can do to sign an autograph now and then. No creativity left up there." She thumped her head with her forefinger. "Do you write, then?"

"No, I'm not a writer. I'm more of a musician."

"That's unusual. Most of the young women who come calling like you are writers or would-be writers. They're looking for the magic words or something, as if I can bestow creative imagination on them with a touch, like knighthood. What is it you're expecting to get then, from this visit?"

Again, Harper balked. "I just wanted to meet you. You've given me so much pleasure with your work. I don't expect to get anything, particularly."

It was hard to imagine this squinting old woman as the Hilda Perry of Harper's imagination, the eccentric who traveled the world with a colorful entourage of fascinating characters, who took and cast off lovers of both sexes with alarming frequency, many of them renowned artists like herself. Her love affair with the poet Catherine Gardiner, at least as reported by biographers, had been nearly epic in its ferocity.

The legendary Hilda Perry was a rollicking spirit. Harper had been enthralled with her ever since reading an article about her several years earlier. The list of her lovers, or her alleged lovers, had captivated Harper's imagination. Since then, she had thought of Hilda Perry as the model of the free spirit, as a woman leading the kind of life that Harper herself would have liked to lead—rich, full and devil-may-care.

"You've lived such a fascinating life," Harper said. "So exciting."

"Do you think so?" Hilda asked, sipping her tea. "And, yet, here I am—old, alone, sick and forgotten."

"Hardly forgotten," Harper objected.

"You know, these days, I am just as likely to hear someone say, 'I thought you were dead,' as anything else." Hilda refilled Harper's teacup. "Since you don't write, I guess you aren't looking for advice on how to become a published author. And you aren't going to toss me a manuscript to read, thank God! So you're just a very enthusiastic admirer of writers?"

"Not just writers. All artists."

"I see. You're an art groupie." Hilda smiled thinly.

Harper recognized that she was being mocked, but she didn't think it was malicious.

"Art has become my religion," she replied. "The relationship between the artist and her art is where I think you can find the best lesson for how to live a meaningful life."

"Ah, well, better than being a Baptist, I guess."

"I was raised Catholic."

"So was I." Hilda raised her cup in a salute. "My condolences."

Amused, Harper said, "Thanks."

"I'm not sure I'm following you, though. How can an artist teach you to live a meaningful life?"

"I think artists are the only people living authentic lives," Harper said sincerely. "I think art is the only way you can be in touch with your true self. There are truths that can only be experienced through stories, images or music. All of the other ways we interact with one another, like conversation or work or even sex, are imperfect and inevitably removed from the reality of our souls."

"What do you mean by 'soul,' exactly?" Hilda asked.

Harper smiled. "Of course you wouldn't let that go without a challenge. I used the wrong word. I should have said 'mind' or 'self.' 'Soul' is an artifact left over from my days of religious brainwashing."

"No, no," Hilda said, putting down her cup. "It was the word you chose without overthinking it, so, following your own train of thought, it's the right word, isn't it?"

"Oh, sure, I see your point. Well, then, the soul that I'm referring to would be the part of you that is you and not someone else. It's the part of you that is so difficult to show someone else, for all sorts of reasons, but primarily because it's unique, so no one else can really experience it. They don't know how to look at it. They usually see you in the context of their own reality, how they see the world, and that distorts you to fit the expected

79

model." Harper stopped to take a breath. Hilda waited patiently, so she continued. "So art allows a person to strip away conscious thought and create something that expresses that authentic identity. Does any of this make sense? Am I rambling?"

"You are sort of rambling, but I think I understand. So that's what you think I'm doing when I write, expressing my authentic self, revealing my soul, so to speak?"

Harper nodded.

Hilda raised one eyebrow. "The irony is that 'art' is the same word as 'artifice,' and that's what poetry and prose and painting and music are. One of the definitions of art, in fact, is 'that which is not nature,' something not found in the natural world. Works of art are inventions, and so one has to question whether they can ever possibly express this authentic self that you're talking about."

Harper sighed admiringly. "Then what am I trying to say?"

"I can't tell you that! But I think the non-verbal arts, like fine art and music, are better at expressing actual emotion than the written or spoken word, so in that sense, I agree. As a musician, you must know that music is a more natural expression of feeling than speaking. It doesn't get filtered through language, which is inherently flawed, being an arbitrary system of symbols. I love words. I love the English language, don't get me wrong, but it's a dimension removed from actual thought. It's unnatural. Even a master at stream of consciousness like James Joyce can't do more than hint at what our minds are doing. There is no way to create a sentence that properly displays the process of thinking, feeling and remembering several things at once."

"Music can't do that either," Harper observed.

"No, it can't. And it doesn't try to. Art, any type of art, creates order out of a naturally chaotic reality. That's the point of art, isn't it? It doesn't show you the ugly, twisted, complicated stuff as it really is. It tames it into something else, something we can look at dead-on without horror." Hilda paused and smiled, a benign expression that seemed out of place in her emphatic speech.

"For my money, though," she continued, "the only way to

reveal yourself honestly to another person is to be unconditionally in love." Hilda studied her for a moment, then asked, "Have you ever been in love, Harper?"

Harper thought briefly of Eliot, dismissed that thought and shook her head.

"Too bad. Someday, when you are, you won't need any art or artifice to share your soul with another person. I spent my life falling in and out of love. All of those books there in your bag aren't my attempt to share my authentic self with the rest of the world. They're my inability to keep all of the rantings, ravings and exultations of my heart to myself."

Harper would have liked to write that down, but it seemed rude to actually do so. She hoped she could commit it to memory.

"Haven't you ever noticed," Hilda said, her voice low but clear, "that a poet writes her first poem when she falls in love for the first time? It doesn't have to be with another person. It can be with a puppy or life or a flower. But it's love, that overwhelming joy or pain that can't be contained. It requires expression. It bubbles over like a boiling pot, and then you have art. Art, in its purest form, doesn't give a damn if there's anyone out there looking or listening. If it were alone in the universe, it would still express itself just the same, howling into the dark cold emptiness of space."

Harper, awestruck, said nothing.

"Yes, it's all about love," Hilda said in summation.

Wow, Harper thought. *Is she right*, is *it all about love?* She herself had no prospects for falling in love. Eliot had moved to Washington where he'd gotten a teaching job, leaving her more or less free to find other romantic interests. They had vowed to continue their relationship from a distance, getting together when they could, but she didn't really think that would happen. Nothing serious had come of it, but when Eliot found out she was seeing other men, he had become furious. "I'm not going to wait here chastely for you like Penelope," she had responded. "I'm not your wife." With no real choice in the matter, Eliot had agreed to her terms, and they had embarked on what Harper described as "a free and open liaison," a situation that delighted her.

So she had loved, but she really had never been in love, not in the way that the poets described it. She was definitely open to it, though. She turned back to Hilda with an expression that she hoped would convey her appreciation of the older woman's insights.

"Are you straight or gay?" Hilda asked her.

Harper was taken off guard.

"Most of the young women who seek me out are lesbians," Hilda explained. "I just wondered."

Harper, completely recovered, said, "'As long as they know how to use it, it doesn't matter much to me what they come equipped with.'"

Hilda laughed loudly, an open-mouthed chortle that filled her face with delight and gave Harper a glimpse of the woman she had expected to find here. "You know, I never actually said that. The biographer made that up!"

Harper grinned, pleased with herself for remembering the quote and entertaining her host.

"But I might have said it," Hilda quipped, "if I had thought of it."

Hilda sipped her tea. A small, wry smile played across her face before she turned her attention back to Harper and the present. "That biographer was tenacious. She was young and full of ambition. She chased me around the world that summer. What was her name?"

"Lillian Fields."

"Ah, yes, Lillian. Oh, she was so obnoxious! That was the summer Catherine and I were on our trip to Egypt."

"Catherine Gardiner?"

"Yes. You know her, do you? She lives out there somewhere near you, near San Francisco."

"I know of her, of course. I've never met her."

"Catherine is one of the few people who still writes old-fashioned letters on lovely stationery. Every couple of months,

I get such a letter from her. Which is something, you know, because she's still a young woman and has adapted to computers and e-mail and who the hell knows what else. She writes a beautiful letter. I keep them all. I think Catherine is well aware that some day some biographer will publish them in a book. She writes them as carefully as she does her poems, I've no doubt. The language of a poet is so self-conscious. Well, that's what we were just talking about, wasn't it?"

Harper nodded enthusiastically as Hilda let out a short laugh and her face lit up.

"Can you imagine if they'd had computers a hundred years earlier and we had stories like 'The Purloined E-mail' and the collected e-mails of Edna St. Vincent Millay, complete with smiley faces?"

Harper laughed too. "No, I can't imagine."

"It was Lillian, you know, who broke us up, right there in the desert at the foot of the pyramids."

"Really?"

"Oh, yes. That time anyway. We broke up so many times. It wasn't on purpose. Just circumstances. Let me tell you this story. It's a good one."

The two women chatted about Hilda's books and her adventures until, it seemed, Hilda had worn herself out. In the end, Harper felt that Hilda had enjoyed her visit. She couldn't have been happier with it herself. She had been granted an audience with a true sage.

Eventually, Hilda smiled tiredly at her and said, "So, let me sign your books, and then you can be on your way."

With an unsteady hand, Hilda wrote in blue ink on the flyleaf of the Lillian Fields biography. "To Harper. May you find the song your soul wants to sing."

Chapter 10

JUNE 19

"O my love is like a red, red rose," Harper sang, accompanying herself on the piano, "that's newly sprung in June; O my love is like the melody that's sweetly played in tune. As fair art thou, my bonny lass, so deep in love am I; and I will love thee still, my dear, till all the seas gang dry."

"That's a lovely song," Joyce remarked.

"Harper," Roxie complained, tucking her long legs under herself, "isn't that supposed to be a love song? You played it so slowly and mournfully, it sounded like a dirge!"

"It's supposed to sound like bagpipes. They're always sort of mournful. You know, castle wall in the Highland mist and all that."

"Maybe, but we're not playing a funeral. This is supposed to be fun. Where's the humor? Where are the drinking songs, for God's sake?"

"All right, all right," Harper said. "How about this one? 'It's all for me grog,'" she began. Joyce and Roxie joined in right away. The song was a favorite they'd used before.

"Oh," they sang, swaying side to side, Roxie holding up her wineglass, "it's all for me grog, me jolly, jolly grog. It's all for me beer and tobacco. For I spent all me tin with the lassies drinking gin. Far across the western ocean I must wander."

"Yes!" Roxie said. "We'll do that one for sure."

"Let's do a round," Harper said. "We already know 'Heigh ho, nobody home.' How about that?"

"Heigh-ho, nobody home," sang Roxie. Harper and Joyce came in one and two lines later with "meat, nor drink, nor money have I none" and "Still I will be merry," stretching "merry" out for several notes.

They managed to sing the round about six times before losing their rhythm. Roxie poured herself another glass of chardonnay. She seemed to be enjoying herself. Harper was glad to see that. Perhaps the worst period of mourning her husband was over, although she had never actually observed Roxie mourning, other than at the funeral. There, her tears had been silent but continuous. Her sons, smartly dressed in suits, had been seated on either side of her, appropriately somber, clutching her hands. Later, at their house, Roxie had seemed solemn but not distraught. In every conversation they had had since that day, the only sorrow she had voiced was over her sons having lost their father. She expressed no self-pity, and Harper admired that.

"Do you really think we should do that one?" Joyce asked, sliding to the edge of the couch to reach for a cracker and a slice of cheese.

"I had my heart set on a round," Harper said.

"Are there any others?" Roxie asked.

"Row, row, row your boat," Joyce suggested.

"That's really not appropriate," Roxie said. "We need something from the period."

"Well, there's this one," Harper said, paging through her book of old English folk songs. "'Why doth not my goose.'"

85

"Oh, I don't know that one," Joyce said, clearly intrigued. "Let's try it."

"'Why doth not my goose,'" Harper read, "'sing as well as thy goose when I paid for my goose twice as much as thine?' That's four lines. I'll go first, then Joyce, then Roxie will come in on the third line. Ready?"

They tried it, going around about three times before Joyce burst into laughter and rolled back on the sofa. Roxie started snickering too, breaking off in the middle of her line.

"Why doth not my goose," Harper finished by herself, "sing as well as thy goose when I paid for my goose twice as much as thine?"

"Because thy goose is cooked!" announced Roxie, sending Joyce into convulsions of laughter.

"What the hell is a goose doing singing anyway?" Roxie asked, and Joyce started snorting, doubled up and unable to breathe.

"So, I guess you don't like this one?" Harper asked.

"Au contraire!" Roxie said. "I love it. I want to do it. What about you, Joyce?"

Joyce sat up, holding her stomach, tears on her cheeks. "Me too. Let's do it."

"Okay, then," Harper said. "I think that makes four songs. Probably enough. So we have our program."

"Before we call it a night," Roxie said, "play us something with a little more heft. I love to hear you play, Harper. It always sounds so effortless. It's like music is your native tongue."

"Thank you," Harper said. "Okay, then, some serious music it is. Here's one I've just learned recently."

Harper played as Roxie sat back in her chair with her eyes closed. Joyce sat at attention, watching Harper's hands on the keyboard. The piece was short and over in a few minutes. Harper put the cover over the keys and pushed herself back from the piano.

"God, Harper," Roxie said, opening her eyes, "you practically gave me an orgasm."

Harper laughed. "You're a woman who knows how to

appreciate music." She stood and slid the bench into its nook.

"That was nice, Harper," Joyce said. "What was it?"

Harper looked inquiringly at Roxie.

"I don't think I know that piece," Roxie said. "It sounds like one of Felix Mendelssohn's *Songs Without Words*. But there are so many of those, I don't know them all."

"Very good," Harper said. "You're close. It *was* Mendelssohn and it was one of the *Songs Without Words*. But it was not Felix."

"What?" Joyce asked. "Is this a riddle?"

"Fanny Mendelssohn!" Roxie blurted.

"Fanny Mendelssohn!" Joyce exclaimed, before slumping and saying, "Never heard of her."

"Exactly," Harper said. "Not many people have."

"So what made you dig that up?" Roxie asked.

"Somebody reminded me of her recently. Got me curious. I've been listening to her work. In many ways, it's almost indistinguishable from her brother's. Makes you wonder who influenced whom. She was the elder of them, after all. Some people think she invented the form for these piano pieces, although he, of course, has traditionally been given credit."

"That's like what we always say about if Shakespeare had a sister," noted Joyce. "But Mendelssohn actually had one?"

"It's the usual story. She was a woman, so she couldn't become a professional musician, or, at least, she was told that she couldn't. In fact, some of her work was originally published under her brother's name, just to get it published."

"In a way," Roxie said thoughtfully, "all of her works were songs without words, weren't they?"

"You mean because her voice was unheard?" Harper asked.

Roxie nodded. The three of them were silent for a moment in what seemed to Harper a tribute to Fanny Mendelssohn.

"By the way, Harper," Roxie said, "will you be able to come play for my classes again this year?"

"Sure. I always enjoy that."

"So do they. Much better to listen to you play the cello than to me droning on about diatonic triads. That thing you do where you make animal sounds, do that again, okay? That's so funny."

Harper, remembering how Roxie's sophomore class had cracked up at her chicken and howling cat, smiled. "Maybe this time I can figure out how to get a goose in there."

Joyce started giggling again. "Oh, Harper!"

"Before I forget, girls," Harper said, "I've got the most fantastic costume for the faire this year. Let me show you my new doublet."

She ran to the music room closet and pulled down a royal blue velvet doublet with gold thread and gold buttons. *This is going to look wonderful over a white linen shirt*, she thought. Both Roxie and Joyce enthusiastically agreed when she held the garment up for them to admire.

"So you're going as a boy again," Joyce noted.

"Yes. My breeches and hose and everything else, I'll reuse. I just need to get a matching hat to go with this."

"I'm going as a man this year too," Roxie said.

"Really?" Joyce said. "So I'm the only girl in this troupe?"

"Apparently," Roxie said, snorting loudly.

"I need to get home," Joyce announced. "Can you e-mail these songs to me? I'll try to memorize them before the faire. I'll have to get a new bodice because I dumped wine all over myself last year. Had to throw that one out."

Harper walked Joyce to the door, where they hugged good-bye. She returned to Roxie, who was draining the last of the chardonnay into her glass.

"Do you like the program?" Harper asked.

"It's wonderful. Should be a lot of fun."

"You're in no hurry to get home tonight?"

"No. The boys are with Dave's mother this weekend. House is empty."

"Why don't you stay here then?" Harper offered. "You probably shouldn't drive home anyway."

Roxie's dark brown eyes rested momentarily on Harper, then she leaned back in her chair and said, "Thanks."

She seemed lost in thought. Was she thinking about her

husband? Harper wondered.

"Anything exciting going on with you, Harper?" she asked.

"Uh, no, not really. Well, this isn't exciting necessarily, but Chelsea called me a week ago."

Roxie raised her eyebrows. "Oh?"

"I didn't talk to her. She left a message. I think she wants to get together."

Roxie shook her head. "Harper, haven't you learned your lesson with that woman?"

Harper shrugged. She had no friends who were not aware of the devastation she had felt when Chelsea left her, of how her spirit had been broken for months afterward.

"What she did to you," Roxie said, "it was horrible. She served her purpose, now let her go. There are so many gorgeous, fascinating women in the world. You're one of them, and you deserve someone who will cherish you."

Roxie finished her wine and set her glass on the table a little harder than she probably intended. "Put on that doublet," she said. "Let me see it on you."

Harper put the garment on over her blouse and buttoned all but the top button. Roxie unfolded her legs, rose from her chair and stood admiring the costume. "I've always loved the way you look in these things," she said, her voice a note lower than usual. "So handsome. So sexy."

Roxie put her hands on the doublet, running them up over the shoulders, then clasping them behind Harper's neck. Her eyes, liquid and intense, were focused on Harper's mouth. She tilted her head sideways and leaned down to press her lips to Harper's, kissing her sensuously with a bit of tongue. Harper, stunned, held onto the kiss until Roxie released her.

"You're so damned cute," she said with a sigh. "What woman wouldn't want you? Don't waste any more emotion on Chelsea. If I wasn't in love with somebody else, I'd make a play for you myself."

Harper was dumbstruck.

"I wasn't the best wife to poor Dave," Roxie said, as if in

explanation for what she had just done. "I thought you might have figured it out by now."

"You're gay?" Harper asked.

Roxie nodded. "We stayed together because of the boys. Avoided custody problems and all that. But now there's no reason for me to hide it any longer." Her voice was casual, as if she were commenting on the weather.

"Wow," Harper said. "I don't know what to say. For how long—"

"Eight, nine years. My partner, her name is Elaine, and I have been together about four. Dave knew all about this, of course. He had his own romances, all very discreet."

"My God," Harper said, "you've had an entire, secret life that I knew nothing about."

Roxie nodded. "Yes, but all that's changed now. No more secrets. Elaine is moving in with me this fall. I want to tell you all about her, Harper. She's a cop. Oh, my God, when she's in her uniform—"

She fanned herself with her hand. "Well, I am a sucker for a uniform. Maybe you should take off that doublet." Roxie looked Harper over, raising an eyebrow suggestively. "We'll talk in the morning, okay? So how about showing me to my room? I'm beat."

Though it was after midnight before Harper was settled in her bed, she was unable to sleep. Roxie was gay? Not only that, but Roxie had known she was gay for the entire time Harper had known her. And she had never suspected. She had thought she knew Roxie, but she had known only a small part of her. The rest of it was a sham. The part of her life where her heart lived its most vibrant moments had been concealed. She must have lived through such emotional upheavals during that time—falling in love and losing love, perhaps more than once—and she had endured all of that in silence.

What must it have been like for her, thought Harper, *when I came to her with my happy news of Chelsea two years ago and then, a few months later, with my heartbreak, asking for sympathy?*

There were so many times that Roxie must have been holding back. Five years ago at the Renaissance Faire, for instance, when she had chanced upon Harper with her arms around that girl. Hadn't she wanted to confess something then? And when they went to the gay pride parade four years ago and Harper asked her why she was flirting with that police officer. *Oh!* Harper thought with sudden understanding, *that must have been Elaine.*

Roxie was in love with that cop, and yet she had looked Harper in the eye and lied about it. Harper couldn't imagine doing that. She didn't think she was capable of that kind of duplicity. She was disappointed that Roxie had not trusted her, had not considered their friendship stronger. *What kind of a friendship was this if it was based on so many false assumptions?*

At least Roxie wanted to talk now. In the morning she would hear the entire story and their friendship could begin again.

Good Lord, thought Harper, rolling over to try to sleep. *Joyce is going to crap her pants when she finds out that all of her friends have gone lesbian on her.*

Chapter 11

SUMMER, FIVE YEARS AGO

There weren't many opportunities to play medieval musical instruments in public, but the Renaissance Faire definitely provided one. Every summer for the past several years, Harper had taken one of the instruments from her collection, dressed in increasingly authentic costumes and spent a long day entertaining the crowd. Roxie and Joyce usually joined her, bringing Joyce's polished voice and Roxie's superb Cockney accent to the party.

Harper was dressed as a boy this year. Her small breasts were simply not suited to the cinched bodices that Roxie and buxom Joyce wore. Besides, she enjoyed dressing as a boy. Clad in a tightly laced doublet, a Robin Hood-style felt cap, billowy off-white shirt and brown flannel breeches, she definitely looked the part. A leather flask filled with wine dangled from her belt. When she wasn't playing it, she carried a mandolin by a leather strap over her shoulder.

Joyce was in yellow and Roxie in green, both of them sporting many-colored ribbons and flowers in their hair and on their sleeves. Joyce had painted a red rose on her right breast, which bulged above the top of her bodice.

"Ah, kind sir," Joyce begged, stopping a wealthy merchant with a huge yellow feather in his hat, "I'm so thirsty what with all the dust and the singin'. Could ye spare a drop of ale for a poor wanderin' minstrel?"

He laughed cheerily and handed her his mug. "Here ye go, ye wretched creature."

She turned the mug up, unceremoniously pouring the contents down her throat.

"Hey, there, go easy," he complained, grabbing the mug back. "A drop indeed! Come here, my pretty wench." He took her roughly in his arms and kissed her, grabbing her ass through the thick cloth of her skirt. "Ah!" he said, releasing her. "Meet me later, lass, at the wishing well." He winked and walked on.

"Fun's fun," Harper said, "but you're asking for trouble kissing strangers."

"He's no stranger," Joyce replied. "That's Lloyd Harkins, my accountant. And it's not the first time he's kissed me." She grinned. It wasn't that much of a stretch, Harper thought, for Joyce to play the part of lusty maid.

"I tried to get Dave to come," Roxie said, referring to her husband. "But he has no interest in dressing up and playacting. Thinks it's silly. It wouldn't hurt him a bit to loosen up and be a little silly once in a while."

Harper laughed, thinking of Dave in a Renaissance costume, stockings on his legs, baggy breeches on his lanky frame. "It's hard to imagine Dave dressing up, I have to say. But if you had brought him, it would have at least given you a fellow to play with."

Roxie grabbed Harper's belt. "Oh, we've got a fellow. Little 'arper 'ere. Isn't he cute?" Roxie hugged her playfully and kissed her cheek. In her normal voice, she said, "I should have been a boy. This skirt is damned uncomfortable and insufferably hot."

"Oh, the summertime is coming," sang Harper, strumming the mandolin. "And the trees are sweetly blooming, and the wild mountain thyme grows around the purple heather."

Joyce and Roxie joined in for the chorus, Roxie playing her small wooden flute. When their song was finished, Roxie announced, "I'm hungry. Let's go find some food."

Leading the way, Harper played the mandolin and sang, Joyce's tambourine rattling behind her. "Will ye go, lassie, go? And we'll all go together to pull wild mountain thyme all around the blooming heather. Will ye go, lassie, go?"

Joyce had a rich contralto voice, well suited to these country lilts. Roxie's voice was so-so, but her ability on the flute was outstanding. They made a fine trio, and although this was mainly for fun, all three of them took the effort seriously, practicing before the event, for instance.

They succumbed easily to the hawkish speech of a food merchant and each bought a toad-in-the-hole, sitting on bales of hay to eat them. "This is awful," Joyce said after two bites.

"Authentically awful," Harper told her. "That's part of the fun. Go with it."

Joyce, disgruntled, finished her lunch in silence. Harper washed hers down with a good portion of the wine in her flask. As they ate, they watched the revelers. There was a mock fight between two fat women and a man in a pillory begging passersby for water. An itinerant bard was spouting sonnets, doffing his hat at the ladies and kissing hands. On a nearby stage, a band featuring a drum, two bagpipes, a bass and a dulcimer played Celtic instrumentals.

Sufficiently rested, Harper stood, brushed the crumbs off her pants, and said, "I want to have my fortune told."

"I want more beer," Roxie announced. "We'll meet up again in an hour right here, okay?"

Harper struck out on her own under the oak trees. Soon she came to a lane of merchants and weekend mystics of all sorts. Under a striped yellow and white lean-to, a woman with scarves around her head, wearing flowing Madras cotton robes, sat at a small round table covered with gold cloth. She beckoned to Harper with a many-ringed hand. Harper sat down across the table from her. The woman was not as old as her mannerisms suggested. She was close to Harper's age, in fact.

"How are you enjoying the fair, my dear?" asked the divinator.

"It's great. A lot of fun."

The woman introduced herself as Madame Zelda. She spoke with flourishing hand and arm gestures, long red fingernails slashing the air. "So, will it be a tarot reading?"

Harper nodded.

"Have you had a reading before?"

"Once. Several years ago."

"You must open your mind, my dear, if this is to work. Are you willing to do that?"

"Yes," Harper assured her.

"Good. What is it that you want to know? Do you have a question?"

"Well, the obvious thing, I guess, would be something about my love life. Am I going to get married or meet someone new or end up alone and unloved."

Madame Zelda smiled and let Harper shuffle the cards. With exaggerated deliberation, she turned up ten cards, one at a time, and arranged them in a precise pattern, pronouncing, after each, its role, until the cards were on the table in the form of a cross with four alongside.

Madame Zelda sat quietly contemplating the pattern for a moment. "Here is the Fool, " she announced. "He's a free spirit and represents an adventure into the unknown. The Fool's journey requires the ability to act on impulse, to take a chance."

Harper liked the sound of that. "To follow your heart?" she asked.

"Yes, exactly." Zelda continued. "We have the King of Swords. The man in your life, perhaps. The King of Swords is an intellectual, a master of reason and logic."

"Well," Harper remarked, "that would have to be Eliot."

"Your boyfriend?"

Harper nodded.

"Here we have the five of wands. That suggests discord between you. There's a struggle of purposes. You don't want the same things."

This is getting eerie, Harper thought.

"The next card, the eight of cups, suggests a dissatisfaction with the status quo, the need to go on a journey of self-discovery. What you are currently experiencing," continued Madame Zelda, "is growing uncertainty. I see by these cards that you can expect this situation to worsen in the near future. I'm afraid that you and your boyfriend may be heading toward trouble. And here, the Tower, an interesting card. The Tower represents a crisis or upheaval, your world being thrown into a state of chaos."

"That's scary," Harper remarked.

"It doesn't have to be. It can be the beginning of something new and wonderful. The Hanged Man here tells you to give up control, to surrender to the change, let yourself be vulnerable. If you can do that, you may be able to find a greater happiness than you've ever known."

The fortune-telling continued in this manner until all of the cards had been explained. Madame Zelda paused, looking into Harper's eyes. "If this is about your man, the cards are saying that you will separate. But eventually, you will find a new happiness, much greater than this one. The cards indicate so strongly that you need to make a change that you may not want to be merely open to it. You may want to initiate it."

Harper paid the woman, mulling over what had been foretold. It didn't upset her, the idea of breaking with Eliot, especially if the result was greater happiness. She wondered, as she strolled a shady path, what this new lover with such huge potential would be like. She knew there was no magic in fortune-telling, but she definitely believed that the seed of an idea, planted in an open mind, could grow and influence events.

Resuming her role of wandering minstrel, she played her mandolin among the craft booths, singing, "Sigh no more, ladies, sigh no more; men were deceivers ever; one foot in the sea, and one on shore, to one thing constant never." She stopped in front of a jewelry booth, singing to a group of women. "Then sigh not so, but let them go, and you be blithe and bonny, converting all your sounds of woe into 'hey nonny, nonny'."

Nearby, a sultry female voice said, "A pretty song, sir." Harper turned to see a young woman regarding her with round sienna eyes from behind the jewelry counter. She wore an ankle-length orange skirt, white blouse, cobalt blue bodice and a garland of daisies over her long black hair.

"Thank you," Harper said, hanging the mandolin over her shoulder.

"Tarry a moment and view my wares." The young woman's hands were clasped in front of her, her breasts bulging above her bodice in the manner of these costumes. Her eyes stared purposely. Her voice was deep and musical.

Harper looked at the jewelry to humor her. Predominantly sterling silver. Plenty of New Age symbolism—crystals, dragons' claws, wizards and the like. Several pieces of the same type hung from chains around the girl's neck.

"Have I anything to suit your desires, kind sir?" asked the girl, the tone of her voice suggestive, so much so that Harper looked up to see if her expression matched it. The girl smiled coquettishly, averting her eyes.

"Perhaps," Harper said, playing along. That was what she was here for, after all, play. "Have you anything else to show me?"

A seductive smile appeared on the girl's face. "Come around the counter, handsome fellow. I have some wares that I keep out of sight. I'm sure they will intrigue you."

What game is she playing? Harper wondered. *And do I want to play?*

No harm in finding out, she decided. She walked around the counter to where the girl stood. They were face to face now behind a sparkling table of silver baubles and transparent crystals, sheltered only slightly by the structure of the booth from the eyes of passersby.

97

The girl looped a finger in the leather thongs that crisscrossed Harper's doublet and kept it tight across her chest.

"What did you want to show me?" Harper asked, almost whispering, a nervousness overtaking her.

"Come inside." The girl nodded toward the tent opening beside them, tugging gently on the thong. "You won't be sorry."

They stood so close now that their clothing brushed together. *She must know that I'm a woman*, Harper thought. *I haven't disguised my sex that well.*

"Saucy wench," Harper said, suddenly emboldened by the wine and the costume. She slipped an arm around the girl's slim waist, clasping her tightly. The girl let herself fall against Harper, not resisting. Her breasts were mesmerizing, her dark eyes enchanting, her lips sumptuous. Harper could imagine kissing them. As she allowed this image into her mind, a pang of desire gripped her. The girl obviously wanted to be kissed. Harper wanted to kiss her. *So why not?*

A boisterous greeting rang out, shattering the fantasy. "Harper, there you are!"

She jerked herself away from the girl to see Roxie, beer in hand, on the other side of the counter. Harper forced a smile.

"Perhaps the pretty youth will buy a bauble for his sweetheart?" said the girl, casting her hand toward Roxie with a wry smile. Harper hurried to join her friend, glancing back as they moved on to see the dark head turned in her direction. She struggled to regain her composure.

"What was that about?" Roxie asked.

"I'm not sure. I think I was being propositioned."

"Sorry I interrupted," Roxie said, arching her eyebrows. "You might have had quite a lark."

"You don't think I would have..."

Roxie laughed. "My God, Harper, sometimes you're so provincial."

Harper balked. *Provincial?* she thought, finding the word distasteful.

"I'm not," she said, indignant. "I'm not the least bit

provincial."

Roxie looked momentarily puzzled. "Harper, I'm just teasing you. Lighten up."

Harper recognized the confusion in her mind. She tried, but failed, to laugh off the incident. For the rest of the day, images of the girl's lips and bosom interrupted her fun. Lying in bed that night, unable to sleep, she was plagued by the memory of the desire that had gripped her in the presence of that dark-haired temptress.

The next morning, driven by those images, Harper put her costume on again and returned to the faire by herself, making her way directly to the jewelry booth. She had no plan. She only knew that she had to see the girl again, to try to understand her feelings. And there she was, just like yesterday, standing behind the counter, her demeanor jovial, her smile, which she flashed to each of her customers, flirtatious. Harper watched for a few minutes from some distance, unnoticed. The girl sold a necklace and then her booth was clear of visitors. Harper approached, wondering if the girl had been trifling with her and it had meant nothing, if she played this seduction game with everyone.

As soon as the girl looked up to see Harper, it was obvious that she recognized her. "Ah, sir," she said, "you have returned. You saw something here that you liked, after all?"

Harper felt nervous in a way she hadn't anticipated. "Yes," she said. "Very much. Are you going to invite me in?"

The girl laughed her musical laugh and said, "No, not today." She jerked her head toward the tent opening and scowled, and Harper realized that there was someone inside the tent. Just then he emerged, a bald man with massive arms and tattoos on his neck.

"Zoë," he said, "where are those yellow zircons?"

"In the red tool box, the big one," Zoë answered.

"I looked there. I've been through it three times already."

"All right. I'll look." Zoë turned to go into the tent.

"Wait!" Harper said, too loudly.

Zoë turned back to look at Harper and shook her head almost

imperceptibly, frowning. Then she slipped into the tent. The man smiled at Harper. "Is there something I can show you?"

Harper shook her head and left, feeling disappointed but not really knowing what it was she had come back for. She wanted to kiss that girl, Zoë, she knew that, but beyond that...? She had no idea.

Chapter 12

SUMMER, SIX YEARS AGO

The heavy wooden door swung open a few moments after Harper rang the bell. Mary Tillotson's gorgeous custom-built house would be the setting for Harper's project in the video production class she was taking. She tried to squeeze in at least one class a year, generally something in the arts, to keep herself engaged and current. Her instructor, Bob Lerner, had assigned them the daunting task of producing a half-hour show, subject open. Harper had struck upon this idea after seeing one of Mary's watercolors hanging in the school cafeteria. A biography of a charismatic and successful local artist, that's what she'd do. Couldn't miss.

Harper was only a little surprised to see Chelsea Nichols in the doorway greeting her with a bright smile. Over the past two years she had become Mary's satellite, at least on campus. Whenever Mary came into view, you could be sure that Chelsea was not far off.

Harper's contact with her had been slight, limited to helping her find reference material on the occasions she came into the library. In almost every case, the presence of Mary could be discerned in her activities. "We're reading Eudora Welty," she would say about one of her English classes. "Mary says I must read her autobiography, *One Writer's Beginnings*."

Harper wondered what it would be like to have a disciple. The rumor mill was going full force again, of course, regarding Mary and her predatory sexual forays among the female student body. Harper hadn't heard Chelsea named but assumed it was her presence that was fueling the gossip. Shock, horror and titillation accompanied the rumors, spread primarily by male professors, many of whom, given the opportunity, would certainly have taken their own turn with such a pretty young coed. But the idea that a woman should do such a thing filled them with self-righteous indignation. Harper found the rumor mongering extremely repulsive, but that didn't keep her from being intrigued by the real-life situation.

So finding Chelsea here at Mary's house threw Harper off for just a second. Adjusting quickly, she noticed that the twenty-three-year-old's long, sunny-blond hair was tinged slightly green, the result, no doubt, of hours spent in the enormous pool she had glimpsed on the north side of the house.

Chelsea, the epitome of health and youth, wore shorts and a cap-sleeved shirt, revealing tanned arms and legs that were smooth and muscular. "Hi, Harper," she said familiarly, hooking a loose strand of hair behind her ear. "Come in."

Harper followed Chelsea into a huge living room, ornately decorated with furnishings from a jumble of styles—Victorian, Oriental, Edwardian, Early American, Scandinavian and Shaker. The walls were almost obscured by paintings, dozens of them, all sizes and styles. Small statues and curious ornaments occupied the tables. A baby grand piano stood on a raised landing on one side of the room in front of heavy, forest green drapes, closed against the afternoon sun.

Harper turned to see Chelsea grinning at her. "Cool, huh?"

Nodding, Harper said, "Very cool."

"Wait here. I'll get Mary."

Chelsea left the room. Harper put her movie camera and notebook on a table, careful not to jar a smooth soapstone carving which resembled, abstractly, two intertwined female bodies. She walked around the room's perimeter, studying the paintings. There was a Jackson Pollack, all splatters and blue and black lines, hung beside a canvas heaped with fleshy female bodies that Harper recognized as a Rubens. She wondered briefly if these were reproductions or originals.

Above the fireplace was a huge (at least five feet long) impressionistic reclining nude. The face, though lacking detail, was obviously Chelsea's. The painting was an intriguing work— soft tones of blue and pink, swaths of gray. The head was thrown back, golden hair streaming down behind, the face in profile, eyes closed. The breasts, sharp triangles, were thrust upward, and the back was arched, leaving a curving gap between the figure and the surface on which it reclined. It could easily be interpreted as a woman in the throes of passion.

"Do you like it?" asked Mary from behind.

Harper turned to see Mary and Chelsea in the doorway. "Yes," she said. "Captivating."

Chelsea stood beaming. For what was she so pleased with herself? Harper wondered. For being young and beautiful? For being Mary's lover?

"It's quite recent," Mary explained, stepping into the room. She placed herself in the center of an Oriental rug about twenty feet from the painting, her gaze absorbing her creation. Harper waited, but Mary continued to stare for a moment longer before saying, "I'm delighted with it. Do you see how, if you let it take hold of you, it moves?" As she made this observation, she raised a hand toward the work, her head tilted upward, her face blissful. Had she been wearing white robes instead of jeans and a silk blouse, Harper would have described her as saintly. Even dressed as she was, she seemed to emit a nimbus-like glow.

"Oh," laughed Mary, abruptly, "I'm such an egotist!"

"With absolute justification," Chelsea remarked, her expression adoring. Harper wondered how long Chelsea had been installed in this house. It had to be less than a year, she decided, based on her observations of the two of them on campus. The rumors had escalated about six months ago, spurred on, perhaps, by the news of cohabitation.

"Yes," Harper agreed. "It must be wonderful to be able to create something you love, to make a work of art that seems to have a life of its own. I admire and envy that in artists."

"But, Harper," Mary objected, "you're an artist too. You're a musician."

Harper laughed nervously. "Maybe, but I'm not an artist in any sense that I think of when I use that word. I love music, but to be an artist, I think you have to have that drive to do it, the inability to not do it."

Mary sighed wistfully. "That drive, yes, it's vitality itself. Though it can be a tormentor." Mary dropped onto the sofa with one of her legs bent underneath her, then beckoned with her hand. "Come here, Harper, and tell me what you've got in mind." Then, to Chelsea, she said, "Darling, how about getting us all a cognac? Does that suit you, Harper?"

"Yes, that would be nice." Harper sat on the other side of a coffee table that supported an immense Grecian urn. "I'm not sure how to go about this. Dr. Lerner suggested that we approach this project as though it would actually be televised."

"You mean it won't?" Mary asked indignantly.

"The best ones might, on a local cable channel. But I'm an amateur at this. It's only been two months since I first held one of these cameras. Please don't expect too much."

Mary leaned forward, her eyes intense and focused. "I always expect too much. If you're going to produce a film about me, I want it to be exceptional. I'm going to make sure it is. Yours will be the best one."

Chelsea distributed three glasses among them, then stood behind the sofa, behind Mary, in a possessive pose. There had to be almost thirty years between them, Harper thought. A case of idolatry, obviously, although Mary was, in her way, exceptionally charming. Harper herself found Mary interesting and attractive. It was easy to see how a student might develop a crush on her. And for Mary? What was the attraction of this girl? Being worshipped, especially by an apostle as adorable as Chelsea, probably needed no further explanation.

"I have a couple of students in the studio," Mary said. "I thought you'd like to film me working with them. I want to be sure, though, that I'm allowed to see the final product before Lerner does. And that I get to cut anything I don't like."

Harper agreed.

"What is your theme going to be?" Mary asked. "What is the focus?"

Harper hesitated. "I guess it's pretty straightforward. I'm just going to feature some of your work, listen to you talk about it. The focus, I suppose, is simply to show what a brilliant artist you are."

Mary grinned and tilted her head slightly. "Flattery will get you everywhere," she said flirtatiously. Harper flushed. "But try to be more objective, dear. Let's focus on my unique vision as a painter. We aren't simply putting up a PowerPoint show of my paintings and saying, 'Oh, aren't these interesting.' You've got to get an angle, and I'll be happy to talk to you at length about my vision, what makes me Mary Tillotson, and why I'm not, for instance, Constance Hooper. Do you see?"

Harper felt intimidated, vainly trying to remember anything she could about Constance Hooper, another contemporary painter, and then deciding it didn't matter, that she'd gotten the point. Mary obviously wanted this to be more than a project to satisfy a class assignment. Harper glanced at Chelsea, who was looking at her with an inquiring, amused expression. She's going to challenge you, she seemed to be intimating.

"Yes, I understand," said Harper, "I really appreciate your taking the time to do this. Some of the students in my class are filming their dogs, you know."

"I'll make time for anyone who is serious about art," Mary said. "You are serious, aren't you? I mean, this class you're taking, you must have some aspiration that involves filmmaking."

Harper hesitated. She hadn't given it that much thought. She searched for something to say besides, "Well, no, I just thought it'd be interesting."

Mary, not waiting for her answer, said, "I have no intention of being the subject of a mediocre student project, like somebody's dog. If I'm the star of this show, it has to be the real thing. I don't give many interviews, Harper. I agreed to this because you're a friend and colleague. So, you, in turn, must make this a shining testimonial to me."

"I'll do my best," Harper said. "I understand you don't want it to look like an encyclopedia entry."

Mary nodded and sipped her cognac. "Or Who's Who in the art world. I want it to be me. It should reflect who I am in every aspect, right down to the choice of font for the credits. Oh, and will you have music?"

"Yes, of course."

"Fabulous. Classical?"

"Yes, that's what I know best. And I think it suits you."

Mary looked satisfied. "Okay, then. Look, Harper, if I'm going to entertain you with my art, how about entertaining us with a bit of yours? Play something for us."

"Oh, yes," Chelsea urged, "play for us."

Harper, taken off guard, said, "I didn't bring my cello."

"You can play that, can't you?" said Mary, waving toward the baby grand.

"Yes, actually, I'd love to play that." Harper went to the landing and pulled the stool out, sitting before the magnificent instrument.

"Do you need music?" Mary asked.

"No," Harper said, uncovering the keys. "I've been practicing Beethoven's *Appassionata*. I can play that. Maybe the first movement."

Chelsea pulled the drapes open. Light poured in, shining

almost blindingly off the luminous black surface of the piano. She then ran over to Mary, plopping down next to her on the sofa.

"*Appassionata*," she repeated. Her eyes flashed with delight. She placed her head in Mary's lap, looking childlike.

"Yes, a perfect selection," Mary agreed, laying a tender hand on the girl's head. What a charming tableau they created in that pose. Harper would have liked to have filmed that, but Chelsea was not to be a player in this documentary. It was strictly about the art, not about the artist's life. That was the agreement.

Harper waited for the two of them to settle into stillness before beginning the piece. As her fingers touched the keys, she heard with elation the richness and perfect tone of the instrument. Immediately, she was alone with the music, her body melding with the keys.

Let it play itself, she reminded herself. *Let your body become the music. Forget fingers, lose the sensation of touch. The music is all.*

She had learned this technique while studying Zen. Yield and overcome. It was supposed to be a way of reaching enlightenment, but she had never managed to master the technique completely. She had, however, found a means of adapting it to music.

Halfway through the piece, Harper glanced over at Mary and Chelsea to see them smiling affectionately at one another. Harper smiled too, marveling at the power of love, basking in the power of music. As the last note subsided, she lifted her hands from the keys, euphoric.

Chelsea leapt up from the couch, applauding.

"Glorious," Mary said, also clapping.

"That was so beautiful," Chelsea said. "I wish I were musical. I don't know how to play anything."

"You have your own talents," Mary said, looking appreciatively at Chelsea. "But I agree that an ability to make music is enviable. It's so universally appreciated. If I weren't a painter, I think I should like to be a musician. Music is the art of movement. It's alive in a way that paint on canvas can never be. It lives in multiple dimensions at once, in time and space, attaining a real-world depth that a master of perspective can merely imitate on a flat surface. And at the same time, it's ephemeral, passing out of existence almost as soon as it comes into it. It exists only for that moment that it strikes your eardrum. For that reason, music is more precious and more mysterious than a painting."

Harper wished that her camera was already on. She hoped that Mary would come up with something equally quotable when it was.

"I'd settle for either of those talents," Chelsea said.

"You, darling, are a wordsmith," Mary countered. "There is nothing more powerful than the written word to elucidate an idea. The writer has a level of control over her audience in a way that no other form of art can attain. A piece of music can evoke a mood, like joy, but has little influence over the finer strains of feeling in the listener, who may respond with wistfulness, for example. But a poet who leaves that kind of latitude available to the reader is just a sloppy poet."

Harper noticed that she and Chelsea were listening in the same rapt manner to Mary's observations.

"Words and music accomplish similar goals," continued Mary, "but they're almost the antithesis of one another. They spring from different parts of your psyche. You would have to be an extremely exceptional individual to be able to give life to your emotions through *both* language and music. However," Mary said, exuberantly, "bring together a composer and a lyricist and, well, you've got a show, haven't you?"

Chelsea laughed at that, glancing from Mary to Harper, her eyes shining. Her enthusiasm was blithe and unpretentious. Mary responded to Chelsea's delight with a serene and natural smile. Apparently they had quite a bit to offer one another, Harper thought. Despite the cynical gossip about Mary taking advantage of a child, this relationship could be viewed with a lack of skepticism if a person would allow it, and that's how Harper was inclined to view it. She wasn't a skeptic. If it looked like love, then it probably was, and who was she to question that?

Chapter 13

JUNE 21

Wilona greeted Harper with a crushing hug in the doorway of her house. "How was the drive?" she asked.

"Long. I could sure use something wet and cold."

Wilona served her iced tea. From the kitchen window, Harper could see several birdhouses hanging from tree branches and a copper birdbath occupied by two blissful sparrows. On the shelf outside the window, a nuthatch pecked at loose seed. Gorgeous framed photos of birds, trees and old fence posts lined the hallways of Wilona's house.

The last time Harper had been here, it had been December, a year and a half ago. The pine branches had been heavy with snow, a fire had crackled in the living room and she had settled heavily into this retreat like a bear into its winter den. She had come with the excuse of making a documentary. But, four months after losing Chelsea, she was in need of a refuge more than a project. Between interview sessions and filming Wilona in the snow with her camera, they talked about abstractions like happiness and personal fulfillment. Or Harper sat quietly with a book and a cup of hot chocolate, lost in her own thoughts. There was opportunity here for quiet introspection. During that week, Wilona's healing presence had enveloped her like a cloud. By the end of the visit, she had felt more fit for the world.

Today the landscape around the house was painted in noisier hues, but the atmosphere within was the same. It was an extension of Wilona herself, a mantle of warmth spreading out to envelop the house, its contents and anyone inside. Harper felt safe and welcome here.

As she took the first swallow from her glass, a boy appeared in the kitchen doorway, as if he had materialized out of thin air. He had made no sound. He was slight, maybe eleven or twelve, with a close-cropped Afro. His face was turned to Harper, but his eyes looked past her.

"Andrew," Wilona said, seeing him there. "Come here, baby."

He walked toward her and let himself be engulfed by her arms. Then she turned him to face Harper and said, "Harper, this is my grandson, Andrew. This is the lady I told you about. Her name is Harper. She'll be visiting us for a few days."

The boy extended his hand and said, "How do you do?"

He still didn't seem to see her. Harper suddenly realized that he was blind. She stepped toward him and took his hand, shaking it firmly. "Nice to meet you, Andrew."

"Now you go change your clothes for dinner," Wilona told him. "Your shirt has grape jelly stains all over it."

Andrew hurried out of the kitchen.

"Grandson?" Harper asked, bewildered. "I didn't even know you had a son. Daughter?"

"Daughter."

"Really? I made a documentary about your life, and it never came up that you had a daughter and a grandson."

"The documentary wasn't about my life. It was about my

work."

Harper heard what Wilona said, but it was still not making sense to her.

"My daughter is at a religious retreat in the Colorado Rockies," Wilona continued. "It's just an excuse to escape her responsibilities, as far as I'm concerned. I've had Andrew a few times before, but I think this time it's for good."

"Is that okay with you?" Harper asked.

Wilona nodded. "Better than okay. I love that little guy. And he deserves as good as he can get."

"But you've always been such a free spirit," Harper said. "Coming and going as you please, traveling all over the world, pursuing your art."

"'Free spirit'?" Wilona repeated, obviously amused. "Harper, I've always had things that came before my art. For me, photography was an escape, but only in the sense that it allowed me to flee in my imagination, not for real. My life has always been grounded in the here and now. When I was fourteen, my mother developed a slow-growing brain cancer that took away her hearing and the use of her legs, caused horrible seizures and eventually killed her when I was nineteen. For all those years, she was helpless and I had to do everything for her, which, believe me, wasn't pretty. Then I got pregnant with my daughter and spent the next eighteen years raising her as a single mother. She's bipolar and has never been able to support herself for more than a few months at a time, so even as an adult, she's needed a lot of help. Then there was Andrew. That girl couldn't even look after herself, so you can imagine what our lives were like when she ended up having a baby. Even if he hadn't been blind, he would have been too much for her, although when she's on her meds she functions okay."

"I had no idea," Harper said, stunned. "What about all those talks we had about what's important in life? Why didn't it come up?"

"But you remember, don't you, that we were mainly talking about you and Chelsea? You needed to talk about that. Besides,

111

I don't like to dwell on my problems. I don't want to seem to be complaining. It's more fun to talk about photography, and you, of course, have always been most interested in my life as an artist, so that's what I try to be for you. But I've never been a free spirit and that's okay with me. I'll continue my work. I've always found a way to do that. Andrew can come along. You'll see that he's a pleasure to be around. He's a joyful child."

Harper felt a little battered. In the course of a few minutes, her entire view of Wilona's life had been upended. Wilona hadn't changed, obviously. Harper's view of her had just been wrong, wrong in the most fundamental way. She had imagined Wilona as carefree, concerning herself with no one's needs but her own. In Harper's view, the art had been the single focus, the thing that defined Wilona. She was a photographer. Now it was obvious that the focus had been too narrow. *What does this mean?* Harper wondered, feeling disoriented.

When dinner was ready, the three of them ate in the kitchen, birds twittering through the open window. Wilona pulled the crust off her bread and left it on the sill for the birds. Andrew, listening, named each bird as it sang—sparrow, blue jay.

"I hear a woodpecker," he said at the end of the meal.

"Really?" Wilona asked, cocking her head to listen. "I don't hear it."

"Do you hear it, Harper?" Andrew asked.

Harper strained to listen. "Yes, I do. Very faint. Your hearing is remarkable."

"That's true," Wilona said. "And my hearing is getting worse and worse. Andrew is becoming my ears."

"And you're my eyes," he said, grinning.

"That's right," she agreed.

"Do you like to listen to music, Andrew?" Harper asked.

"Yes!"

"Music is a big part of his life," Wilona said.

"Oh, do you play an instrument?"

He shook his head.

"I wish I could teach him," Wilona said, "but I know nothing about it. This fall I'm going to enroll him in a class, though. If there's space available."

After dinner, Andrew showed Harper his CD collection and MP3 player and they listened to some of his music. He had memorized an extraordinary number of songs and could sing them perfectly in tune. His musical tastes were varied but were clearly influenced by his grandmother, as evidenced by a preponderance of old-school rhythm and blues. On her way from Andrew's room back to the living room, Harper paused to admire a photo of a cardinal. Andrew stood beside her and said, "This is my favorite."

Startled, Harper asked, "The photograph?"

"Yes. I like the way the shadows from the leaves change the color on the bird's feathers."

Harper turned to catch Wilona's eye. She was sitting in a rocking chair, rocking just a couple of inches to and fro. She grinned. "I describe them to him," she explained. "He has a finely detailed mind image, a more detailed image than you probably have."

Harper looked back at the photo, trying to imagine what Andrew's mind image of it was like. Up until this moment, she had thought it sad that Andrew had never seen one of his grandmother's stunning photos. Harper wouldn't have been surprised if Andrew had turned to her then and said, "You still have much to learn, Grasshopper."

Quite frequently, Harper closed her eyes while playing music, but she'd never thought about why. She supposed it was to allow herself to see the music as Andrew did, as he saw the photograph, without any visual interference. It wasn't easy to do because even when you closed your eyes, you tended to see images of piano keys or notes. To see the music itself required a more concentrated blocking of the visual. Harper had learned to do that, over time. She could see the music itself when she worked at it—waves of colors, gliding, flowing, marching, bouncing.

"That cardinal is going into my next book," Wilona said.

"Oh, I meant to ask you about that." Harper sat on the sofa

113

next to Wilona's chair. "How is it coming?"

"All of the photos have been chosen. We're working on page layout and narrative. I'm hoping to see it in print by winter. I wanted to talk to you anyway, Harper, about this one."

"Oh?"

"I've made a pitch to my publisher to include a DVD with the book."

"A DVD? What would be on it?"

"Among other things, your biography of me."

"My video? You want to sell that with your book?"

"Yes. My publisher thinks it's a good idea. Usually we just have a foreword or introduction in the book with some biographical information and a photo. This would be something more intriguing, I think, and now that a few people actually know who I am, there might be some interest in me as well as the photos. At least my publisher thinks so."

"Yes! I mean, you're well-known now. People are curious about the artist. Sure. I think it's a wonderful idea. But are you sure it's good enough? Are you sure you don't want to have one professionally made?"

Wilona smiled affectionately. "It's good enough. It tells exactly what I want to tell people about my technique and my relationship with my subject. Would that be okay with you, then, to use it?"

"Okay? Absolutely."

"Good. I know you haven't really had any aspirations like that. From what you've said, you're doing this just for the pleasure of it, but I assume you have no objection to commercial success. Maybe we can get you a small piece of the royalty split." Wilona laughed good-naturedly. "A very small piece."

"That's not necessary, but I won't turn it down. It would be kind of nice, you know, to be a part of a commercial product like that and such a beautiful one as well."

"Well, thank you. We're quite the mutual admiration society here!"

Just before sunset, Wilona suggested a walk. Her house

occupied a clearing in a sparse conifer forest. The smell of pines and the lacy afternoon sunshine filtering through them left Harper feeling peaceful. She breathed deeply, absorbing the fresh spirit of life in the woods. They ambled alongside a shallow brook. Harper peered into the water of the stream, sometimes seeing the surface mirror of it, sometimes looking through that to the rounded rocks below. In the sound of the water rushing over boulders, she heard a marimba, accompanied shortly by maracas. It was a light, regular rhythm, a pleasant, calming tune.

Harper was feeling humbled. First, she had discovered that Roxie had been living an entirely different life than she'd understood. Now she had discovered that Wilona too had a much different life than she'd imagined.

She wasn't the only one for whom Roxie's lifestyle would be a revelation, though. There was no way she could have known about that. It had been a secret, after all. She didn't know why Roxie thought she could have guessed. Still, it bothered her that their friendship had turned out to be so superficial. At least that's how it seemed to Harper now. After all, if they had been as close as Harper thought, Roxie couldn't possibly have kept so much of her emotional life hidden.

And now Wilona... Obviously her senses were flawed. It was as if she were color blind. Or partially deaf. There were whole ranges of the lives of her friends that she didn't hear, that were beyond her upper and lower registers.

This has been going on a long time, Harper realized, thinking about Peggy, another good friend she hadn't really known. She wondered who else she thought she knew, but didn't. Chelsea came to mind, of course. She had been so certain that she knew Chelsea's feelings. Was it possible that she was wrong about that too, that Chelsea had never had the depth of feeling that she had thought? Maybe it had only been about sex for Chelsea. Maybe it still was.

More disturbing than the lack of awareness about the true inner lives of her friends was Harper's sudden doubt in her ability to know herself. *Is my view of myself as flawed as my view of other people?* she wondered. She had been thirty-six, after all, before she recognized that she was a lesbian, despite numerous hints along the way. Not only had she been involved in a phony relationship with Eliot for nearly seventeen years, but she had also spent decades searching for spiritual and emotional fulfillment without having a clue about how that might manifest itself. She had given equal validity to all comers in that arena, congratulating herself for her open mind.

Perhaps her mind wasn't quite so much open as vacant, she thought. *Is there* anything *I really know about myself? About my desires and my passions?*

There was the music. That seemed certain enough.

And there were her feelings about Chelsea, even if Chelsea's feelings were unknown. One thing she knew about herself with certainty was that she wanted Chelsea. She had never stopped wanting her.

The snap of a twig caused her to jump. She had forgotten Wilona, who now stood a few paces behind her, watching her with an inquiring gaze.

"Is there something on your mind, Harper?" Wilona asked. "You seem distracted."

Harper turned to face her. "Chelsea called," she said. "I think she wants to see me."

Wilona frowned, causing deep furrows to appear in her forehead. "Oh, girl, you can't let her do that to you. If you do, you're some kind of masochist."

"I have to listen to my gut," Harper said.

"Your gut?" Wilona shook her head. Her dark eyes were troubled. "You're going to do it, aren't you, no matter what anybody says?" She took a small camera from her jacket pocket. "Hold still there. I want a picture of you before that girl destroys you for good." She snapped the picture.

When they got back to the house, Harper sat on the back porch near the copper birdbath, turned on her cell phone and dialed Chelsea's new number. She had already memorized it, she realized. She also noticed that her hands were trembling. The phone rang three times and then the voice mail message began, Chelsea's cheerful voice instructing her to leave a message. Harper hung up, disappointed. She would try again later. Now that she had finally decided to call, her desire to talk to Chelsea was fierce.

Chapter 14

SUMMER, TEN YEARS AGO

Using a heavy-duty staple gun, Harper covered an exterior wood-framed wall with moisture barrier material. This was her job for the next couple of hours. Eliot was working on the other side of the house, mixing cement for the front steps. There were about a dozen volunteers today, and the little house was going up fast. This was Harper's first time working with Habitat for Humanity, and she was loving it. The camaraderie among the crew was energizing.

This was the perfect thing to do with a few weeks of summer vacation. It would change someone's life for the better. Harper had assumed that you had to go to Africa or South America to do this sort of thing, like the summer she had spent in Oaxaca, but it turned out that there were destitute people everywhere, even in California. Still, it was too far from home to drive every day, so they were staying in a hostel along with some of the other volunteers.

Eliot came by to look at her handiwork, his UCSC T-shirt filthy with concrete dust and splatter. "Very neat," he announced, then laughed. "Your tidy rows of staples."

"Yes," she said, standing back to admire her work.

"You do realize that nobody will ever see them. I mean, siding goes on top."

"Yes, I know that."

A shock of brown hair fell over his forehead. "So you don't have to be quite so uniform is what I mean. Just so it's tacked on thoroughly."

"This is how I do it," she said, and then more precisely, "This is how I *prefer* to do it."

"Okay." He shoved his hands in the pockets of his shorts, still grinning. "Maybe we should put you on some of the finish work, like painting or baseboards or something. You're such a perfectionist!"

"And maybe you should go back to mixing cement."

"All right," he said, leaning in to give her a kiss on the cheek.

When the van arrived with lunch, Harper took a break and sat in the shade of the house with a hot dog and beans on a paper plate and a plastic cup of Pepsi. Wilona Freeman, a sturdy black woman in stretch pants and sandals, lowered herself with care beside Harper, holding a similar plate and cup. A woman of about forty-five, she had volunteered with Habitat several times before.

"Thank God," she said as her butt hit the ground. "My feet are killing me." Wilona grinned broadly. "Harper, that's your name, right? First or last name?"

"First. My mother's maiden name is Harper."

"Well, how do you do, then, Harper. I'm Wilona." She nestled her cup down in the grass securely. "From Placerville. You know where that is?"

"Sure. Been through it lots of times. Seems like an interesting place to live. What do you do there?"

"I'm a photographer."

"Really," Harper said, putting down her hot dog. "Is that what you do for a living, then?"

"Yes. I've been lucky. Had some good breaks. Some fairly steady work for a couple of magazines." Wilona told her about her photographs and her two published books. Harper made herself a mental note to see if the books were in the library when she got home. If they weren't, she assured Wilona, they soon would be.

She asked Wilona a lot of questions about her craft, her technique, her subject matter. Wilona seemed happy to talk about her work and about her travels, journeys around the globe in search of material. She had been practically everywhere, and she had lots of intriguing tales, more than enough to keep Harper enthralled for the duration of their project.

"Yes, I've traveled a lot," Wilona said. "But one of the best things about photography is that you can find something interesting just about everywhere, even in your own backyard. All around my house, I have bird feeders hung in the tree branches. I like to take pictures of birds, especially hummingbirds because they're always in motion. The precious little things are just a blur or a flash of light to the ordinary camera lens. They can be quite a challenge. I like a challenge."

"I'd love to see some of those," Harper said.

"If you find those books, you'll see them. There are a couple of hummingbirds in there, both of them taken right outside my house."

"Do you live alone?" Harper asked.

"Yes, just me and my birds. Don't need anybody else."

"Never married then?"

Wilona shook her head, wrinkling up her nose in distaste. "Not for me. I never wanted a man around telling me what to do."

"You mean you wanted to maintain your freedom, your autonomy?"

"Exactly."

"But you had lovers?" Harper only realized after she asked it that it was an extremely personal question. But Wilona didn't seem to notice.

"Oh, the men have come and gone over the years. Some of them stay around a while. Who's keeping track?"

Harper gazed admiringly at her lunch mate. Here was a free spirit, she thought. This woman was living her special, unique life, perfectly suited to her artistic temperament. She did what she wanted to do, on her own and fearlessly.

For the remainder of the project, Harper sought Wilona out at breaks and sometimes after the day's work was done and listened to her talk. She seemed so secure about her place in the scheme of things. She didn't seem to have any unfulfilled longings or regrets. Harper had always been drawn to women who lived that way.

Wilona's home was close enough that she could drive in each day. In addition to working on the house, Wilona was also taking photographs, chronicling its progress.

The official record for Habitat for Humanity, it would be presented to the homeowner. She also took a flattering photo of Harper, hammer in hand, nailing a railing in place on the back stairs.

"Now you have a memento," Wilona said, presenting the framed print to her on the last day of the job.

By the time the house was finished, they had become good friends.

Chapter 15

JUNE 22

Harper and Wilona set out Tuesday morning to find Carmen Silva. They drove north through the Sierra foothills with the windows down, enjoying the cool morning air.

"Thank you, Wilona," Harper said. "I really appreciate your help on this. I think my weak area all along has been the visuals. Your contribution here is going to make this one much more professional."

"Oh, it'll be fun," Wilona answered. "By the way, how did you hear about this woman anyway?"

"My first encounter with her work was an accident. I was visiting a friend in the hospital, and I saw this fantastic rug hanging in the stairwell. It stopped me short. It was such a fine piece, you know, and so remarkable. There was a card on the wall with her name on it. At that point, I didn't know anything about her, of course, not even if she was living. It took me a while, but

I eventually tracked her down. I've seen two more of her pieces since then, both equally impressive."

By asking directions from a boy on a bicycle, they finally found the little shack they had been searching for. It stood beside a dirt road, a tiny pink stucco house with a door of white peeling paint and two open windows facing the road. Lined up on wooden racks outside the house were several rows of colorful blankets for sale.

They got out of the car, Wilona loading herself up with camera equipment. Harper carried the tripod. She knocked on the front door, which was slightly ajar.

"Come in," called a thick, commanding voice from within.

Harper led the way into a room that seemed to belong to another place and time. She felt transported. What she saw first was the old woman, sitting on a three-legged stool, squat and huge, Buddha-like, her face deeply lined, tiny eyes straining toward Harper, a rag wrapped around the top of her head, no evidence of hair. Next she saw the children, two boys and a girl, sitting on the floor facing the old woman as though they were students or disciples. The room held four looms and several woven blankets, including one in progress on the loom at which the old woman sat, a pattern of red, blue and purple. Along one wall were simple shelves of wooden planks crowded with spools of yarn in all imaginable colors.

"Hello, Mrs. Silva. I'm Harper Sheridan. This is Wilona Freeman. It's so good to meet you at last."

The old woman roused herself, but did not stand. "Okay, you kids, scat!"

"No, wait," Harper said. "Are these children related to you?"

"No, they're just kids from around here."

"Let them stay," Harper said. "Okay, first we'll get set up, and then we'll have a chat. How's that?"

The old woman shrugged. "Okay with me. You can talk to me, but don't try to change me. Just don't try."

"I wouldn't think of it." Harper watched the old woman for a moment, then said to Wilona, "Set up your equipment. When

123

you're ready, we'll start."

Carmen Silva turned back to the work on her loom. She passed the shuttle through rapidly, her feet, clad in scuffed leather sandals, working the treadles, her hand pulling the reed with a thwack against the yarn. She worked in a regular rhythm, the clack of the pedals and thwack of the loom creating a kind of music with a predictable beat. The children sat watching her, one of them holding a calico cat. Harper, anxious to preserve the scene, whispered to Wilona, "Get a couple minutes of this, just as it is now."

Wilona nodded and quietly began filming. Harper started to create the story in her mind— an old woman who wove beautiful textiles of excellent quality, a woman who did nothing but weave, whose passion for decades had been weaving. Even if there had been no video series to perpetuate, Harper decided, she would have come to see this woman and listen to her life story.

Wilona filmed the scene before them, sweeping across the room to where the mesmerized children sat, then back to the loom and the methodical rhythm of the weaver. Harper sat on a stool near Mrs. Silva, studying her face. Gently, so as not to disrupt the mood, she said, "Mrs. Silva, we're ready."

The old woman stopped weaving and turned her attention to the camera.

"Why don't you just tell us about yourself, about how you got interested in weaving and how you live."

Like most people, Mrs. Silva seemed pleased enough to be the subject of interest.

"Well," she began, her voice deep and slightly raspy, "it started long ago, thirty years ago. When my grandmother died, she left that behind." Mrs. Silva gestured toward one of her smaller looms. Wilona panned over to the loom Mrs. Silva pointed to. "She used to make the most beautiful cloth on that thing, but I never paid that much attention. I was young. I was stupid. She showed me how to use it a couple of times, but I didn't like it much."

Mrs. Silva's small eyes looked almost black. She picked up a photo from the table by her side and showed it to the camera.

"This is her." The woman in the photo could have been Carmen Silva herself. Their ages were similar.

"After she passed, I didn't know what to do with that damned thing. I gave it another try and, what d'ya know! I just sort of took to it. Then I got better at it. People started buying the stuff I made. Some people say that my stuff is just as good as hers was." She shrugged. "I've got four looms now, as you can see. I'm still weaving. It's just what I do. All the time. I never tire of it."

Harper knelt nearby, enthralled. "Tell us what your life is like," she said, "day to day."

"I mostly stay here," Mrs. Silva explained. "Usually, if it's not too cold, I leave the front door open. People pass by, coming and going. Sometimes someone comes and buys something. Or brings me things, like food, or just comes to talk."

Laying offerings at her feet, Harper thought.

"The children come and watch. Sometimes they help with the yarn. Sometimes I send them out on errands. I can't get around much anymore. Bad knees. I used to go to church on Sundays, but not anymore. Sometimes Father stops by." Her fingers went subconsciously to the silver cross around her neck.

Harper listened, captivated. Mrs. Silva became a kind of mystic to her. She was a woman doing what she must do, as if she were designed by nature or ordained by God to do this. She reminded Harper of Sister Josephina. Their minimalist lifestyles, of course, were similar, but more than that, there was such a sense of rightness about them. They both suited their lives so completely. No complaints, no unmet needs. At peace and in harmony with the universe. Harper was envious.

They spent two hours with Mrs. Silva, listening to her talk about her life and her weaving. She proudly displayed her work for the camera. Before they left, Harper purchased a shawl with white and green designs over a black background. The pattern was intricate like so many of Carmen Silva's creations, not simple geometric shapes of lines and zigzags, but complicated, imaginative motifs that testified to a truly artistic mind at work. Harper caressed the fine wool as though it possessed some magical power, as if it had absorbed some of the passion of its creator. She felt that it might be able to instruct her.

On the drive back, Wilona said, "That went well. We can look at the film tonight, do some editing."

"That would be great. I was hoping you'd want to help with that part. What an inspiring woman!"

"What does she inspire you to do?" Wilona asked.

Harper glanced at her friend. Wilona waited expectantly.

"Uh," Harper said, turning her gaze back to the road, "I don't know. Something like what she's doing, I guess. Something that I could feel a real passion for."

"But you don't know what it is?"

Harper sighed. "No, I don't know what it is."

"Well, from what I've seen, you seem to have a passion for admiring other people's passions." Wilona laughed.

Harper didn't really think that was funny. "I'm just trying to understand them. I want to know how a person knows what to do."

"In your case, don't you suppose it would have something to do with music?"

"I guess so."

"Maybe, instead of trying to emulate other people, you should look more carefully at what you already have in yourself. You can't absorb somebody else's passion, no matter how much you admire it. It's a hackneyed bit of advice, I know, but, dammit, girl, seek within."

"'Seek not the truth in another's heart,'" Harper quoted. "Yes, I'm aware of the hackneyed advice. Doesn't mean I can follow it."

"Okay, enough with quotable quotes, then. How about stopping right up here? We can have our picnic."

Harper pulled into the park Wilona had spotted, and they carried their lunch to a shaded redwood table. As Wilona unpacked baked chicken, pasta salad and strawberries, two squirrels appeared nearby, standing on their hind legs, looking expectantly at the possibilities unfolding before them.

126

"Do you remember when she was telling us about her grandmother," Harper said as she ate, "about how she had tried to get Carmen interested in weaving, but the spark didn't catch?"

"Uh-huh."

"But after her grandmother died, she suddenly discovered she had a passion for weaving after all."

Wilona waited, her dark eyes placid.

"This is going to sound nuts to you."

"Go ahead." Wilona's eyes twinkled in anticipation.

"While she was talking...at the time, I mean, I had the idea that when her grandmother died, her spirit moved into her granddaughter, and that's why she became the weaver. She didn't inherit the talent and the passion genetically. She inherited it spiritually."

Harper caught a small smile playing across Wilona's lips.

"You don't really believe that, do you, Harper?"

"I don't know."

"Couldn't it just be that she was older, so it was more interesting to her then? Hard for a child to devote the kind of time and concentration necessary to learn a skill like that."

Harper considered this. "Yes, I suppose. And maybe losing her grandmother stirred something in her, to keep it alive, you know?"

"Maybe. She loved her grandmother, obviously. I think that makes more sense than the heebie-jeebie ghost idea."

Harper laughed. "But don't you think it's interesting anyway, that the granddaughter would have the same talent and drive as her grandmother?"

Wilona raised her eyebrows, her mouth full of chicken, and said nothing.

"This reminds me of something," Harper said. "Mary Tillotson used to teach a class called 'My Mother, My Muse.' It was about channeling the artistic impulse of your female ancestors into your own art."

"Sounds like a fun idea for a class. A little New Agey."

"Probably. But interesting to think about. What is the source of the artist's vision? When we talk about that abstract concept, the Muse, what do we really mean? Is it all just genetics, the way our brains happen to be wired? Or is there something more mysterious at work?"

"You know I don't have much of a mystical bent, Harper. I think it's all just the luck of the draw. A chance arrangement of genes and a particular selection of personal experiences."

"Don't you think there's anything predetermined?"

"You mean by God? You know I don't believe in—"

"No, I don't mean by God. I mean, don't you think some things would be true for each of us regardless of our personal experiences?"

"Well, some things, but they're genetic and they aren't determined before you were conceived. I'm thinking of things like your being gay or my mother getting cancer or Andrew being blind. I don't think Carmen Silva was destined to be a weaver, if that's where you're going with this."

Wilona pushed a container to Harper's side of the table. "Have some strawberries," she said. "I picked them this morning while you were asleep."

Harper took a strawberry and watched a scrub jay above them while she ate it. "These are wonderful." She took another.

Wilona was silent for a moment and then said, "Harper, I think there's something wrong with the way you look at other people's work."

"What do you mean?"

"Well, I saw it here today with Carmen, and I've seen it before in your comments about my photography, for instance. It even shows up in your documentaries. It lends a tone of reverence to your films and that's great. I mean, I certainly appreciated it in the one you made of me, but I thought it was just a technique you were using for the films. I didn't realize at first that it's how you really see things."

"I don't understand. What technique?"

"The assumption that the passion for the art preceded the practice of the art, as if it's manifest destiny that Carmen Silva is

128

a weaver and I'm a photographer."

Harper glanced over for a second to see Wilona nodding to herself.

"When I was twelve," Wilona said, "my uncle gave me a camera for my birthday. I hadn't asked for it. Had never thought about taking pictures one way or another. He just thought I might enjoy it and cameras were becoming inexpensive and commonplace at that time. So, of course, I took some pictures. Later, when my mother was ill, I took a lot of pictures of her. It was sort of an obsession. I knew she was going to die. I think I thought that I could stop the cancer by taking its picture, freezing it in its tracks, you know. I mean, I didn't really think that, but I fantasized it. The camera and the photographs became really important to me during those years. That's how it started. By chance. It wasn't something I was driven to do before I did it. That's my point. The passion grows out of the practice, not the other way round."

Harper said nothing. She had always assumed that people who were driven to do something like paint or write had always been driven to do it, that the drive was innate to them from birth, like Mozart. But most people weren't like Mozart.

"I can see I'm going to have to start over completely," Harper said at last, "and redo that documentary about you because I've gotten absolutely everything wrong."

"Oh, no!" Wilona said emphatically. "You didn't get it wrong. It's a beautiful testimonial to the photographs. I love it. What I said before is still true. It's about my work, not about my life, and that's okay. There's nothing wrong with that film. It's a true work of art."

"So I'm an idiot savant?"

Wilona laughed. "I wouldn't go that far. But, you know, you seem to be in total awe of other people's work without understanding that it's *work*. The films that you're making are art. They're beautiful. But they're work too, aren't they? You spend long hours editing content and dubbing in words and music. It's the same for me and the photos. It's not like the hand of God is on my shutter button."

"But not everybody with a camera can do what you do."

"No, you're right. There's got to be a predisposition to it, but whether I end up being a photographer or you end up being a cellist is largely a matter of chance. It's what you do with the talent after you realize that you have it that makes you an artist. How did you end up playing the cello, by the way?"

"Oh, well, I hadn't planned that. I wanted to learn the violin. I had this high school music class, and the first day we were going to actually play instruments I was late because I missed the bus and had to get my brother to take me to school. By the time I got there, everyone had picked out their instruments, and all of the violin positions were taken. So the teacher said, 'Why don't you grab that cello, Harper, and give it a try?'"

Wilona smiled in a self-satisfied way and said nothing more.

Chapter 16

SUMMER, TWO YEARS AGO (JUNE)

The summer of Harper's thirty-sixth year was turning out to be more interesting than most. Much more. A huge transformation was taking place, a transformation that had been approaching for a long time. She was ready for it. She embraced it.

For the last sixteen years, summers had, at least in part, meant Eliot. But, this, this would be the summer of Chelsea. Eliot was now relegated to her past. By ten thirty this morning, he was out of her life. By eleven, she was on the phone with Chelsea, ready for a new beginning.

"He's gone," she reported.

"Eliot?" Chelsea asked. "Gone for good, you mean? Or gone for the season?"

"Gone for good. He just left. I told him it was over."

"Wow! I didn't think you'd really do that after all these years."

"It was time I did. It was just clinging to the past, for both of us."

"Are you okay?" Chelsea asked.

"Yes, fine. I feel such a sense of...relief, I guess I have to say. And hope for the future."

"Good. I was worried that you might have second thoughts. Since I'm sort of responsible—"

"Oh, no, you're not," Harper said. "Not at all. Don't think that. I needed to do this, regardless. You were just the catalyst. Whatever happens now, I'll always be grateful to you for that, for giving me the push in the right direction."

"No regrets."

"No regrets. Absolutely not."

"Can I come over?" Chelsea asked, sounding suddenly shy.

"Yes, of course! Why do you think I called?" Harper laughed lightly. Her voice was calm, but her body was in a state of frantic euphoria. Today would be the culmination of weeks of gentle wooing between them.

"See you in a few minutes," Chelsea said.

"Can't wait."

Harper switched off the phone and took a deep breath, relishing the delirious tension in her body. *At last!* she thought, closing her eyes so that she could conjure up an image of Chelsea's hesitant smile, an expression she had grown to adore. That shyness, it wasn't lack of confidence. It was lack of presumption. Chelsea took almost nothing for granted, it seemed. Harper found that refreshing and endearing.

She had known Chelsea for six years but still did not know her well. Until recently, she had known her only as Mary Tillotson's student lover, an interesting young devotee of the woman of arts and letters. For most of this time, Harper had thought of her as simply an extension of Mary. But lately Chelsea had emerged as an individual. She was no longer the impressionable young coed that Mary had taken under her wing. She was a twenty-seven-year-old woman who had come into her own.

After being a rare visitor to the university library since her graduation a few years earlier, Chelsea had begun to appear again in recent months. She was back in school, she told Harper, working on her master's in education.

They had started talking, first about books and writers, poets and painters. They had long, sometimes antagonistic, discussions that left Harper feeling stimulated and drained at the same time. During one of these talks, Chelsea mentioned, in passing, that she was no longer with Mary, that Mary had "kicked her out" and that she was living alone in an apartment. After that, their conversations turned more toward the personal.

One day in early spring they went out for a drink, a date that ended up lasting several hours. By the second hour, Harper had felt comfortable and familiar enough to ask a question that had been on her mind for a while—after six years with Mary, what had gone wrong.

"Mary doesn't comprehend the principle of exclusivity," Chelsea told her.

"You mean she cheated on you?"

"It's probably not fair to say it that way. 'Cheated,' I mean. Because that isn't how she would see it." Chelsea smiled sadly. "Mary actually has a very loving heart. She loves everyone. Almost literally. She thinks of sex as just another aspect of human relations, not something to be denied or suppressed. It's something to be given as a gift to out-of-town visitors, like a fruit basket."

Chelsea's voice had a tinge of bitterness. She had obviously been hurt. "In a way, I admire that. It's honest and free, but it isn't something I want for myself."

"That doesn't seem unreasonable to me," Harper said. "Most people expect fidelity in a relationship. I guess things were different in the beginning, then."

"Not for very long, actually," Chelsea said, "but I was so smitten, I took what I got, you know? I let her make the rules. It was a classic case of hero worship. I put her on a pedestal. But as I got older, there was no way she could live up to that image, of course. I hate to admit it, but I'm a cliché."

"So you don't love her anymore?" Harper asked.

"The relationship is over. I can't give her what she wants, the unquestioning adoration. She thrives on that. She isn't able to adapt to something on a more equal footing. She'll always see me as a student. No, it just doesn't work anymore, even if I could overlook the occasional dalliance." Chelsea took a sip of her merlot, looking thoughtful. "Which I can't."

Harper was aware that Chelsea hadn't answered her question about love. She had to conclude that Chelsea still loved Mary. She also accepted the idea that the relationship was unsalvageable. What Chelsea was saying fell in line with what Harper herself had observed over the last several years.

"The others—" Harper asked tentatively, recalling campus rumors that went back to the beginning of her own career, "—are they students?"

"Oh, no!" Chelsea laughed. "No. Mary has a thoroughly maternal relationship with her students, and she doesn't cross the line."

"But, you?"

Chelsea looked embarrassed. "That was my doing," she said. "I forced my way into her life. She resisted, believe me. Her students do adore her, and plenty of them desire her. She's fended off dozens of students, men and women, and she knows how to do that. Her attitude about them is that they're *messy*— her word. No, I was a rare exception." Chelsea narrowed her eyes at Harper. "Look, can we talk about something else, something more interesting?"

Harper found the subject of Chelsea's relationship with Mary extremely interesting, but she said nothing more about it. The rest of the time was spent on more lighthearted topics. She found herself talking about her family in Cape Cod and her idyllic New England childhood. They also talked about music. On that subject, Chelsea said, "I'm an imbecile when it comes to music."

"Oh, I doubt that."

"No, it's true, even though I go to the symphony and all that.

I like music, but I don't really get it, if you know what I mean. Of course I like pop music. But classical, it can be a little tedious... sometimes. Sometimes it's wonderful. Your cello solo that time, that was wonderful."

"Thanks. You don't have to like everything. Even I don't like everything."

Chelsea smiled. "But opera, that just has to be the worst! I will never figure that out. Mary loves it. I went a couple of times for her sake, but it just seems so ridiculous to me."

It was nearly impossible, Harper realized, for Chelsea to have a conversation without mentioning Mary, despite her own request to avoid the subject. That wasn't surprising. Practically her entire adult life had been spent under Mary's wing.

Harper studied Chelsea as they talked, absorbing details of her appearance—her skin with its fine blond hairs, a nose slightly flattened at the end, the smile which lifted only the right side of her mouth, and her light, pleasant laugh. Glimpses of her diminutive round ears and the tiny scar under her left eye mingled with the faint whiff of a blooming tea rose in the planter box below the open window. An interleaved memory of sight and smell insinuated itself into Harper's subconscious, producing sensory echoes that resounded in her mind often after that day.

She found herself waiting for Chelsea to appear in the library, looking up from whatever she was doing when she heard the swoosh of the automatic doors opening and feeling disappointed when it wasn't her. Chelsea's face appeared in her mind involuntarily, along with bits of conversation or the way Chelsea hooked her hair behind her ear, unhurriedly, with her index finger. These images came to her as she hung clean kitchen curtains or mowed the lawn. They came often and unexpectedly and left her feeling warm and happy. She started mentioning Chelsea to her friends, even Eliot, often just to repeat something clever she had said. And, as springtime waned, she began to wonder if there was any possibility that she and Chelsea could be more than friends.

By May their friendship had moved unopposed into that

realm of desire that had always been mysterious and alluring to Harper. Understanding and unafraid, she allowed Chelsea to move deeper under her skin. They went to dinner together, then to a chamber music concert and then to the theater to see Mary Zimmerman's play *Metamorphoses*. Harper had always had a special love of Greek mythology and Chelsea, with her Morrison education and years of devotion to a woman in love with all things classical, proved the ideal companion for this event.

During the performance, they exchanged smiles with one another over special moments in the action, wordlessly conveying their enjoyment. Afterward, they went out for dessert, sharing a piece of Kahlua cheesecake at a round, rickety table in a noisy diner.

"The pool was practically a character in the play," Chelsea remarked. "And not always the same character. It was sometimes benign, sometimes threatening. It was the one constant. Always there, but you never knew what part it would play."

Harper nodded. "You're right. Surprisingly versatile, considering that, as a prop, it never really changed at all."

"The staging, the costumes, everything, that production was just gorgeous to look at."

Harper sipped her decaf, watching Chelsea's eyes. She looked lovely tonight, dressed in heather gray slacks and a cute embroidered jacket over a silky azure blouse. She wore gold hoops in her ears, and her sunny hair was swept up and pinned haphazardly on the back of her head, leaving her neck bare.

"Which story did you like best?" Chelsea asked.

"Orpheus and Eurydice, I think. It's such an intriguing idea, isn't it, that you could go into the underworld and bring back a loved one who's died. To cheat death, it's something we've all wished for at one time or another."

"Yes, a universal fantasy. I have to agree with you about that one. It was very moving. So full of suspense as he led her back up to the world of the living."

"I know! I found myself gritting my teeth while they did that slow march out of Hell."

Chelsea poised her fork over the last bite of cheesecake and looked inquiringly at Harper, who nodded assent. Chelsea took the bite. "He just had to believe she was following him. It was an incredible leap of faith."

"You could feel his agony. He wanted desperately to look, to see if she was still there or just to see her."

"And, then, of course, when he turns and looks at her, your heart just sinks."

"Even though we knew he would," Harper added.

"Yes, we knew he would, but somehow we hoped he wouldn't. We wanted a happy ending."

"We always do."

Chelsea nodded. "Yes, people do so want a happy ending!" She poured milk into her coffee, then asked, "Could you do it?"

"Not look, you mean?"

"Yes. Just trust, blindly."

Harper thought for a few seconds and then said, "Yes, I could."

Chelsea shook her head. "I don't think I could. I'd look. Wouldn't be able to stop myself."

"You can't make the leap of faith?"

"I've never been very good at faith."

"Even when it comes to love? In that case, what else is there but faith?"

Chelsea smiled crookedly. "Well, maybe a couple of things, but you're right. Believing in love is largely a matter of faith."

After dessert, Harper drove Chelsea home, parking outside her apartment building.

"I had a great time," Chelsea said, her expression conveying more than her words. "I really like you, you know?" She touched Harper's arm briefly, then slid out of the car on the passenger side.

"I'll call you," Harper said. "Maybe we can do something next weekend."

Harper recognized that they were now dating, that they were no longer two friends "hanging out." She also knew when she

137

invited Chelsea to her house for dinner a week later that she was inviting her to the next stage.

That Saturday, Chelsea arrived with a basket of nectarines she had picked from her parents' tree, a gift of summer fruit. She wore her hair in a ponytail, exposing her small ears with their gold hoops and the tufts of light hair down either side of the back of her neck, hairs too short and wispy to be pulled into the elastic band. Across the top of her nose ran a random pattern of light freckles that hadn't been there the last time Harper saw her. As the weather warmed, the freckles emerged from their winter dormancy. Her hair seemed lighter too, as if it were absorbing summer sunlight.

Chelsea placed her hand on Harper's more than once during dinner, smoothly guiding their evening toward the physical. Harper had already told Chelsea what she needed to know, that, although certainly not naïve about sex, she was inexperienced with women. She had never even kissed a woman, though that time with Peggy, in college, had gone well beyond kissing. That had been seventeen years ago, but it was close to the surface of Harper's consciousness once again. Chelsea's experience, Harper knew, was also limited, though in a different way—but in this particular dance, they seemed to have agreed, she was leading.

After dinner they sat in patio chairs on the redwood deck, sipping a crisp Riesling and eating nectarine slices while the lively tones of Vivaldi serenaded them from inside the house. The night was warm with only an occasional slip of a wind cutting through the heavy air. They were both tired of talking, it seemed. They sat side by side, enjoying one another's company in silence, watching the night sky and listening to the faint tinkling of a neighbor's wind chimes, an odd, but not unpleasant, percussive addition to Vivaldi. At one point Chelsea reached over and took hold of Harper's hand, clasping it easily between them, casting an uncomplicated smile at her. Harper felt calm and happy and strangely as if the two of them had been sitting here like this, contented and familiar, for years. She felt, in fact, as if they were already lovers.

As their magical evening concluded, they stood just inside the front door, looking at one another wordlessly, an air of expectation between them. Chelsea put her hand to Harper's cheek, caressing her gently as she moved closer. Her eyes were full of portent. *She's being careful and polite*, Harper realized, *because this moment is a powerful memory in the making, a moment to be cherished.* Chelsea took Harper lightly in her arms and kissed her tentatively. As soon as Harper felt those soft lips gently pressing hers, she gladly abandoned herself to the feeling. She'd been imagining this for several weeks already.

They kissed one another tenderly for several minutes during which neither of them spoke. Harper tasted sweet nectarine juice on Chelsea's mouth, a flavor that diminished as they continued kissing. Chelsea was a wonderful kisser. Harper felt immediately comfortable and natural with her, their mouths meshing perfectly in a leisurely, luxurious communion. She felt Chelsea's hands on her back, their breasts and thighs touching. Everywhere their bodies intersected, there was heat and a heightening of senses.

Chelsea's lips grazed her neck, her ear, her collarbone, so tantalizingly soft and sensuous. Harper, her eyes closed, felt as if she were being transformed into music. She felt like a Mendelssohn sonata drifting through the room. Ironic, she thought, remembering how Chelsea professed no musical talent. And yet she was masterful at playing Harper.

Chelsea could have done anything she wanted to at that point. Harper was completely under her spell. But she said good night instead, leaving Harper's body craving more, leaving a promise of something extraordinary yet to come. Long after Chelsea had gone, Harper felt the splendid sensation of her mouth.

She knew why Chelsea hesitated. It was because of Eliot. She was waiting for Harper to be done with him. She didn't want to be involved in a triangle. She was moving cautiously. If Harper had felt any doubts at all about what she should do next, Chelsea's marvelous kisses would have easily dispelled them. But she had no doubts.

The following week Eliot arrived for his summer visit. Harper had told Chelsea, weeks earlier, long before she had tasted those velvety lips, that she planned to break up with him this summer. She didn't want to do it on the phone, though. She wanted to do it in person. So she let him come as planned, but, soon after he arrived, she told him what she had been rehearsing for months.

"You can't see me in your future," he said, repeating the gist of what she was trying to explain. "Is that what you're saying?"

"That's right. There's no future for us. We've known that for a long time. I don't want to invest any more of my life in something with no future."

"I thought that's what you liked about it," he objected, "that you didn't have to invest anything. You know, the lack of commitment, the free and easy good times. You've said as much, that you didn't want to be tied down or deal with expectations."

"Yes, I know, but I've been feeling differently lately. It doesn't feel right to me anymore. It feels hollow. I think I need something more substantial."

"Harper, I've been trying to persuade you for years now to get married. You can't get any more substantial than that."

"I'm sorry, Eliot, but I just don't see you as a part of whatever substantial means for me."

"So you don't love me anymore?"

"As a friend, Eliot. I love you as a dear, old friend."

"Since when?" he asked.

"Honestly, it's always been that way."

As Eliot slept in the guest room that night, Harper considered the sixteen years of summers that he had inhabited and felt a vague sense of loss. She was buoyed, though, by the tremendous potential of this new summer. And, although he was disoriented, she knew he would be okay. Better than okay. He had a life already that didn't include her. This breakup felt anticlimactic to her. She thought it would probably be similar for him, once he got over the sting.

After breakfast the next day, Eliot hugged Harper goodbye and left. It was a sad moment, the end of an era. But by the time she had dialed Chelsea's number to report that he was gone, the sadness had completely left her.

Now, an hour later, as Chelsea's Honda appeared at the curb, Harper couldn't have been happier. She was ecstatic, in fact. Eliot was completely forgotten as she watched Chelsea approach. She moved like a waltz from the street to the door. Her hair, loose, bounced over her shoulders as she stepped up the walkway. She was radiant. She fell into Harper's waiting arms, the sun's heat clinging to her skin and clothes. They clutched one another tightly, their mouths coming anxiously together.

They kissed with unrestrained desire. Finally, Harper pulled away and took Chelsea's hand, leading her into the bedroom. They sat on the bed and resumed kissing. Neither of them had uttered a word since Chelsea's arrival. They had been talking for months. There was nothing to say now except through touch.

Chelsea pulled off her shirt and slipped out of her bra, tossing it on the floor. There was a faint tan line slung low across her chest. Her firm breasts were as round as peaches and looked just as luscious, their relaxed nipples the color of bubble gum. Harper touched them softly, feeling silk. As her thumb passed over a smooth aureole, it clenched into prominence—an invitation. They removed the rest of their clothes rapidly.

There was something in her that had been waiting all her life for this moment, thought Harper, holding this woman in her arms. It had been lying semi-dormant, not peacefully as in a dreaming sleep, but fitful and impatient, goading her. And it had taken her all this time to understand what it was that she had been heading toward.

Chelsea lowered Harper to the bed, lying on top of her. Taking hold of Harper's mouth with hers, she kissed her so deeply that Harper could feel desire sweeping across her entire body.

Chelsea's hands moved over Harper's curves, caressing her with exquisite, lingering touches. Her mouth rhapsodized Harper, softly, sweetly. Her fingers touched every part of Harper's body as if she were a blind woman reading the libretto of her soul.

Harper touched Chelsea too, marveling at how soft and sleek she was, how like satin her skin felt against fingertips and lips.

With sensitive abandon, she let her mouth follow its own course—along Chelsea's shoulder, then down between her breasts, along the side of her waist to the bone protruding at her hip, and then into the tender spot at the top of her thigh where honey-colored hair tickled her nose. Facing toward the footboard now, Harper kissed the pale skin below Chelsea's navel, letting her tongue glide along the tan line low on her stomach.

Chelsea turned on her side, pulling Harper's hips close to her face, then stroked her, gently and lightly at first, with her fingers, but gradually more insistently, deepening the sensation, and Harper's body found and matched the rising tempo. She gripped Chelsea's body more tightly as the heat grew between them and her desire swelled. She felt Chelsea's hot breath between her legs and then felt her warm, wet mouth nuzzling into her. As her tongue slid up and back down like a bow on a violin, Harper buried her face in Chelsea's soft inner thigh and let herself be overwhelmed.

Chapter 17

SUMMER, TWO YEARS AGO (JULY)

The summer of Chelsea, with its long, languid nights of lovemaking, proceeded happily through June and into July. When the time came in late July to travel east, Harper went reluctantly. She and Chelsea hadn't been apart for more than a day up until then, and she was still drowning in the ecstasy of this woman's company.

"I'll be here when you get back," Chelsea told her, urging her to go. "I'll just want you more."

"I'll only stay nine days," Harper promised.

Those nine days passed by rapidly with frequent phone calls from Massachusetts to California and from California to Massachusetts. Harper, thoroughly preoccupied with her newfound joy, told her brother all about Chelsea on the day of her arrival. She was relieved to have a confidante. Danny, she knew, wouldn't be alarmed or judgmental. He was momentarily surprised, but that soon gave way to the anticipated interest and support.

Harper wasn't able to hide her overwhelming happiness from the rest of her family, although she tried, making her phone calls away from the house or late at night when everyone was asleep. Since Chelsea was three hours behind, this was ideal. But her mother was watching her, it seemed, growing more and more suspicious, because mothers can sense the moods of their cubs without being told. And it probably didn't look all that nonchalant the times Harper's cell phone rang and she bolted from the room like a spaceship going into hyperdrive.

Alice waited until the third day to ask, "Who is it that you're so preoccupied with, Harper?"

"A friend," she said evasively.

Her mother eyed her in a way that made Harper feel small and vulnerable, as if she were five and being asked, "Who spilled milk all over the dog?"

"Girl friend," Harper said shyly. Although she had correctly predicted Danny's response to her love for a woman, she wasn't sure how her parents would take it, despite their political support for gay rights.

"I see," Alice replied, looking steadily at Harper. "Someone special?"

"Uh-huh."

"Does she have a name?"

"Chelsea." Harper slid the photo she'd been carrying out of her cell phone case and handed it to her mother.

Alice looked at the photo carefully for a moment, then handed it back. "She's darling," she said cheerfully. "A darling girl! Thank you, Harper, for sharing this with me." Alice reached for Harper, giving her a warm hug. She then turned toward the oven where she was baking lasagna and appeared to be finished with the subject.

Harper was perplexed. Maybe her mother hadn't understood.

"Mom," she asked, "is that it? You don't have any questions?

You aren't going to ask what happened to Eliot or why I'm dating a girl?"

Alice turned back to face her, looking puzzled. "I assume it's because you like her. And what do you mean about Eliot? Has something happened to Eliot?"

"I broke up with him, of course. This is a big deal, Mom. I've changed, you see? Dumped the old boyfriend. Dating a girl." She gestured vaguely. "Something sort of different going on here."

Alice gazed at her silently, pressing her springy hair down with one hand, as if holding it on her head. *Is she finally going to get it?* Harper wondered, waiting.

Alice removed her hand from her head. "Are you trying to tell me that you and Eliot were actually a couple all these years?"

"Well, of course! What did you think? I've been seeing him since college, for God's sake. I mean, no, we weren't married so, in the eyes of the Church, I guess—"

"No, that's not what I meant." Her mother pursed her lips tightly, then said, "I'm sorry, Harper. This is very strange. I didn't realize he was really your boyfriend. I thought we were all just pretending that he was your boyfriend, that you weren't comfortable being open with us."

"What!" Harper stared, unbelieving.

"I thought you've been with women all along. I was hurt, actually, that you never felt you could talk to me about what was really important in your life. I hated it, in fact, going along with this whole Eliot thing. Do you realize that I've been to a dozen PFLAG meetings over the years talking about my gay daughter who simply refuses to come out to me?"

Harper collapsed into a chair. "I don't understand. Why did you think Eliot was a front?"

"Well, it started in high school, of course, with Peggy. Everybody knew she was a lesbian. The two of you were inseparable, and then you ran off with her to California. You were extremely melodramatic about it. You said that if we wouldn't let you go to California with Peggy, you'd kill yourself. What was I supposed to think?"

All of this was true, Harper realized, except the part about everybody knowing that Peggy was a lesbian. *She* hadn't known. The other kids hadn't known. The boys she dated hadn't known. It had apparently been obvious to some of the adults, though.

"Did everybody think this?" Harper asked. "Danny and Neil?"

"I don't know what everybody thought. We didn't talk about it. We never told them. We thought that if you weren't comfortable coming out to your family, we had to respect that."

"You might have said something during all these years," Harper said, still in shock.

"I guess I thought we had an understanding," Alice told her. "At PFLAG, they told me to be patient and let you come out when you were ready."

"Wow, I can't believe this."

"Well, dear, the good news is that your parents adjusted years and years ago to your being gay, so there's no adjustment period needed now."

It took a few days for Harper to get used to the idea that in her parents' eyes, she had always been gay. But her mother was right, she didn't have to worry about what negative impact it might have on her family relationships. Nothing changed. Even Neil, who hadn't been a part of this decades-long conspiracy, who had always thought of Eliot as his future brother-in-law, didn't seem particularly surprised or disturbed. In the only mention of it between them, Neil hugged her and said, "I'm glad you're happy, Harper." Their parents, having taken a pro-gay stance for such a long time in their effort to be supportive of Harper, had apparently prepared the entire family well for the coming-out day.

After that day, Harper's sexual orientation became a non-subject. She didn't know what Neil and Kathy told their children, if anything. Only Sarah, who was about to turn fifteen, was old enough, anyway, to have any real understanding of such things. She was just coming into an age where she was starting to stand out to Harper, to look like an individual. She was moving out of

146

the amorphous body of her nuclear family to assume her own identity.

Harper only realized this a couple of days later while walking in the woods behind the house. A cushion of verdant grass lay over the ground, kept moist by the canopy of leafy branches above. These few acres had been one of her favorite places as a child.

Harper strolled slowly, thoughts of childhood ripe in her consciousness. When she heard a childlike voice call her name, she looked to see Sarah sitting with her back against a tree trunk, a book on her knees. Her hair, a light shade of brown, hung straight from a center part down upon her nearly flat chest.

"Hi," Harper said.

"Were you daydreaming, Aunt Harper?" Sarah asked.

"Yes, I was. What are you reading?" Harper picked up the book to read the jacket. *Les Misérables*. She handed the book back. "How far have you gotten?"

"About halfway. Have you read it?" Sarah stood, tucking the book under her arm.

"Yes, it's a classic. In fact, I saw a play based on it, in San Francisco."

Sarah sighed. "How wonderful to be able to go to the theater. How wonderful to be able to go to San Francisco."

Those are things I take for granted, thought Harper. She put her arm around the girl's shoulder, and they began walking slowly together. "Have you ever seen a play?"

"Just school plays. You must know a lot about books, Aunt Harper. You must know about every book that's worth reading."

Harper laughed. "I wouldn't claim to."

Sarah was tall for her age and lanky, much as Harper had been as a teenager.

"Daddy says you've been to Europe," Sarah said.

"Yes. I've been to England, Ireland and France. Oh, and two weeks in Italy."

Sarah looked up at her with awe. "Could you tell me about Europe?" she asked. She had the same romantic views of Europe

Harper remembered in herself. "Europe," the word itself, inspired romance.

They went down to the dock to talk. Her niece was intelligent and sensitive, Harper discovered, courageous and full of conviction. She was alternately timid and bold. And she was infatuated with learning. Harper was enthralled.

"Could you make a list of books for me to read?" *Give me the keys to the kingdom*, Harper heard her say. She was touched that Sarah thought she had those keys to give.

"I'd be happy to." She looked closely at the girl. "What do you want to do with your life?" she asked.

"Everything!" declared Sarah in exultation. "Just like you. I want to go away to college, travel all over the world, meet all kinds of people, live in exotic places like California or Zimbabwe."

Harper laughed. *What an extraordinary image she has of me. I must seem brilliantly avant-garde, probably because she's filling in all the gaps with her imagination.*

"And I would like to have a monkey named Cleo who rides on my shoulder wherever I go," added Sarah, satisfied with herself.

"That sounds sublime," Harper remarked.

Sarah's eyes widened. "Sublime," she repeated, caressing the word with her tongue.

The two of them sat at the end of the dock, their legs dangling above the water.

"Do you write?" Harper asked.

"Oh, yes. I definitely want to be a writer. I write short stories and epic poems."

"Epic poems? Like Homer and Virgil?"

"Exactly!" Sarah said, looking astonished.

"So, is your hero male or female?"

"Female, of course."

"Of course! Not the least bit conventional, though. I'd like to read something of yours, if you wouldn't mind."

Sarah grinned. "I'd be happy to have your opinion," she said rather formally.

Harper looked out across the water, watching the sea gulls.

"Have you heard of Boudica?" she asked. "The ancient warrior queen of old England?"

"Warrior queen?" asked Sarah, obviously intrigued. "Like Xena?"

"Well, yes, but a real person. Come to think of it, she appeared on *Xena* in a few episodes. You might enjoy reading about her since you write epics. She led an army against the Romans in the first century A.D. She became a legend. There's a statue of her in London."

"Have you seen it?"

"Yes. We can look it up on the Internet this evening if you want. Also, there are poems about her and novels and movies too, if you're interested."

"I'm very interested," Sarah assured her.

"I thought you might be. You might also be interested in another ancient heroine of Ireland. Her name was Maeve. She was a queen who could run faster than a horse. She had a dozen husbands and innumerable lovers, most of them kings, and she carried birds and animals on her shoulders."

"Oh, my God!"

"Yes, your monkey Cleo reminded me of her. She's also the subject of an epic poem, *The Cattle Raid of Cooley*, which I can send you to read."

"You really do know everything, don't you, Aunt Harper?"

"No, Sarah, but I've been practically living in a library for a long time now. I couldn't help but have picked up a few things."

"Well, neither of my parents even has the slightest idea what an epic poem is."

"No, your father was never much for the humanities. He's a math and science guy, like your grandfather. And your mother, I hear, was the same way."

"I wrote a poem about Persephone the other day. Neither one of them even knew who she was. I was just like, what? Are you serious?"

Harper smiled.

"You know who she is, right?" Sarah asked.

149

"Yes." The challenge on Sarah's face prompted Harper to tell the tale. "Persephone was the beloved daughter of Demeter, goddess of grain and crops and the cycles of the Earth. Hades abducted her and made her his queen. Demeter was so distraught that the Earth quit turning and life came to a standstill. In the end, Persephone was allowed to return to Earth for a season each year, reunited with her mother, prompting a period of flourishing abundance."

"Spring."

"Yes, spring. And when Persephone returned to the underworld each year, the earth was plunged into a period of cold barrenness."

"Winter." Sarah smiled, delighted. "I knew you knew it."

Harper nodded.

"I love that story," Sarah said.

"It's a good one," Harper agreed. "It reminds me of a book I had as a child, a book about the Greek myths. It had all these fabulous illustrations in it. Actually, I think that book is still here in the house. If we can find it, I'd like you to have it."

"Thank you!"

Harper was enjoying the role of mentor. She didn't think she'd ever been one before. The closest she came was helping students in the library. This felt different, probably because Sarah was younger and more eager.

"Sarah," she said, suddenly struck with an idea, "I don't know what your parents would think of it, but there's no reason you can't come to visit me in California. You're old enough to travel alone, as long as I meet you at the airport. We could have a lot of fun. We could go to San Francisco, anywhere you want, and Santa Cruz and Monterey. We could go to the theater." Harper said this last word with an upper-class British accent while throwing her hand above her head with flair. "What about spring break? You get a week off then, right? I do too."

Sarah looked at her as if she were some kind of supreme being. The next thing Harper knew, she was running toward the house screaming for her mother. Harper stayed where she was,

150

watching the sun set, smiling distractedly. She hoped Neil and Kathy would give their permission. It would be fun taking Sarah around to see the sights for a week or so. She was so hungry for knowledge and experience.

Harper watched a lone rowboat glide silently across the water toward its dock. Her thoughts turned to Chelsea as she imagined Sarah's spring visit. She was sure that Chelsea would enjoy it just as much as she expected to. Sarah was so open and enthusiastic. It would be a joy for the three of them to ride a roller coaster in Santa Cruz and a cable car in San Francisco. Maybe they could drive up to Mendocino too where Chelsea's brother had a summer home. Sarah would think the drive up the coast highway was awesome. Didn't everyone?

A flood of possibilities came to mind as Harper imagined the three of them sightseeing. The list of places she thought of mingled with the list she already had in her mind for just Chelsea and herself. There hadn't been time to do any of these things yet, and she wanted to do everything with Chelsea. Even ride a cable car! They had both done that, of course, but they had never done it together.

She took her cell phone out of its case and called Chelsea's number. She answered on the second ring. "Oh, Harper, I was just thinking about you."

Harper lay back on the wooden planks of the dock and pressed the phone closer to her ear.

"Miss you," she said, staring up into a pale blue sky.

"Me too. Tell me about your day."

Chapter 18

JUNE 23

Andrew held Harper's guitar uneasily. She reached around the chair he was sitting in, placing his fingers on the strings and showing him how to use the pick. Then she had him play a chord and change his fingers, then play another, until he understood how the different sounds were made.

Wilona watched them from her rocking chair across the room. They were taking a break from working on the documentary, a task that was proceeding smoothly. Having made four already, Harper knew what to do, how to put together the story. With Wilona's expertise, the film editing was going much more quickly than Harper ever could have done on her own.

So, after playing a couple of songs on her guitar to entertain them, Harper had asked Andrew if he would like to try it. He had responded eagerly. His face lit up each time he touched the strings and made music. *This is what Roxie does for a living, every day*, thought Harper. It seemed like rewarding work, though she knew that Roxie's students were not all nearly as cooperative as Andrew.

"That's wonderful," Harper told him. "You're a natural-born musician!"

They continued the lesson until Andrew had learned the C, G and F chords. After an hour, Wilona suggested that it was time for him to get ready for bed. To Harper's surprise, he agreed. "My fingers have had enough for today," he said, returning the guitar carefully to Harper before leaving the room.

"Thank you for that, Harper," Wilona said.

"Oh, you don't need to thank me. It was fun. I've never tried to teach anyone to play before. Of course, he's an eager student. Makes it easy. When I first took piano lessons as a child, I was a terror. My poor music teacher..." Harper laughed, remembering what a petulant student she had been. "You were right, he's a joyful child."

"That's enough to teach us all a lesson, isn't it?"

Harper nodded.

"I think I'll go to bed too," Wilona said, pulling herself up from her chair. "I'll see you in the morning, Harper, and we can finish up that film work."

Once the rest of the household was quiet, Harper went to her room and phoned Chelsea again. There was no answer. In fact, the phone went to voice mail after only one ring, indicating that it was turned off. Harper hung up, then, after a few minutes, called again. This time she left a message. "Chelsea," she said, "this is Harper. I got your message. I'd like to talk to you too. Call me back on my cell. I'm not home right now."

Harper placed her phone on the bedside table, then read a book for a half hour, occasionally glancing at the phone, as if doing so might encourage Chelsea to return her call. Finally, tired and discouraged, she turned off the lamp. She lay in the dark with a window open to a warm, still night gloriously filled with stars, one of the tremendous benefits of being away from the city. A faint odor of pine came in periodically on the breeze.

Starry skies like this reminded Harper of nights lying in a sleeping bag beside a mountain lake, one of those inspirational experiences that makes you feel so alive and so in tune with nature.

Whenever Harper contemplated a sky like this, deep in the night, she heard music—sonorous, profoundly resonating harmonies synchronized with the orbit and rotation of celestial bodies, united like the instruments of an orchestra under the direction of a grand maestro.

Harper and Chelsea had never gone camping. They'd never gone fishing or snorkeling, never gone to a museum or even to a movie together. Everything had happened too fast. Their weeks together were frozen in time at the first flush of love, suspended at the core of transcendent zeal, before it had a chance to lose any of its luster. In that respect, it was perfect, an untainted grand passion.

If Harper were an artist, she would have wrestled that summer into a painting or a novel or a song. An artist had that power, to transform the too-intense sting of life into an object of beauty. What sort of poem had Chelsea written, she wondered, to lessen the ache of that wound?

For Chelsea had been hurt too. Harper had been wrong about a lot of things, but not about that, surely. Chelsea's tears that day, the day she said goodbye, they were genuine. After all of her second-guessing of Chelsea's intentions, she was back to believing again. Harper knew that her gut could always be trusted, and her gut told her that the bond between them had been real.

It was nearly midnight. She tried not to draw any conclusions about why Chelsea wasn't returning her call. *She'll call tomorrow*, she reassured herself, drifting into a fitful sleep.

Chapter 19

JUNE 24

But Chelsea did not call, and Harper had to conclude that she wasn't going to. After all, it had now been two weeks since her original message. Who knew what had prompted the call in the first place? Maybe it had been a momentary lapse of judgment. Perhaps the summer heat had had the same effect on her as it had been having on Harper, reviving in them both a driving need for one another. If so, Chelsea had clearly managed to master her desires.

Harper prepared to return home. Her documentary was already taking a semblance of its final shape. The background music, which she would choose on her own, would be added later. She thanked Wilona and said goodbye to Andrew, wishing him luck with his music.

It was nearly three o'clock when she pulled into her driveway. The first thing she did when she got inside the house was to pick up the phone to see if there was voice mail. There was. Had Chelsea called here instead of her cell phone? No, it was her mother, reporting that Sarah was still missing and the police were doing nothing at all about it.

Harper guiltily realized that she had completely forgotten about the family emergency while she'd been away. *Shit!* she thought. *How could I have forgotten that?*

She needed to call them, but first... She switched on the air conditioner to relieve the stuffiness in the house and went to the kitchen to get a soda. She stiffened at the sight of a note taped on the refrigerator door. The note was written in a script she didn't recognize. Someone had been in her house while she was gone. Nobody had a key, except... No, Chelsea had given hers back.

Then she saw that the note was addressed to "Aunt Harper." Sarah? It had to be. She flipped the paper over to check the signature. It was! She read the note quickly.

Aunt Harper,

Surprise! I came for a visit. Arrived here Monday afternoon and hung around waiting for you, but after a while, I let myself in. You should get a better lock on your bedroom window. Don't worry. I didn't break it.

I helped myself to your food and stuff and hung out until this afternoon (Tuesday). I hope you don't mind. Since you didn't come home last night and I have no idea where you are or when you'll be back, I think I'll take off. Nothing to do here. Can't even surf the Web because of the password on your computer. Don't know your cell number either. Should have gotten that before I left. Stupid, I know.

Sorry, I don't have a phone. Dad took it away months ago. I'll find a way to call, though, in a couple of days to see if you're back. For now, I want to see the sights. I'm going to Disneyland!

P.S. I saw the pictures of Chelsea in your guest room. I heard Mom and Dad talking about her once, a while back, about how she's your girlfriend. She's really <u>sublime</u>.

Sarah

The word "sublime" was underlined emphatically.

Harper stared at the note in her hand for a moment, letting this information sink in. Sarah had been here Monday and then left on Tuesday to go to Disneyland? Today was Thursday. Harper's head was spinning.

Why did Sarah come here? Harper wondered. *And where the hell is she now?*

When she had recovered enough to act, she called her brother and gave him the news. Neil was ecstatic at first.

"Oh, thank God she's safe," he said. "So where is she now?"

"Like I said," Harper explained. "I don't know. Her note said she was going to Disneyland."

"Disneyland. Isn't that way down by L.A.?"

"Yes. Nowhere near here. She probably didn't realize that. It would be at least six hours by car."

"So how could she get there? Would she take a bus? Jesus, would she hitchhike?"

Harper didn't know how to answer that.

"So what you're saying," Neil continued, in an accusatory tone, "is that you've lost her."

"Well, technically, I didn't actually have her."

"But she was there, she was there to see you, to seek out your help."

"I had no idea. I'm sorry, Neil. She did say she'd call me in a couple of days."

"But it's been a couple of days. That was Tuesday. Now it's Thursday. She hasn't called. Nobody's seen her or heard from her. Anything could have happened. Oh, God, Harper, I wish you'd been home."

"I do too. At least we know more than we did before. And her note sounded very cheerful. No mishaps along the way, apparently. She's a resourceful child."

Neil grunted begrudgingly. "I'll call the police and tell them."

After hanging up, Harper got her suitcase out of the car, then returned to the refrigerator for the soda she'd been after, noticing that several were missing. It looked like Sarah had also helped herself to that expensive imported gouda. *I hope she appreciated that*, Harper thought, opening the freezer with the aim of satisfying her hunger with a pint of strawberry ice cream. Gone. Oh, well, she thought, reaching for a Lean Cuisine spaghetti instead, Sarah had probably done her a favor with that one. She had just stuck the frozen dinner in the microwave when her doorbell rang. Thinking that it was Sarah returning, she ran to the door and pulled it open without even looking through the peephole. It wasn't Sarah. It was a female police officer. *Oh, God*, Harper thought, a hundred imagined disasters trampling each other in her mind.

"Good afternoon," said the officer. "Are you Harper Sheridan?"

Harper nodded, scanning the police cruiser at the curb. It was empty.

"I'm here about your niece. To take a statement," she added quickly. "To help us find her." She stuck out a hand. "Officer Wakely."

"Come in," Harper said, standing aside.

Officer Wakely stepped inside with a confident stride, taking a rapid glance around the room before turning back to Harper. "You're Roxie's friend, right?"

"How did you—"

"Elaine. That's me."

"Elaine? Oh, you're—" So this was Roxie's girlfriend. Harper took a closer look at the officer. She was not very tall, but she looked strong and solid. She looked tough, like a woman who could take care of herself in any situation.

"Figured it was you when I saw the paperwork," Elaine said. "How many people in this town are named Harper, right? I mean, first name. Can't say I ever knew your last name. Roxie just says, Harper, you know, when she's talking about you. Your brother called his local force. They called us. I'm here to verify the details."

"Sure."

"By the way, I'm glad to finally meet you. I've seen you play with the symphony. I usually go, if I'm not working. Wouldn't normally be my cup of tea, you know, but it's important to Roxie. I can usually get a half hour nap in, if I'm lucky."

Elaine grinned to let Harper know that was a joke, but Harper suspected there was some truth in it.

"About your niece," Elaine said, "no idea where she might have gone?"

"Besides Disneyland, you mean?"

"Yes. We got that. Of course, we've alerted the Anaheim police. Any friends or relatives nearby? Or in Southern California?"

"The entire family is back east. Other than me, I mean. As far as her friends go, I really wouldn't know."

"Can I see the note?"

Harper retrieved it and handed it to Elaine, who read it slowly. "She knows about Chelsea, I see."

"Not really. I mean, her information is out of date."

"A couple of years out of date. I guess they don't talk that much about your love life back there."

"Not as much as you and Roxie, apparently."

Elaine smiled, then handed the note back to Harper. "Sorry."

"No, that's okay," Harper said, waving at the air. "Of course she's told you about that."

Elaine nodded sympathetically.

She must know a lot about me, Harper thought. *And until a week ago I didn't even know she existed.* As they sat down at the kitchen table to go over the facts of the case, Harper couldn't help thinking about how bizarre this whole situation was.

Once Elaine had the information she'd come for, she made her way to the front door. "I'm sure we'll be seeing one another again, Harper. Hopefully when it isn't business. Meanwhile, we'll see if we can find your niece."

"Thank you. Tell Roxie hi for me."

Elaine winked and let herself out.

Chapter 20

SUMMER, THREE YEARS AGO

As a cellist, Harper was primarily interested in the Baroque masters. She was particularly fond of Corelli. So when she found out that the summer concert series included two Corelli works, one a cello concerto, she decided to sign up for it. Normally, she only played the regular season because there were so many summer conflicts. She hesitated briefly—she and Eliot had plans to go hiking and camping in Olympic National Park in Washington—but chances didn't come that often for a solo, as she explained to him when she called with the change of plans. He was irritated at first but then agreed to come down so he would be there for the performance, something that wasn't practical during the school year.

On the Sunday afternoon of the concert, Eliot was seated in the fourth row of the center section. She waved to him before the performance began, then adjusted her blouse collar and took her seat with the other cellos. Eliot had already had to endure endless rehearsals at home during the week he had been in town. He was good-humored about it, though, and even hummed along some of the time.

The entire program was inspired, with the overture to Rossini's *The Italian Girl in Algiers*, Haydn's *101st Symphony* and Corelli's *Concerto Grosso no. 4* to finish. When the time came for her solo, Harper took a chair at the front of the stage next to the violin section. "Knock 'em dead," she heard Roxie whisper. Maestro Guthrie stood on his platform, tall and tuxedoed, sweat glistening on his forehead. It was his custom to give a brief introduction to each piece, especially during the summer series when the audience often contained people new to classical music.

"Arcangelo Corelli," he said in a commanding voice, "was a major Baroque composer who was hugely popular in his time and died a rich man. He was also an accomplished violinist. As a composer, one of his greatest contributions is a group of twelve concerti grosso. This is a form for a small group of soloists and a larger orchestra."

Harper was grateful that she didn't have to speak. Her mouth was dry, and her mind was racing in incoherent circles.

"Tonight we will be playing *Concerto Grosso no. 4 in D Major*," Guthrie continued. "You might keep in mind as you listen that Corelli had a profound influence on Vivaldi. You will also hear something reminiscent of Bach's *Brandenburg Concertos* here. Those came later, and were based on a similar form. Our own Ms. Harper Sheridan will be performing on the cello."

Guthrie turned to face the orchestra, giving Harper a brief smile of reassurance as the lights went down. As he stood there stiffly, his baton at attention but motionless, it felt to Harper as if time were standing still. The musicians held their breath, then as a unit began to play.

After that, there was nothing but the music. Harper no longer saw the audience, but only the sheets on her stand and the conductor, whose violent motions occasionally sent beads of perspiration flying her way. Then, after a few seconds, she saw nothing but the music itself.

Playing the cello wasn't like playing the piano. It wasn't like any other instrument she had played. She adored its voice, so rich and deep, full-bodied like dark chocolate. She also liked the way it felt, its shape and intimate physical presence. Playing the cello was not an activity of the hands alone. It was a whole body experience. Cradled in her arms like a dance partner, its body between her legs like a lover, it responded to her embrace by sending its chords deep inside her. As she played, she imagined that there was music coming out of her own body too, an echo from her instrument.

By the time the music ended and the conductor waved his baton at her to take a bow, Harper was completely spent. There had been no mistakes, which was all she had really hoped for. But beyond that, the performance had been magical. She couldn't have been happier, and the wide grin on Guthrie's face suggested that he felt the same way. He stepped off his podium and hugged her, whispering next to her ear, "Magnificent, Harper." Roxie grinned proudly at her.

The applause continued, giving Harper the opportunity to focus again on individuals. Eliot was standing, clapping like a lunatic. Mary and Chelsea, seven rows back as usual, were smiling and clapping. Harper was glad to see them, glad that they had shared her special moment.

In the lobby, Harper shook the hands of the patrons as they filed out, waiting for Eliot to appear. Before he did, though, Mary and Chelsea edged through the crowd to her side.

"Glorious!" Mary pronounced. "Congratulations, Harper."

"Thank you." Harper felt flushed and vibrant.

Chelsea beamed at her. "It was the best piece," she said. "That Haydn thing was just boring by comparison."

Mary looked shocked. "Boring? You're calling Haydn's *Clock Symphony* boring? Chelsea, you're simply hopeless when it comes to music. I don't know why I waste my money on your ticket."

Chelsea frowned and looked embarrassed.

"If you're going to criticize a masterpiece," Mary continued, "and one assumes that you're calling the performance into question, not the composition, then at least choose more evocative words. Wearisome, perhaps, or lackluster."

"I don't see any reason to be pretentious," Chelsea said. "Boring is a perfectly good word. Everyone knows what it means and it describes my feelings precisely."

Mary looked exasperated. "Well, then, have it your way."

After five years of mindless adoration, it appeared that Chelsea had developed a mind of her own. Harper couldn't help but feel slightly amused.

"I think they call it the *Clock Symphony* because you're looking at the clock the whole way through." Chelsea chuckled shortly at her quip. "My point, though, was that I really enjoyed Harper's performance."

"I'm glad you liked it," Harper said, still euphoric.

"It was such a happy tune," Chelsea elaborated.

"Happy tune!" Mary repeated with disbelief and then, realizing that Chelsea was goading her, frowned and said no more.

Harper and Chelsea grinned at one another in a moment of collusion. Then Harper caught sight of Eliot about thirty feet away, looming above a sea of silver hair. She waved to catch his attention. She turned back to Mary and Chelsea, saying, "Sorry. I just wanted to let my boyfriend know where I was."

"Your what?" Mary asked loudly, crinkling her nose.

"My boyfriend," Harper repeated, wondering if Mary was getting hard of hearing or it was simply the din of the room. Mary and Chelsea looked at one another with perplexed expressions.

Chelsea looked in the direction Harper had waved. "That one there?" she asked. "The tall guy with the long brown hair?"

"Yes," Harper said. "That's Eliot."

As he reached her side, he kissed her cheek and said, "You were fantastic, honey. Just fantastic. I hope you know how good you are."

"Oh, God, I was so nervous," Harper replied, then made the

introductions.

"Oh, I know you," Eliot said, shaking Mary's hand. "I mean, I've seen Harper's film. You're the painter."

"That's right," Mary said with a beatific smile. "And that reminds me, Harper. I'd like to use that film at my gallery exhibit. I want to have it playing continuously on a television monitor. I'll need your permission for that. We'll be glad to pay whatever fee you'd like to charge."

"Oh, no," Harper said. "You can consider the film yours, really. I'm just glad you think it's good enough to use."

"Well, you know that I never tire of listening to people talk about me or my work, so of course I love it." Mary beamed in that mock-innocent way she had.

"So how long have you two been together?" Chelsea asked.

"Oh, wow, about sixteen years," Eliot said. "Is that right, hon?"

He slipped an arm around her waist. For some reason, the gesture made Harper uncomfortable. It was just a bit too possessive.

"Since college, yes," she said.

Chelsea looked astonished. "Oh, then quite serious, I guess."

"Eliot teaches at Washington State," Harper explained, as she was accustomed to doing. "We only see each other in the summer."

"What an interesting arrangement," Mary exclaimed. "Even I might be willing to have a boyfriend under those circumstances." She laughed.

Chelsea rolled her eyes, then said, "Congratulations again, Harper. It was really special."

When Mary and Chelsea had gone, Eliot turned to Harper and asked, "Are those two a couple?"

Harper nodded. "It's a teacher-student thing."

"Ah. Now, that, I understand."

"I guess you've been around that block, haven't you?"

He smiled tactfully and didn't answer. Harper didn't care what he did or with whom when he wasn't with her, as long as

164

he was safe and responsible. Generally speaking, they got along smoothly. Eliot was easygoing and agreeable. They hadn't had a fight in years, but the last time they did it was over his need to have her to himself. His inclinations were toward ownership, and she was adamantly against that. He was always trying to corral her, but so far she'd managed to sidestep his attempts.

Harper had arranged her entire summer this year around the symphony schedule. That meant making a late July visit to Cape Cod that was just twelve days long, a little shorter than usual. A week after her solo, Eliot went to visit his sister and Harper settled into her parents' home, relishing the peace and comfort that she always found there.

Coming to visit really felt like coming home, not just to a place, but to a state of mind. She and her brothers had been born and had grown up in this house. The moment she caught sight of it each summer, its white wood exterior, brick red shutters and dormer-style second-story windows exerted on her a calming effect that was almost mystical. Sleeping in her childhood bedroom was soothing too, even though almost everything there had been changed in the intervening years. Just two things remained from her childhood—the white dresser with its gold accents and curvy legs and a wooden plaque on the wall next to the closet. The plaque contained a Biblical quotation from Job that Harper still considered valid advice:

But ask now the beasts, and they shall teach thee;
and the fowls of the air, and they shall tell thee:
Or speak to the earth, and it shall teach thee:
and the fishes of the sea shall declare unto thee.

Through the years, whatever affiliation she made with a philosophy or religion, Harper had continued to believe in the truth and wisdom of nature, specifically her own nature, the part of herself that operated on instinct like an animal. Her intellect seemed faulty, as proven early on by her inability to master calculus and later by her complete mystification at the experiment known affectionately among physicists as Schrödinger's cat. She could never get beyond the horror of a cat being killed in a box, even if it was just a theoretical cat. Eliot was so fond of this theory that he had named his own cat Schrödinger. Harper suspected there were a lot of cats with that name.

During her stay, her brothers visited as usual and Harper spent hours relaxing on the boat or doing nothing on the wide porch behind the house. She and Danny often sat there in the evening as the sun set, talking or just listening to birds. Occasionally, she played Danny's guitar, folk songs, usually, so everybody could sing. The guitar was Harper's first one, which she had given her brother when she got a new one, hoping to interest him in playing. It hadn't taken, so the guitar sat idle, waiting for her return each summer.

The piano was still here too, the piano she had lessons on as a child, and she usually played at least one evening for the gathered family. Her mother also played once in a while, the only other member of the family who was musical. It had been Alice, in fact, who had forced piano lessons on Harper when she was just seven years old in the vague belief that girls had to cultivate such talents, as if they were living in a Jane Austen novel. Harper was grateful later, of course, for the lessons and the gift of music, something she knew that she would treasure for the rest of her life. She was grateful too that her mother's outdated notion of how to make a girl marriageable hadn't extended to lessons in embroidery and English country dance.

Lazing in an Adirondack chair on the porch, Harper admired the blues and lavenders of her mother's hydrangeas lining the edge of the lawn as the deepening shadows enriched their hues.

"How's Eliot?" Danny asked, pushing his glasses up on his nose with one finger.

"Okay," she said noncommittally. "Wearisome, perhaps, or lackluster." Harper smiled to herself, remembering Mary's suggestion to Chelsea about Haydn's 101st. Somehow, it seemed to apply.

"Huh?" Danny asked, suddenly paying attention.

"Oh, it's just getting old, I think."

"Really? Even though you only see him a month out of each year?"

"Yes, even though."

Danny was quiet for a moment, then said, "Were you ever really in love with Eliot?"

"No," Harper said quietly. "I don't think so. Not in the way you mean." She decided to move the focus off herself then. "How about you? Any romantic prospects?"

"Nope. It appears that my most intimate relationship is still with God. Which is extremely ironic, since I'm not even sure I believe in God anymore. But, lately, when I do imagine God, the image in my mind is female."

"Female?"

"A feminine force, anyway. There's so much evidence to support that view. You have to dig, though, because of the thousands of years of misogyny aimed at purging the female divinity from Christianity." Danny threw his feet over the edge of the railing. "Several of the heterodox texts contain references to a feminine divinity. And, of course, the religions that were replaced by Christianity, so many of those were structured around a goddess. You know all that, though."

"Yes, I've read a few books in my time."

"There's evidence to suggest," he persisted, "that the Trinity originally was comprised of the Father, the Mother and the Son. The Holy Spirit was a term referring to the feminine god. And many archeological finds mention God's consort, Asherah."

Danny was speaking in an intellectual manner about a subject that Harper had never approached intellectually. Her own experience with religion, with all of the religions she had sampled, had not been intellectual at all. It was a spiritual pursuit, an attempt to feel a sense of oneness with God or the Earth or the cosmos. She had sat with her eyes closed, trying to obliterate the contents of her mind, in order to reach a state of spiritual fulfillment. She had no experience with Danny's approach, a spiritual life based on reasoning. So she just listened.

"The idea of a female component to the Trinity was rejected

167

by the fathers of Christianity, who couldn't conceive of an equality between the sexes, especially for gods. So they widowed the male god, made Christ's mother a sexless woman and made Christ a sexless man. Sex was literally purged from human experience of the divine. And where it was acknowledged, it was usually considered base and shameful. Obviously, Western civilization has never recovered from that attitude."

"No wonder you were defrocked," Harper remarked. "Your approach to religion seems determined to undermine the faith. I don't even know how you ever toed the line enough to become a priest in the first place."

"I wasn't defrocked. I left. Besides, you know that's how to get people to think. I never did appreciate any parishioner who hadn't arrived at faith through suffering. The others are sheep. Who wants them?"

"Christ is the good shepherd," she reminded him. "The sheep are the ones the Church counts on for its foundation."

"Sure, but they don't offer any challenge. They just hold out their hands and wait for the priest to put the religion package in them. That isn't how a priest earns his keep. Or it shouldn't be. We should help them to discover God for themselves, to achieve a truly won faith, or it means nothing. I believe it requires a lot of time and often a lot of mistakes to really know who you are, to confront your true inner self."

"So are you talking about self-knowledge or faith in God?"

"What's the difference? That's my point. If I were God..." Danny looked skyward, then back to Harper with a grin, "I would have no patience nor any use for the faith of those who were ignorant and untested. If a person isn't in touch with his or her self, then what are they offering to God or to anyone, for that matter? Even a friend or a lover. It's hollow. Undependable."

Danny stroked the small mustache, a new addition to his face that was still a little jarring to Harper. The goatee of the previous summer was gone. "Harper," he asked, "were you ever tempted to a life of religious devotion?"

"Um, yes, once. Remember the summer that Eliot and I went

168

to Mexico to do disaster relief work?"

"Yes. Oaxaca, wasn't it?"

"Right. I met a woman there, Sister Josephina. I admired her so much. I thought she'd found the perfect life for herself, a life devoted to helping the poor with no focus on herself at all. I very briefly wondered if that life, her life, would give me the same kind of satisfaction that it gave her."

"And your conclusion?"

"I wasn't really able to stay and find out, but I don't believe it would have worked for me. It was right for her. Not really my scene."

"It's interesting, isn't it, how everyone has his or her own calling? How each one is different?"

"Yes. It makes it hard to figure out what's going to work for you. But I sort of knew already that the religious part of a life of religious devotion wasn't for me."

Danny laughed. "Sort of a dilemma, that. Maybe our religious views aren't so different after all."

Harper sat quietly thinking. It was dusky out, and insects had started to circle around the porch light. "The thing is, Sister Josephina is happy. That's what it all boils down to, finding a way to live peacefully, in harmony with the world, without the feeling that something's missing. And if you're really happy, why do you need to look any further? That's all anybody really wants."

Danny smiled his wide, thin smile. "You're probably right, but happiness is an elusive beast."

"Yes, it is. And so we all wander around looking for the song our soul wants to sing."

"That's very poetical. What kind of song would that be? Some old country-western ballad? Jive-talkin' boogie? Maybe that song from *West Side Story* we used to sing when we were little, remember, dancing around the house in our underwear?"

Danny jumped out of his chair, twirled around and sang two lines from "I Feel Pretty," causing Harper to laugh loudly.

She shook her head. "No. It's a song without words."

Danny stopped dancing. "Really? Why is that?"

169

"The soul doesn't speak in words. You should know that. That's your line of work, isn't it?"

"I can't recall ever having a conversation with anybody's soul, not directly, bypassing their mouth. Thinking about it, though, I guess you're onto something." He leaned down to her, close to her ear. "Well, hello in there, Harper's soul. You have any requests? Got a song you want to sing?"

"You're such a kidder, aren't you? It's just a metaphor for finding what will make you happy."

Danny leaned against the railing and gazed at her through the dimming light. "I don't think most people even know what would make them happy. What makes you happy, Harper?"

She thought for a moment, remembering the Corelli solo, how transported she had felt while playing. "Music makes me happy. And love. I'd like to fall in love. Everyone is happy when they're in love."

"Yes, that's true." Danny smiled broadly at her. "So, let's do it," he said, "let's fall in love!"

He extended a hand toward her and pulled her from her chair, then the two of them danced across the porch singing "I Feel Pretty" at the top of their lungs and laughing.

Chapter 21

Harper wasn't surprised when her mother called her early Friday, just as she was taking that first precious sip of coffee. She curled up in her easy chair, her cup close at hand on the little table beside it.

"No, Mom," she said, responding to her mother's questions. "Believe me, I will call you or Neil as soon as I know anything."

"I just can't believe she's in California. How did she get there?"

"I don't know. Maybe she's not alone."

"What do you mean?"

"Maybe somebody drove her. Maybe she took off with somebody."

"You mean a boy?"

"Well, that would be the most likely thing. Doesn't she have a boyfriend?"

171

"Do you think Kathy and Neil would know if she did? She doesn't tell them anything. The police questioned her friends, but they claim to know nothing."

Harper listened while her mother described the months of rebellious behavior that had led up to Sarah's flight. She managed to drink a third of her cup of coffee without saying a word.

"Why did she come to you?" Alice asked.

Harper set her cup down beside her open address book. "I don't know."

"Are you sure? You're not in cahoots with that girl, are you, Harper?"

"Are you kidding me? Of course not. Why would I—"

"You always had a rebellious streak yourself."

Harper flung her feet to the floor. "Mom! That's ridiculous. Of course I would tell you. I know everyone is worried. Honestly, I'm telling you everything I know."

"All right, then."

A few minutes later, Harper hung up. As she picked up her coffee cup, the address book caught her eye again. It was open to the "N" page. There were three entries there, her dentist, the Norcal Shakespeare Company and Chelsea Nichols. Why was it open? She hadn't called any of those numbers. The address and phone number listed for Chelsea were for Mary's house, after all. Maybe she'd opened it to write in the new number for Chelsea? But the new number wasn't there.

She sat in her chair for a few minutes, staring absently at the book as she finished her coffee. What if it was Sarah? What if she had been looking for Chelsea's name? She thought Harper and Chelsea were still together. Looking her up would have made sense, given that assumption.

If Sarah had called or visited Mary's house, though, she would have discovered right away that she wasn't going to find Harper there. She would have come back, wouldn't she? Or gone on to Disneyland, maybe.

There was a chance, Harper realized, that Sarah had contacted Chelsea or Mary. If so, the police should be informed. She dressed and set out for Mary's house. She could have phoned, she knew, but doing so would rob her of the chance to see Chelsea and ask her why she had called and left that message. The possibility of seeing Chelsea again was, she had to admit, as compelling as the need to solve the mystery and drama of her niece's appearance and subsequent disappearance.

Minutes later, her stomach in knots, Harper rang the bell, hoping Chelsea would answer. After a moment, the door swung open. Her stomach lurched. Damn. It was Mary. She had hoped to avoid Mary altogether.

"Ah, hello, Harper," Mary said exuberantly, a wide grin on her face. "What a surprise! What brings you here? Old times' sake? Wanting to rub salt into the wound?" Her voice, though cheerful, was not welcoming.

Harper, confused, said, "I don't know what you mean."

Doubt flickered across Mary's face, but she recovered quickly.

"I'm looking for my niece, Sarah, actually," Harper explained. "She's missing and I thought she might have come here."

"And why would she do that?"

"Well, because she thought, uh…" Harper stopped, unable to find a way to explain.

Mary opened the door wider. "Come in."

Harper gazed quickly around as she stepped inside but saw no one. "Have you seen her, then?"

Mary, closing the door, said, "Yes." She waved her hand to indicate that Harper should follow her. "Fascinating girl. We've been having a wonderful time."

"You mean she's here now?"

"Yes. She's out by the pool." Mary walked rapidly through the kitchen toward the back door. Harper followed in a state of confusion.

"Such a quick intellect and a feisty spirit," Mary said. "Reminds me of Chelsea when she was young…and impressionable."

"Is Chelsea here?" Harper asked, remembering suddenly.

Mary stopped abruptly and turned to face her, the amusement

173

gone from her face. For the first time in all the years Harper had known her, she looked old. Deep lines creased each side of her mouth, and her dark hair was spattered with gray with one dramatic lock of silver swept back from her forehead.

"Chelsea hasn't been here since April," she said. "Are you going to tell me you didn't know that?"

Harper, stunned, shook her head. "I—no, I didn't."

Mary studied her for a long moment, her expression flat and unnerving. Then she turned and pushed the back door open, leading the way to the pool where Sarah was lying in a lounge chair, wearing a skimpy pink bikini and reading a book. If Harper hadn't expected to see her niece, she wouldn't have recognized her. For one thing, her hair was now bleached blond and quite short. Harper had never seen her without long hair.

She had turned into a woman overnight as well, it seemed. *No wonder they're having all of this trouble with her*, Harper thought, taking in the long legs, ripe bosom and flat, tanned stomach. She was a voluptuous creature. She looked up from her book and broke into a wide smile.

"Aunt Harper!" She sprang from her chair, ran up and flung her arms around Harper, then stood beaming at her, her expression that of an excited child. A tiny diamond in the left side of her nose sparkled as she moved. "You guys are back."

"I got home yesterday," Harper said, confused by the "you guys."

"Is Chelsea here? I want to meet her."

Harper glanced at Mary, who averted her eyes.

"Have you been here since Tuesday?" Harper asked.

Sarah nodded.

"No Disneyland?"

"You know, I had no idea Disneyland was so far away! I went to the library and looked it up. Besides, I used up my life savings coming out here, so I had no way to get there. I decided to find Chelsea instead. I figured she'd know where you were. That's how I ended up here. Mary said I could wait for you here. I've been having a great time. Mary's a painter. Did you know that?

She does these amazing impressionistic scenes. She promised to paint me. Don't you think that would be cool? Oh, and the things we eat around here are just amazing. I've had so many things I've never had before. We had caviar! And Mary let me have a glass of champagne last night."

Harper cast a sharp glance at Mary, who shrugged. Sarah was still speaking, rapidly, excitedly. "Oh, God, Aunt Harper, she knows so much about literature. Have you seen her library? I could just die. Nobody has a library anymore. I love it. I could live in there for years."

Harper looked from Sarah to Mary, exasperated.

"What could I do?" Mary asked, adopting a mocking tone once more. "The little orphan came calling. She had nowhere else to go, poor thing." Mary stepped toward Sarah and put her arm around her shoulders. "And since she was a relative of my good friend Harper, I had to take her in, didn't I?"

Harper felt herself growing angry. As calmly as she could, she said, "Mary, can we go inside and talk?"

"Of course." Mary gave Sarah a squeeze, then released her, saying, "Go back to your book, darling."

Mary offered Harper a seat in the living room. The walls were still covered with that incongruous collection of art, including the painting of Chelsea, which was hanging where Harper had first seen it, above the fireplace. It had been six years since she had been in this room.

"What did you want to talk about?" Mary asked shortly. Her expression was unfriendly.

"What the hell is going on here? What have you been doing with my niece?"

"What do you think I've been 'doing' with her?" Mary asked defiantly. "Discussing the finer points of iambic pentameter?" She looked incredibly pleased with herself.

Harper leapt out of her chair. "She's only sixteen!" she exclaimed.

Mary, her voice perfectly calm, said, "Too young for iambic pentameter? I think not."

175

Harper, confused, said, "What?"

"Surely you're familiar with iambic pentameter?"

Harper realized that Mary was playing with her, which made her even angrier. She forced herself to speak calmly. "Why have you kept her here?"

"Kept her? God, Harper, you make it sound like I abducted the girl. I hope that, despite what it sounds like, you aren't accusing me of anything improper."

Mary's glare was challenging. This antagonism was upsetting to Harper. There was a time when she had hoped she could be friends with Mary. Now they were practically enemies.

"No," Harper said, sitting again. "I'm not accusing you of anything. I just don't understand what's going on."

Mary's expression relaxed. "Sarah showed up at my door Tuesday afternoon, looking for you, babbling incoherently. She assumed she would find you wherever she would find Chelsea, she said, and this was the address she had for Chelsea." Mary pursed her lips. "Well, I assumed the same thing. I assumed you and Chelsea were together, that she had gone to you as soon as I turned her out. It's what she does."

"I haven't seen her," Harper said softly. "I didn't know she had moved out." She felt awkward talking to Mary about this, but Mary was the best source of information she had at the moment. "You and Chelsea, then, you're split up?"

Mary looked at Harper dispassionately. "She's no longer living here. But if I should want her to come back, she would do it in an instant. All I have to do is ask. You know that, don't you?" Mary's voice was calm, but forceful.

Harper dropped her gaze to her hands in her lap.

"But why are we talking about Chelsea?" Mary said, her tone lightening. "I thought you wanted to talk about Sarah. I decided to invite her in, and she just stayed. Nothing very mysterious about it. I did consider that it was a sort of joke on you at first, but, then, after a few hours, I was just enjoying her company."

"I'm still confused. Who does she think you are? I mean, in relationship to Chelsea?"

Mary shrugged. "I believe she has some idea that I'm her aunt or something like that. I don't know. To be honest, Harper, we haven't been talking about Chelsea."

"So what have you and Sarah been doing, other than drinking champagne and eating caviar?"

"It was just a tiny glass. No harm in it. She deserves to sample the finer things in life. We've had quite a bit of fun. We've been listening to music and talking, mostly about poetry and fiction. And, yes, iambic pentameter. She showed me some of her writing. She's not very good, but she is enthusiastic, and she's well read."

"How good could she be at sixteen?"

"Right. My students are usually a little older than that, and that particular couple of years can do wonders for them. But she has this poem called 'Passing Through,' which is dreadful and utterly irredeemable, full of puerile rhymes and heartwarming sentiments. You decide for yourself, but you'll agree with me. Said she wrote it on the train on her way across country." Mary clasped her hands together with an air of solemnity. "Are you going to take her away now?"

"Yes." Harper stood and walked toward the kitchen. Mary followed.

"You couldn't maybe leave her here for a couple of days?" she asked.

"Why would I do that?"

"Why not? She's enjoying herself. She loves to read, and I have books. She told me there isn't a book anywhere in your house. What kind of travesty is that?"

"I'll take her to the library," Harper said.

It occurred to Harper, listening to the beseeching tone in Mary's voice, that Sarah was providing a much-cherished bit of company for her. Harper needed to get her home, though, and tell Neil that his daughter was safe and under her protection.

Well, Harper thought, steeling herself, *if Mary gets lonely enough she can do as she boasted and reel Chelsea back in.* She pushed through the back door to the patio.

"Sarah, get your things together," Harper called to her.

"We're going home."

Sarah looked up from her book. "Okay," she said, sitting up and slipping on her wrap. "I'll be back to visit," she said to Mary. "I want you to show me that meter thing that Ovid and Homer used."

"Dactylic hexameter," Mary reminded her.

"Yes, that. I didn't even know it had a name."

"And Virgil," Mary pointed out, "in the *Aeneid*. That's why it's sometimes called the heroic hexameter, because it was used for the heroic poems."

"The epics," Sarah said.

"The epics, yes." Mary smiled approvingly.

Sarah held out the book she'd been reading toward Mary.

"Keep it," Mary said. "I have another copy." Her voice was gentle. She was in her element instructing young women in the arts, Harper knew. Sarah must seem like the ideal accidental visitor to her. In just three days, they seemed to have formed a genuine friendship.

"I'll get my stuff from my room," Sarah said, looking from Mary to Harper before slipping into the house.

Mary turned to Harper and said, "She's a sweet girl. What are you going to do with her?"

"Send her back to her parents. What else?" She turned to go back in the house.

Mary caught her arm and said, quietly but emphatically, "Harper, while you have her, teach her something."

On the way home, Sarah talked nonstop about her trip out on the train and about her stay at Mary's house, which started to sound like the most fabulous few days any girl had ever had.

"We went out to lunch yesterday with a friend of Mary's. Her name is Catherine Gardiner. She's wicked cool. Do you know her?"

"Well, yes, I do. In fact, I made a documentary about her. She's a famous poet."

Sarah looked astonished. "Really? I didn't know she was famous. You have the most amazing friends! At lunch, I just sat there with my mouth open, listening to the two of them talking. They don't talk like other people. They talk like they're in a play or something. I've never heard a real-life conversation like it."

I would have liked to have been at that lunch myself, Harper thought. It had been Mary who had introduced her to Catherine Gardiner and who had suggested her as a subject for the documentary series. Harper had been grateful for that. She had been interested in the eccentric poet ever since first hearing about her association with Hilda Perry so many years ago. Harper was amused at the thought of Sarah at lunch with the two of them, these odd, intriguing figures of the modern art world.

"And then they quoted poetry at one another, right there in the middle of dessert!" Sarah continued. "I tried to remember it, but mostly I can't. Something about Julia's clothes."

Harper smiled. "Whenas in silks my Julia goes," she recited, "Then, then (methinks) how sweetly flows that liquefaction of her clothes."

"Oh, my God, Aunt Harper! That's it!"

Harper understood Sarah's amazement. She herself could remember a few times hearing professors speaking in that strange literary tongue, a banter of wits which bore no resemblance to ordinary conversation. Their speech was a kind of game, like chess. Chelsea had absorbed some of that from Mary, and Harper admired and enjoyed it, though she herself was unable to play. She had the knowledge for it, but not the skill.

"I hope you got a picture," Harper said, "because you just had lunch with two prominent artists, and there are a lot of people who would have paid money to have been in your place yesterday."

"I've never even heard of her. I feel like such a freak. I'm sure they both think I'm a total spaz."

"I think Mary believes you're worth saving."

Sarah then spoke about the places she had traveled through on her way from Massachusetts to California and the strange characters she encountered. That was just as intriguing to Harper, though in a different way, since the people she had met

179

in train stations, while also colorful and interesting, were often people at the opposite end of the spectrum. They were equally alien to Sarah, whose life up until now had been sheltered, even cloistered in the bosom of her nuclear family.

"You should write all of this down," Harper suggested. "So you'll remember. All the details of your adventure."

"Oh, I have been! I have a journal. I've taken notes of 'my epic journey' across the U.S.A."

Sarah quit talking for a moment as she contemplated that thought, which she was obviously savoring deeply.

During the silence, Harper's thoughts turned to Chelsea and the information Mary had given her. She had moved out in April and had called Harper in June and asked to see her. Mary had assumed that they were back together. *What did that mean?* Harper wondered. Mary knew Chelsea better than anyone did. If *she* expected her to run to Harper, what other conclusion could there be but...

Harper stopped herself from completing that thought, forcing herself to listen more carefully to Sarah's description of rumbling through Wyoming overnight, listening to elk bugling at sunset and how that had made her feel really far from home, impossibly far, as if she had crossed some divide that was passable in only one direction and there was no longer any chance of turning back.

Chapter 22

JUNE 26

Harper put the cereal bowls in the dishwasher and sat across from Sarah at the kitchen table as she finished her glass of orange juice. Dressed in shorts and a T-shirt, she looked different today. Without all of the cleavage and thigh of yesterday, she looked younger, more like the child Harper knew.

Sarah sifted through the stack of CDs at the edge of the table, then screwed up her face in distaste. "Dean Martin?"

"Not mine. I picked those up for a friend."

"Good."

"Have you ever even listened to Dean Martin?"

Sarah shrugged. "Guess not."

She got up and put her juice glass in the dishwasher.

"What was the book Mary gave you?" Harper asked.

"It's poetry. It's Catherine Gardiner's. She told me to read this one poem in particular, but I decided to read the whole book.

I'll get it." Sarah ran into the guest room, retrieving the book and returning, flipping it open to a marked page. "Should I read it to you?"

Harper nodded and listened as Sarah attempted to read a poem called "Tradition." Harper had read that poem years ago and hadn't thought of it since. Sarah read it too fast and without a lyrical quality.

"What do you think it means?" she asked when she'd finished.

Harper took the book from her. "Listen," she said, and then she read the poem, pausing in the right places so the meaning came through.

Young girl sat
spinning, spinning,
knotting herself into a tapestry
of mothers upon mothers,
a pantheon of mothers
stretched along her coiled thread.
Each one sat
spinning, spinning,
admiring the crimson and the silver
where blood of moonlight mingles
in the fine lines of cloth,
consecrated by unquestionables
While daughters upon daughters sat
spinning, spinning,
weaving a dense web of ignorance
and vainglory
around and through themselves
to please their mothers
Who sat
spinning, spinning,
welcoming the end of their days
with regrets for
the patterns and the colors,

mutely dreaming of unravelings,
But only
wailing, wailing
over the spinning
of young girl who sits smiling
at the flawless absolutes
in the shroud she has made.

Harper looked up from the book to see Sarah gazing at her, her brow furrowed by a look of concentration. "Wow," she said. "You read that so much better than I did."

"Did it make more sense, hearing it like that?"

Sarah nodded and took the book back, then studied the page, silently reciting the poem again to herself with her new insight.

"Read it a couple more times, and then we can talk about what it means," Harper told her.

Sarah continued reading. Harper drank her coffee, thinking about how much she could tell Sarah about this poem and about so many poems and stories and the people who wrote them, if there were more time. "Teach her something," Mary had advised. There was only so much you could teach someone in a couple of days. Not enough to make much difference. To make a difference, you'd have to have more time.

"Sarah, Mary mentioned a poem you wrote called 'Passing Through.' Do you mind if I look at it?"

She went to get the poem for Harper, returning with a piece of paper that had been folded often into fourths and was covered in a scrawling longhand. Harper skimmed it quickly, agreeing with Mary's assessment. It was dreadful, at least in its current state.

"Why don't you read it out loud to me?" Harper suggested. "That makes such a big difference, especially in the author's own voice."

Sarah's eyes widened with delight, and Harper understood that it was because she had used the word "author" to refer to her. Sarah took the poem and read it aloud, lending a singsong

183

rhythm to it that had eluded Harper when she read it. The message was a simple one about passing through the dingy side of small towns without ever knowing anything about them or the people who lived there, people who must have interesting and tragic lives, each one a story worth telling. It wasn't so much "dreadful" as amateurish, a poem that probably wasn't worth a second thought...until Sarah recited it. Because, in her voice, it wasn't a poem at all. It was a song.

"A little stiff," Harper said. "What if you try to sing it?"

Sarah looked astonished. "Well, I did. I mean, that's where it came from. I heard it in my head first. I sang it, like a song. And then I wrote it down as a poem."

"So sing it for me, like you did in your head."

Sarah took a deep breath and then sang the song without looking at the paper. She sang in a pop style with a slightly melancholy tone, and the song had more complexity to its melody than the poem had revealed.

Harper was taken aback. "That's a lovely song," she said. "It's melodic and thought-provoking. Do you read music?"

Sarah shook her head.

"Come here." Harper led Sarah to the piano in the living room. She pulled the bench out, then asked Sarah to sing her song again. While Sarah sang, Harper began to play, picking up the tune. In a few minutes, she had embellished it and increased the tempo, and Sarah was laughing with excitement and a little embarrassment to hear her song transformed like this.

"Let's record this," Harper suggested, "and when I have time, I'll write down the notes for you."

Sarah seemed elated. It had obviously never occurred to her that she could actually write a song. Because she didn't know how to read or write music, she had written an unremarkable poem instead. Now, of course, she wanted to be able to play the song herself. She was all fired up, in fact, to take lessons and launch herself into an entirely new realm of artistic achievement.

After they had recorded the music, Sarah sat at the computer, listening to the instrumental version of her song, singing along

184

with it, pleased with herself. *Okay, Mary,* Harper thought, *I've taught her something. But there's not going to be time, unfortunately, for much more than this.*

"I called your father last night," Harper said.

Sarah looked up. "I figured you would."

"Your parents were very relieved to hear that you were safe."

Sarah shrugged.

"Don't you care that you terrified them?"

"I was just pissed off."

"About what?"

"They won't let me do anything. They took away everything. I felt like I was suffocating. I couldn't go out. I couldn't use the computer. I couldn't watch TV even. They took my phone. If I had stayed there, they would have chained me up in the basement next." Sarah held up her iPod. "This is the only thing I have left, my tunes."

Harper smiled. "So why'd you come here? You knew I would rat you out."

"Oh, sure, but it was an adventure getting here. I had fun. Besides, you promised that I could come out for a visit and I was tired of waiting."

"Sorry about that."

"Well, here I am. Let's party!"

"Your parents have asked me to send you back right away."

"Can't I stay just a little while?" Sarah's expression, pleading and sincere, plucked at Harper's heartstrings.

After pondering it a while, she called Neil again and proposed a new plan. "Let her stay here until my scheduled trip home," she offered. "That's July twenty-sixth. I'll bring her home then."

"Do you really want to have to deal with this for the next four weeks, Harper?" he asked. "You don't know what kids are like."

"We can give it a try. If it gets bad, I'll send her home. I have that luxury."

"I hate to reward her for running away," he said, but in the end, he gave in.

185

Sarah was ecstatic. They sat down with a map of California and a guidebook and began planning where they might go together. Before long, though, Harper's attention drifted back to the question of Chelsea and where she was.

As if reading Harper's mind, Sarah suddenly said, "Oh, but what about Chelsea? Will she be coming with us? I can't wait to meet her."

That's right, thought Harper, startled. *Sarah thinks Chelsea and I are still together*. Mary had not explained anything to her, preferring to avoid the subject altogether.

"Unfortunately," she said, "Chelsea and I broke up two years ago."

"Oh, wow," she responded. "No wonder Mary was so surprised when I showed up."

Harper nodded. "No damage done."

"Oh, that's so sad."

Harper could tell by Sarah's expression that she had given Harper and Chelsea a happy ending in her imagination. *People do so want a happy ending*, Harper thought, recalling something Chelsea had once said.

"So, is Mary Chelsea's aunt or something?" Sarah asked.

"No," Harper said. "Not a relative. They were, uh—"

Sarah's eyes widened. "Oh," she said, understanding. "Oh, shit, that's even worse. Oh, God, Aunt Harper, I'm sorry. I'm such a moron."

"Chelsea has apparently broken up with Mary now too," Harper said.

Sarah perked up. "Really? So she's available? You can hook up again."

"I don't know. I don't really know what her situation is now."

"Why don't you call her?"

"I have, actually, a couple of times. No response."

"Do you still love her?" Sarah asked, her tone almost comically sympathetic.

Harper nodded.

"Well, then, you must go to her!" Sarah said dramatically, her eyes flashing.

Sarah was suddenly no longer concerned about sightseeing, it seemed. She wanted to do something far more interesting—reunite two lovers.

Harper wished she knew if Chelsea still wanted to see her. Even if she did, Mary's threat loomed. Her certainty of her hold on Chelsea was chilling.

"I think she must have an apartment here in town," Harper said, "but I don't have her address."

"Well, she isn't there anyway," Sarah said nonchalantly.

"What?" Harper asked. "Why do you say that?"

"When I asked Mary if Chelsea was home, she said she was gone away on vacation. I thought she meant that she had gone away with you."

"So that's why you were waiting for me there? Why you thought I had come back with Chelsea?"

"Right. Anyway, I asked Mary where. Mendocino, she said."

"Mendocino," Harper repeated. "Her brother has a vacation home there."

"I told Mary I was your niece and that I was looking for you because you weren't home. She was confused. She asked me why I was asking where Chelsea was if I was looking for you. I began to think that maybe it was a secret, you know, you and Chelsea, and that I was outing you guys or something. I mean, I'm still thinking that Mary is her aunt or her landlady or even her mother. So I got freaked out. I don't even know what I said after that, something about you and Chelsea being traveling companions or something."

"Traveling companions!" Harper said, laughing.

"I know, it was so lame! She started asking me all these questions about you and Chelsea, and I told her I didn't know anything, that I'd just arrived from Cape Cod. So then she said I could wait for you at her place. And you know the rest." Sarah looked sheepish. "Anyway, now that you know where Chelsea is, you can go to her."

187

Harper sighed. "I don't know," she said. Sarah's view was so optimistically simple. "Look, I'm going to run to the store. Give me a list of things you like, what you normally eat and drink, you know."

Sarah stayed home downloading some of Harper's music onto her iPod while Harper shopped. Apparently, Mary had introduced her to classical music and now she was totally into it. Her brief stay with Mary, however strangely it had come about, had actually done her quite a bit of good, mused Harper, adding three cans of water-packed tuna to the carton of yogurt and jars of organic green tea already in her cart. Consulting the list, she saw that Sarah had written "caviar" on it. She smiled. *No way, kid.*

She pondered what she should do, if anything, with the information that Chelsea was in Mendocino. She couldn't believe Chelsea had gone by herself to that romantic town. The fact that she hadn't called was probably evidence of that.

Harper's heart was heavy as she drove back home. She wished, more than ever, that she had returned Chelsea's call immediately. Two weeks was time enough for anything to happen—enough even to fall in love with someone else on a wind-swept ocean bluff overlooking a rugged coastline.

Oh, God, Chelsea, she thought, clutching the steering wheel in despair. *Please don't be lying in another woman's arms because I waited to return your call.*

Chapter 23

Sarah had taken charge of the mouse at Harper's computer. They were working together on the background music for the Carmen Silva film. Sarah already knew a bit about editing music files, although the style of music that populated her iPod was entirely different from the sonatas, rondos and concertos they were now trying to fit to the weaving scenes.

Harper had played the documentaries of Mary Tillotson and Catherine Gardiner for Sarah the previous day. She'd been impressed by them and had gained a new appreciation, it seemed, for both Mary's and Harper's talents. Having seen the videos, she finally realized too what a remarkable event she had been a part of when Mary and Catherine had let her tag along for their lunch date. She wanted to be a part of this new film, and Harper was glad to indulge her. It was turning out to be a fun day, even if they weren't making much actual progress.

"I love that!" Sarah exclaimed, hearing *Moonlight Sonata* for the first time. "Can we use it?"

"Maybe," Harper said.

"Who wrote it?"

"Beethoven."

"All I ever knew about Beethoven was da-da-da-dum."

Harper smiled, recognizing the first notes of the *Fifth Symphony*. "Some of his shorter pieces are..."

"Sublime?" Sarah asked, grinning at her own word choice.

"Yes, exactly."

"Didn't you use one of those in the other film, the one about Mary?"

"Yes. I put a bit of *Appassionata* in there. This one is *Piano Sonata no. 14*. It's known as the *Moonlight Sonata*. Very recognizable. I'm not sure if that's a good thing or a bad thing for the film. The music is there to create a mood, not detract from the subject."

Sarah looked thoughtfully at Harper, then rewound the video and started it again. They watched the monitor as Carmen Silva worked her loom. Sarah started playing the music as they watched. "It has the right sound, don't you think?"

"You're right. It lends a hallowed atmosphere to the weaving process. It's almost as if Carmen were playing the music. Her hands move like those of a harpist or pianist. But she's moving faster than the tempo of the music. Can you hear that, how the music is so much slower than her movements?"

Sarah listened again, a serious expression on her face. "I think I get it," she said.

"We might be able to use it in another spot, though. How about this?"

Harper fast-forwarded to a section of film taken in front of the home where all of the blankets were lined up on racks. A series of stills focused on each blanket in turn, showing its colors and patterns for a few moments and then moving to the next one. Harper started the film and the Beethoven sonata simultaneously.

Sarah cocked her head slightly, listening, and Harper thought

190

of Chelsea, remembering that day six years ago when she had played that gorgeous piano at Mary's house. Chelsea's eyes had flashed with delight at the title of the song—*Appassionata*—just as Sarah's were flashing now as she listened to a brilliant piece of music that fit into the scene like a dovetail joint.

This is what Mary gets from teaching, Harper thought, *the sheer delight that becomes so elusive as you get older, except second hand through the eyes, mind and heart of a young person who is receptive and unselfconscious.*

"Aunt Harper, that's so beautiful it almost makes me want to cry."

Harper smiled, more than happy with that response.

"Are you going to use it?" Sarah asked.

"Sure. It's perfect."

Sarah played the piece over three times, satisfied with her contribution. "Will we be able to watch this on TV?" she asked.

"No, I'm afraid not. It will air here on a local channel. That's it. At least for the foreseeable future. But I'll send you a copy of the final product. You can show your family."

"If it's not on TV, they won't care," Sarah said, dejected. "They won't get it."

"Well, maybe they won't. That's how it goes with families. They love you, but they don't always appreciate the same things you do, nor will they necessarily be able to share the things that matter to you. Do you realize, not a single member of my family has ever seen me perform with the symphony?"

Sarah grew thoughtful. "I never thought of that," she said. "It's important to you, isn't it, being in the symphony?"

"Of course, but the reason they don't attend is distance, not lack of interest. The couple of times Mom and Dad have been out to visit, the timing wasn't right. I'd like to share that with them, you know."

"I'd like to come."

"Thank you. Unfortunately, you will be long gone when the season starts in the fall."

Sarah frowned, reminded of her impending return to the

Cape.

"Live classical music is a really different experience from recorded," Harper said. "And on these speakers, well, if this makes you want to cry, you'd bawl your head off if you heard it performed live."

"Can you play it?" Sarah asked. "*Moonlight Sonata*?"

"Sure, I've played it dozens of times."

Harper, getting the point, led the way to the living room and the piano. She played the piece while Sarah sat on the sofa listening. When it was finished, Harper turned around on the bench to face her. "What do you think?"

"Awesome!" Sarah said. "So, that file we were listening to on the computer, was that you playing?"

Harper shook her head, amused. "No. That's a professional recording."

"Oh. But you'll play this for the final cut, right? The background music on the film, it will be you playing?"

Harper hesitated, taken by surprise at this assumption. "It never occurred to me," she said finally.

"No kidding? Why not?"

Harper slowly shook her head, wondering herself why the idea had never entered her mind.

"Grandpa always says what a magical pianist you are."

"He does?"

"Sure! Why do you think he always asks you to play when you're there? Grandma can play the piano, he says, but Harper can make it soar."

Harper felt herself getting emotional. It was true. Her father was always complimentary when she played the piano, but that had been the case since she was young. She had assumed that he was just being encouraging and supportive since she had obviously not been an accomplished pianist at seven or even at twelve. Her piano teachers would be happy to testify to that! But she had gotten better over the years and more serious. Maybe her father's praise had changed somewhere along the way from being merely encouraging to being genuinely admiring.

Sarah's question was valid. Harper had no problem using her voice or her camera skills on her videos, so why didn't she use her music? She had always sought out just the right recording for her films, listening to as many as a dozen versions of the same piece before choosing one for its tone or tempo. She wasn't a world-class pianist by any means, but for the purposes of this video series, did she have to be that good? And she was even better with the cello. If she got Roxie on the violin and one of the violas, they could manage quite a few trios—Mozart, Haydn, why not?

"Oh, Sarah," Harper said, leaping from the piano bench, "what an idea!"

While she set up her recording equipment in the front room, Sarah went back to the computer. As she clicked her way through the classical section of Harper's digital music library, Harper played and recorded the sonata three times. When she returned to the computer, she found Sarah had moved on to something else. She was looking at a tourist guide for Mendocino.

"What are you doing?" Harper asked.

"Just reading about Mendocino. I'm curious about it."

Apparently Harper was not the only one with Chelsea on her mind.

"It's north of here," Harper said, "a little town on the coast with a prominent core of artists and bohemians. It's a lovely place. At least I love it. It reminds me of the East Coast. In fact, it resembles New England enough that *Murder She Wrote* was filmed there."

"*Murder She Wrote*? What's that?"

Harper sighed, feeling old. "An old TV show set in the fictional town of Cabot Cove, Maine."

"What's Chelsea's brother's name?"

"I can't remember. His last name is Nichols, though, same as hers. Why?"

Sarah was intent on her activities now. She was searching through a white pages database of Mendocino. After a few minutes, she said, "Is his name Brandon?"

"That's it!" Harper exclaimed. "Yes, Brandon!"

"So we've found her," Sarah said, obviously excited. She printed a map of the address and handed it to Harper. "Here you go."

Harper stood staring at the piece of paper as if it were the Rosetta Stone. After a moment, she asked, "Was there a phone number?"

"No."

Harper felt flushed and uncertain, still staring at the address. "I don't really know what to do with this."

"Fly to her!" Sarah said, springing up from her chair. "Go to her like Orpheus and drag her back from the hounds of hell!"

Harper laughed, then Sarah did too. Harper found Sarah extremely entertaining, perhaps because she herself was only slightly removed from the same melodramatic bent.

"Orpheus?" she questioned.

"Of course, Orpheus. You remember the book you gave me, *The Greek Myths*? I read the whole thing, twice. There's a picture of Orpheus at the gates of hell playing his lyre."

"Yes, I remember that. He's trying to charm Cerberus so he can pass through."

"That reminded me of you because you're the only person I know who has a lyre."

"I'm glad you read that book, Sarah, and liked it. It was very special to me."

"Well, yeah! Especially because your dad gave it to you and what he wrote in it."

Harper, perplexed, said, "What? What did he write?"

"I've memorized it," Sarah announced, then said, "To my own muse, Harper, who sings so sweetly under the wings of my imagination."

As Sarah said those words, Harper could see them on the inside cover of the book. "Yes, of course, I remember it now," she said.

"I'm surprised Grandpa gave that to you," Sarah said, "instead of a book about quarks or something."

"Well, to his credit, I guess he knew that mythology would

be more to my liking."

"I think you should have the book back now, though. I think you should keep it."

"Yes, maybe you're right, if you're done with it."

"You could use a couple of books in your house anyway." Sarah sat backward on the desk chair, facing Harper. "So, what are you going to do about Chelsea? Are you going?"

"She might not be alone," Harper said, talking to herself as much as Sarah.

"She might not. But she might. It's better to make a fool of yourself than to miss your chance at happiness."

Harper looked sideways at Sarah, wondering if she had read that on some postcard or refrigerator magnet she'd found around the house because it sounded just like all of the advice that Harper had gathered around herself for the last twenty years—the iconic Fool with his reckless pursuit of self-knowledge, the free spirit, the blind prophet, the wandering minstrel and even Orpheus himself, all taking the leap of faith, following the heart, not the mind, into the unknown.

"But I can't leave you here," Harper said. "I mean, we have plans. We're going to San Francisco and Monterey."

"We can do that when you get back. We have almost a month. This is more important."

"Is it?" Harper looked into Sarah's suddenly serious eyes.

"Yes, Aunt Harper," she said. "This is about love. What could be more important than that?"

To a sixteen-year-old, thought Harper, there was nothing more important than that. To a thirty-eight-year-old, to this thirty-eight-year-old anyway...well, yes, there were still not many things more important than that.

"I probably shouldn't leave you alone," Harper said doubtfully.

"I rode a train across the country by myself. I'm old enough to be trusted to be home alone. Even Mom and Dad have left me home alone for a few days. Besides, Mary said she would pick me up any time I wanted to come over for a visit. I really would like

195

to go back and hang out with her. She's really funny."

"Funny? Well, I doubt that she intends to come off that way."

"No, I think she does, actually."

Harper had never thought of Mary as "funny." She was wary of this idea and it must have showed.

"Aunt Harper," Sarah said, sounding mature, "there is nothing to worry about. I'm only interested in boys, believe me, and there are no boys at Mary's house. Couldn't be safer."

She had a point. It was mainly boys that had gotten her into trouble with her parents. And despite their attempts to rein her in, she was nearly an adult. She deserved some responsibility and some trust.

"I'll give you the number of my friend Roxie. I'll let her know you're here and ask her to check on you. You can call her any time if you get worried or need something. And I'll have my cell phone," she said. "Although I suspect the reception is sporadic up and down the coast."

"So you're going?" Sarah looked liked she was going to jump up and down with glee.

"I guess I am." Harper felt an involuntary grin spreading across her face.

Chapter 24

LAST SUMMER

Eliot stopped by to pick up a few of his belongings from the shed, things he had stored there for their summer camping trips. He was on his way to some other woman's house now. He had replaced Harper, quite easily, apparently. This new woman was someone he knew in Washington, someone he had even dated during non-summer months. She had become his year-round companion now. She might marry him and give him kids. *Perhaps they will be blissfully happy together*, Harper thought. *He should be thanking me for releasing him.*

Eliot piled his things on the lawn outside of the shed, his too-long hair covered by a Seattle Seahawks baseball cap.

"Why don't you take both sleeping bags," Harper suggested. "Since they match. You can zip them together. Less useful apart."

"Okay, thanks," he said. "That's helpful."

Harper went inside the house while he transferred his things to his car. She made him a glass of lemonade. When he came in, he gratefully swallowed two big gulps and then sprawled out in a kitchen chair, his long legs taking up nearly half the kitchen. He seemed perfectly at home here. And why not? He had been sitting there just like that for ages.

"You seeing anyone?" he asked.

"No, not really."

He eyed her silently as he drank the lemonade. "It was that girl, wasn't it?" he said, finally. "That girl, Chelsea. It's been nagging at me all year. Last summer I could tell something was up, even before I came down. I just couldn't figure out what it was, what had happened to you. It ate at me for months. And I kept remembering that girl because of the way you talked about her last spring like she was on your mind all the time. You were seeing her, right? I mean, romantically. That's why you didn't want me around."

"Sort of," Harper said evasively.

"Why didn't you tell me? We've always been able to talk about things."

"This was different."

"Because it was a girl?" he asked. His voice was calm, understanding.

"I guess so."

He observed her coolly. "It doesn't really surprise me, Harper. I've seen your heart reach out to women so many times. I always figured that someday one of them would reach back and that would be the end of us. I sort of always knew I wasn't what you wanted."

"That wasn't really why, Eliot," she said. "It wasn't because of Chelsea. We needed to be over anyway. For both our sakes. Whatever this thing was between us for all these years, it wasn't a relationship. It was going nowhere."

"Going nowhere?" He looked surprised. "Because that's the way you wanted it. You know I would have done things differently if you'd have let me. I tried to persuade you to make a life together. But you wanted to be a 'free spirit.'" He said the last sentence mockingly.

"Let's not talk about that now. That happy little domestic scene wouldn't have worked with us and you know it. For a lot of reasons."

He stood up and put his empty glass on the counter. "Well, yeah, the girl, for instance." His voice was sarcastic. "By the way, what happened with her?"

"Gone," Harper said, simply.

Chelsea had been gone for almost a year, at least gone from Harper's arms. But she hadn't left her heart. And the heat of the summer sun brought her sharply to mind, so sharply that Harper could almost feel her skin. She could smell her hair in the heat waves coming off mown grass.

The day after Eliot picked up his camping gear, Harper dialed Chelsea's cell phone and got voice mail. She left a message that probably sounded more desperate than she intended. "I'd like to see you. Please call. I'll understand if you'd rather not, but I just want to talk, that's all."

She knew that Chelsea would call, out of pity or guilt or both. Chelsea was sorry for what she'd done, sorry for pushing her way into Harper's heart and then abruptly leaving. She had said so many times as she was leaving, and Harper had no doubt she was sincere.

Chelsea called the following day. She was wary. Understandably. Harper proposed a picnic, just to talk. No hidden agenda. She suggested Tuesday evening for the free concert in the park. Chelsea agreed. Their phone conversation was brief and guarded.

As Harper packed picnic supplies Tuesday afternoon, her mood was light. When the phone rang, she jumped, alarmed, fearing that Chelsea had changed her mind. It was just a telemarketer. Hanging up the phone, Harper saw, through the screen door, Chelsea's black Honda pull up at the curb. Her pulse quickened. Chelsea's hair, golden light in the sunshine, surrounded her face like a halo. She strode up to the door, one bare knee showing

199

through a sizeable rip in the fabric of her jeans. Harper noted her familiar shy smile with a pang of affection.

She pushed the screen door open, and Chelsea stepped inside, smiling. She hugged Harper close, warmly, but not sexually, and Harper closed her eyes, letting her body feel for just a second the sensations that were like a siren song to her blood and skin. Then Chelsea released her and stepped back.

"Thanks for coming," Harper said. "Everything's ready. Do you want to walk?"

Chelsea nodded. She was silent. Perhaps nervous. They walked the four blocks to the park, carrying a small ice chest and a tote bag.

"It's good to see you," Harper said, searching Chelsea's face for some clue to her feelings.

"You too."

They found a spot on the grass some distance from the musicians and most of the other picnickers and spread out a blanket. Harper had put chardonnay in a Gatorade bottle, which she poured into paper cups.

"Liquor's not allowed in the park," she explained.

Chelsea took the cup and swallowed a mouthful of wine as if it were medicine. She seemed distracted, watching the other people, avoiding eye contact. Harper hoped she would relax.

The nearly white hairs on Chelsea's forearms glittered when a ray of sunlight hit them. Harper was reminded of a singular day the previous summer in a secluded cove they had found by chance, having walked quite a distance from a public beach. After plunging into the surf for a while, they had reclined on their towels on hot sand. Harper had removed Chelsea's bikini top, revealing her gorgeous breasts to the sun. She had traced a finger along the tan line up over the curve of one breast, down into the groove between them, and then over the other, brushing off a few grains of quartz. Chelsea's skin always sparkled in the sun. The fine, blond hairs that covered her caught the light like crystals. Chelsea lay on her back, her eyes closed under her sunglasses, her lips curled into an effortless smile. Her sand-dusted hair was splayed out on the blanket. Looking now at Chelsea's arms in the dappled light under tree branches, Harper recalled this scene in vivid detail, recalled bending her head down to lick the shimmering layer of sunshine from Chelsea's skin.

Delicious memories like these assailed her senses, retelling themselves intensely with sounds and tastes and smells. That day had been one scene in a tale full of promise in which each detail was brimming with meaning and magic. It had been a day full of awe, a day of honest joy like almost every day she had spent with Chelsea last summer.

"How've you been?" Harper asked.

Chelsea turned her attention to Harper. "Good."

"You've got a tan already."

"Swimming."

Chelsea continued to hold herself at a distance. They ate pasta salad and chunks of watermelon in almost total silence as Harper tried to think of a way to draw her out. She yearned to recapture some of the emotional closeness they had had, even if the physical were now denied.

"Are you writing poetry?" Harper asked.

"Not so much right now. Maybe you didn't know, but I finished my master's degree in January. I'm going full time into teaching. Starting next month, I've got a fourth-grade class."

"No, I didn't realize that. I didn't know you were serious about that. I thought the teaching was just something you wanted to have to fall back on, if you needed it someday."

Chelsea picked at the grass absentmindedly. "Originally that's what I planned, but I've been feeling lately like I need to do something more useful. The poetry, it's an indulgence. It's not a profession. I hoped it could be at one time, but it isn't going to be. I can always write poetry, of course, as an avocation. I mean, I can't just be Mary's protégé all my life, now, can I? The time comes when you're no longer the student. You have to become the teacher. In this case, literally."

Harper glanced at the band playing some distance away and then back to Chelsea. "How do you know when the time comes to be the teacher? I mean, there's always plenty more to learn."

"Well, sure. I don't know. I suppose you just want to be pretty sure you know more than the students do." Chelsea laughed, a light, pleasant laugh like the tinkle of a glass wind chime. "There's always going to be more to learn. In that sense, you'll be a student all your life. You can be both."

That's true, Harper thought. You could be both. She hadn't really thought of it that way before. *You still have much to learn, Grasshopper*, she heard in her head.

"I think you'll make a wonderful teacher," Harper said. "I'd never be able to do that. The math alone would send me fleeing out the door."

Chelsea smiled. "I guess teaching isn't for everyone. At least not elementary school. Mary, for instance, thinks it would be absolute torture. She doesn't understand why I'm willingly doing this. Children make her nervous. She thinks they should be put on another planet and segregated from society until they're eighteen and have achieved a certain level of civility. It's sort of funny. She has strong maternal instincts, but they don't kick in for anybody who hasn't grown to adult size."

"How is Mary, by the way?" Harper asked.

"She's well. Working on an exhibition. Opening next month in Santa Rosa."

"Does she know you're here, with me?"

Chelsea shook her head. "She's very touchy on the subject. I thought it'd be better not to mention it. No point getting her worked up over nothing."

Harper, nodding, thought to herself, *Is this* nothing, *then?*

"You're happy?" she asked.

Chelsea said, simply, "Yes." She held her cup out for a refill. She wasn't going to elaborate, which meant that she was being loyal to Mary, loyal to the privacy of their relationship.

A plaintive saxophone solo drifted through the still evening air. Harper was disappointed. She had hoped, more than she had admitted before this moment, that Chelsea and Mary were having trouble, that maybe they weren't even together anymore.

If there were any problems, though, they weren't something Chelsea wanted to share. Harper had to respect that. She let the subject drop.

"How about you?" Chelsea asked. "What schemes have you been hatching?"

Harper thought over the past year. "Well, I'm still working on that video series, you know, the female artists. Got four of them now."

"Good. Really worthwhile project. The one you did of Mary, it's just beautiful. The music, especially. Well, that's where you excel, of course. Do you remember that day, Harper?" Chelsea asked, smiling freely for the first time. "You played the baby grand for us."

Harper nodded. "I remember. I played *Appassionata.*"

"That's such a beautiful piece. Every time I hear it now, of course, I think of you." Chelsea averted her gaze and let her last word trail off almost inaudibly, as if she'd said something she regretted. "So, who are the others, then?"

"There's Catherine Gardiner, thanks to Mary."

"Sure. I knew about that one."

"And Wilona Freeman."

"The photographer?"

"Right. I've known her for years and finally got around to including her this last winter. And Sophie Janssen, the sculptor. One of her larger pieces is in Oak Park. It's a big metal..."

"Pear! Yes, I've seen it. Very sensuous. How do you know her?"

"We met at the dedication ceremony, actually. The symphony performed for that. She's very approachable. Totally down-to-earth and no-nonsense. You'd never guess she was an artist just talking to her."

"Artists aren't all whack jobs, Harper," Chelsea pointed out.

"No, I know that. But they do tend to be a little different, usually."

Chelsea looked amused. "Must have been a challenge for you, then, to make her seem interesting."

203

"No, not really. She's a fascinating woman, despite the sanity."

"So you have a painter, sculptor, photographer and poet, but no musician?"

"No, no musician."

"That seems odd to me. I would have expected you to feature a musician right off the bat."

"I just didn't think of it."

"Sometimes I think you don't value your own art as much as you do other people's. You take it for granted or something, but to the rest of us, musical talent is mysterious and impressive. Maybe one of those soloists they bring in for the symphony would be an interesting subject. Like that oboe player from last season."

"Yes, you're right. I'll keep my eye out, then, for a musician." Harper put a cover on the pasta salad. "Do you want any more of this watermelon?"

Chelsea shook her head. Harper longed to know her thoughts. There was so much that wasn't being said between them.

"Have you been dating?" Chelsea asked.

"Some. A little."

"Women?"

"Oh, yes! After you, what else?" Harper laughed. "I'll always be grateful to you for that."

"Even after how it ended up?"

"Absolutely. It seems like I've been looking for something all of my life, and now I know what it was I was searching for, what my personal truth is, you know?"

"You finally figured out that you're gay, you mean? You make it sound so mystical."

Harper shrugged, recognizing the gentle criticism that had always been a part of their relationship. It was one of the things she appreciated about Chelsea, her insistence on looking at things a little more starkly than Harper was inclined to do.

"So how is it going, then? With these women, I mean?" Chelsea's blue eyes looked searchingly into hers. *What does she want to hear?* Harper wondered. *This wall between us is simply maddening. What would she say if I told her right now that I'm still madly in love with her and I would do almost anything to be lying in bed beside her one more time?*

"Nothing's come of it," Harper said. "Nothing serious. I went to a women's festival a couple of months ago. That was an experience."

"Yes?" Chelsea asked, expectantly.

"I met a woman there, a Turkish tanbur player who called herself Astral. She was fascinating."

"What's a tanbur?"

"Sort of a lute. A stringed instrument with a long neck."

"I can see why she caught your eye, then."

Harper nodded, then said, "We spent the night together."

Chelsea arched her eyebrows. "How was that?"

"Fun. Enlightening."

"Good," Chelsea said with no evidence of jealousy. "Have you seen her since?"

Harper shook her head. "It was a one-time thing."

Chelsea nodded. "You know, I've never done that."

"Slept with a Turkish tanbur player?"

Smiling, Chelsea said, "Had a one-night stand. I sort of envy you that. I tend to fall in love with anybody I sleep with. Irrevocably. Head over heels."

Including me? Harper thought. *Were you head over heels in love with me? Are you still in love with me?*

"I guess it's time to get back," Chelsea said.

They stood in unison and collected their things. They walked slowly, silently. Harper wanted to delay their arrival at her house, dreading the moment when Chelsea would leave.

"So what now?" Chelsea asked. "You've set Eliot free. Not going there again, I guess?"

"No. Eliot has moved on already. I suppose I will eventually find someone. A woman, I mean. You, Chelsea, have shown me the way!" At this pronouncement, Harper made a sweeping gesture across the sky with her arm.

"Oh, come on, Harper, don't make a spiritual quest out of

this too. All I did was pry the lesbian out of you. Simple as that."

Harper liked the way Chelsea jostled her, the familiarity it alluded to. Too soon, they stood on the sidewalk in front of her house. *Is there any way I can make her stay?* Harper wondered. *Am I totally powerless over her?*

"Want to come in?" she asked, trying to sound casual.

"I don't think so. It's been good seeing you again, but I should get home."

Realizing that Chelsea was about to say goodbye, Harper felt panic rising to her throat.

"We can't do this, though," Chelsea continued. "We can't see one another again. I know that neither one of us wants to be just friends. It's obvious to me that nothing has changed. We both still..."

"Yes," Harper said, despairing.

Oh, God, Harper thought, *how I've missed you! And I've missed that crooked smile so much.* She felt her eyes filling with tears. Chelsea looked sad and apologetic. Her eyes began to tear up as well.

"Be happy," she said, then hugged Harper tightly, her hand briefly cradling the back of Harper's head. In that instant, Harper breathed in everything she could of Chelsea. Then her arms were left empty. She watched as Chelsea walked to her car and drove away, realizing that she might never touch her again, feeling hollow inside and letting her tears fall freely.

Chapter 25

JUNE 29

With a suitcase in the trunk, Harper drove the Coast Highway up above San Francisco, through Bodega Bay and further up into the lesser populated sections of the north coast. The highway snaked its way through cow pastures beside the crashing waves of the Pacific. Harper loved this drive. It was a little bit wild, and, in fog, more of an adventure than most people would welcome. But today there was no fog, and the scenery was brilliant. The smell of the sea filled her with happiness. She had no bad memories to associate with that briny smell.

More than once she stopped to consider how rash this journey was. She had no evidence that Chelsea would welcome her. If not for Sarah, she would not be making this trip, she knew. Sarah's romantic fantasies had infected her.

On one of her stops to admire the breakers and the hang gliders along the Sonoma Coast, she phoned Sarah, who answered promptly and reported that all was well.

When she reached Little River, she knew she was almost there. Her heart started pounding more insistently. *It's a long shot*, she told herself, trying to calm down. She might be turned away. She might be spending the night alone wherever she could find a room, perhaps in the backseat of her car because, of course, she had no hotel reservation in a town with a significant summer tourism trade.

There were other potential catastrophes to consider as well, even if she found Chelsea at her brother's house. Chelsea might be angry at being hunted down. Or, worse, she might be with someone else. The closer Harper got to Mendocino, the more likely that seemed to her and the more ridiculous the entire scheme began to appear. She began to panic, wondering how she would handle that situation. Maybe she could just hang out on Main Street until Chelsea happened by, pretending that it was a coincidence, her being here. Everybody ended up on Main Street sooner or later. The town was small. You ran into people like that as they went out to eat or looked into the boutiques and galleries. But, then, how would she explain that she just happened to be passing through? There was no way Chelsea would believe that.

She arrived in Mendocino just after three o'clock. She drove through town, past familiar landmarks, happy to see that things hadn't changed much since her last visit. She parked near the western end of town at the edge of a cliff overlooking the ocean. To the north along this same road tiny houses perched on a thin strip of land, looking like hobbit dwellings, all crowded together and vying for their precious bit of unobstructed ocean view. She glanced at her phone, noticing that it said "No Service." Chelsea might never have gotten her message, she realized. That thought briefly gave her hope.

She stepped out of her car and stretched, facing the waves, breathing in the salt air. The sun was shining brightly, but it was cold here at the edge of the continent. She pulled a sweatshirt out of her trunk and put it on over her T-shirt. Then she looked at her map, determining that Brandon Nichols's house was up the hill to the northeast about three blocks. She looked in that direction, hoping for a sign. All was quiet. Still not sure what her plan was, she decided to walk the rest of the way, favoring the idea of an indirect approach. On foot, if she got a glimpse of Chelsea and another woman, she could duck into somebody's hedge before she was seen. Harper shook her head, wondering at her own lunacy.

She folded the map and shoved it into her back pocket, then walked along the edge of the road toward her goal. This was an impulsive thing she was doing, she knew. Harper cherished her impulsive nature and had been dismayed to find as she got older that she was less likely to give into it. So, she rationalized, even if she didn't find Chelsea, even if Chelsea was here with another woman, this trip would bear witness to her ability to follow her heart. She wasn't ashamed of that.

As Harper climbed the steep hill, her breathing grew labored and the view out to the ocean improved. The exercise had created its own source of heat, so she pulled off the sweatshirt and carried it as she turned down a side street. She walked more slowly now, apprehensive about what she was about to discover. Whatever it was, whichever of the scenarios she had imagined, it was going to be unsettling. There was no possible outcome for the next few minutes other than a huge jolt to her heart. The only mystery was whether it would leave her in despair or in rapture.

She counted the houses ahead, noticing their pattern of address numbers, and picked out the house she was destined for. It was green, pale green like a honeydew melon, and in need of repainting. A small wooden portico sheltered the door. The front windows were closed.

It was quiet. The entire street was silent, in fact. No one was in sight. Harper kept walking. As she came closer to the house, she saw that there was a car on the other side of it. A few more steps and she realized, with a mixture of elation and panic, that the car was Chelsea's black Honda.

This was the first real evidence that Chelsea was actually here. Harper froze in place on the sidewalk in front of the honeydew house. She didn't know what to do next. Ringing the bell seemed suddenly out of the question.

She remembered her earlier plan. Waiting in town for Chelsea to show up, to run into her by "accident," now seemed like a much better idea. She was about to turn around and head downhill when the door of the house burst open and Chelsea came flying down the steps on a skateboard, her eyes focused downward. She was heading straight toward Harper. She looked up as she hit the bottom of the stairs and jerked her board violently sideways to avoid a collision. The board raced off across the street without her. She fell flat on her butt on the sidewalk.

Harper rushed to her side. "Are you okay?"

Chelsea looked bewildered. "Harper?"

Then she stood and stared. "Harper," she said again, breaking into a brilliant smile.

Harper smiled too, then nodded. Chelsea grabbed hold of her, squeezing her in a tight embrace. Harper gripped Chelsea close, relishing the sensation of her body, touching her gleaming hair, pressing her nose into Chelsea's neck and reveling in the smell of her skin. *My body remembers you so well*, she thought, feeling her nerves tightening.

"Oh, my God!" Chelsea said. "I thought I was hallucinating."

Finally, startled back to reality by the barking of a dog, they released one another.

"What are you doing here?" Chelsea asked.

"I came to find you. I called, but I guess there's no reception here. I just decided to come up."

"But... Hey, let's go inside. You can tell me all about it."

Chelsea retrieved her skateboard, and Harper followed her into the old Victorian with its creaking front door and hardwood floors, its floral wallpaper and mustiness. Chelsea obviously wasn't expecting company, Harper thought. She looked disheveled in her worn jeans with threads at the cuffs, dirty sneakers, a gray hoody with a paint stain on one arm.

Chelsea noticed Harper evaluating her clothes. "Yeah, I'm

slumming."

"You're here alone?"

Chelsea nodded. "I decided to get away for a while. Since you didn't return my call, I thought you didn't want to see me. I was feeling pretty blue. This seemed like a good place to squirrel away for a few weeks, do some thinking."

For a moment, they stood silently looking at one another, and Harper could see the emotion rising in Chelsea's eyes. "I'm so happy to see you," she said.

Harper felt her heart pounding in her throat and her fingertips going numb. She too was overwhelmed with emotion.

The outcome of this crazy trip is going to be the best one there could be, after all, Harper realized, taking a step toward Chelsea. They moved into one another, then kissed with urgency, desperation even, and were, within minutes, in bed making love. *It doesn't matter what happens after this*, Harper thought, clinging to Chelsea's naked body. *Whatever happens, it's worth it.*

Harper didn't need any words to tell her that Chelsea's need was deep and genuine. She felt it in hard kisses that left her breathless and in the strength of her embrace. Two years of longing spilled out onto Chelsea's bed that afternoon. But as the afternoon turned to evening and the initial intensity of their passion subsided, Chelsea began to speak. Her words were as reassuring as her hands and mouth.

"I love you, Harper," she said, her lips close to Harper's ear. "I've been falling more in love with you every day for the past two years. I can't tell you how crushed I was that you didn't return my call. You had every reason not to, of course. It took me weeks to decide to make that call. I stared at my phone for hours on end those first couple of days afterward, and then I just couldn't take it anymore. So I came here. Running away, I guess. I thought you were lost to me. I felt so desperate."

"I was just thinking it over, taking my time."

"I didn't expect that. You never seemed like someone who mulls things over like that."

"No, not normally, but you really hurt me before."

"I know. I will always be really, really sorry about that. I made a huge mistake two years ago."

Harper took Chelsea's hand and pressed it to her mouth, then clutched it to her chest. "It doesn't matter now. I just want to live in the moment."

"Okay. That suits me. This is a fantastic moment to be living in."

Chelsea pulled Harper close again and kissed her tenderly as darkness gradually enveloped the room. Harper let herself sink deeper into that place of love and longing that banishes all thought and has no awareness of the past or the future.

Chapter 26

JULY 11

The diffused light of dawn was barely perceptible through the closed blinds of Harper's bedroom. She lay on her side, her head propped up on her hand, watching Chelsea peacefully sleeping, a morning ritual she had been enjoying almost daily for two weeks now. She had reluctantly come home after a heavenly three days in Mendocino, Chelsea following a day later. Here they had resumed their happy reunion.

Harper had feared that bringing Chelsea back to the real world would somehow dispel the fantasy of their newfound devotion to one another. In Mendocino, that fairy-tale town by the sea, they had done almost nothing but love one another and delight in children's pleasures like seashells and ice cream cones. The myth of Orpheus was prominent in her mind as she left. While she trusted absolutely that Chelsea would follow her, there remained, on the edge of her consciousness, the fear that the gods might yet play a cruel joke on her, that they might fling Chelsea into the sea or dash her against a rock and she would be taken away forever like ill-fated Eurydice.

But, no, Chelsea had arrived safely. She now breathed silently and steadily beside Harper, her angelic face perfectly calm, a sheet covering her body except for one flawless shoulder. Harper felt an incredible sense of tranquility. The words she found to express her state of mind—peace, joy, harmony—these were the same words people used to describe a state of grace. She didn't believe that was a coincidence. The thing that struck her most about how she had changed was how completely she had lost her need for autonomy. What she wanted now was to belong to Chelsea and for Chelsea to belong to her, completely and exclusively, all the time and forever. Whatever it was that had appealed to her in the past about independence had vanished. Now, being alone simply meant being without Chelsea, and that meant being less alive.

The smell of fresh paint drifted in from the living room. Yesterday, Saturday, they had spent the day painting it a shade of light sage with off-white trim. Harper felt a twinge of pain in her shoulder from the hours of overhead rolling. Today would be a well-earned play day. She watched Chelsea for several minutes until a scowl passed over her face, wrinkling her freckled nose, and her eyes opened. When she saw Harper, she smiled.

"Good morning," Harper said quietly.

Chelsea reached up and put her arms around Harper's neck and sighed deeply.

"I'll make coffee," Harper said, then kissed Chelsea and slid out of bed. Chelsea sprawled out as Harper pulled on an oversized T-shirt and slid her feet into slippers.

"I'll just stay here," Chelsea said, "and let you wait on me."

"I'll happily do so. Then we can talk about what to do with our Sunday."

"We can do whatever you want. I don't care, as long as we're together."

Chelsea fluttered her eyes dramatically. Harper smiled at her

214

and went to the kitchen. Although she knew that Chelsea was exaggerating a bit, it was still true that they both had few desires to fulfill these days other than their desire for one another.

Harper went to the pantry for the coffee beans, glancing at the calendar on the wall again, focusing on the date circled in red only two weeks away. That was the day she was to fly back East for her family visit. The closer it came, the more it seemed like something to be feared. She didn't want to leave Chelsea. If it wasn't for her promise to return Sarah, she didn't think she would leave. She could send Sarah on alone, of course, but that probably wasn't the responsible thing to do. This fear of hers was not rational, she knew. There was no reason to act on it.

With a silent chuckle, Harper noted again the fortune-cookie saying taped to June 29, the date of her reunion with Chelsea. When she'd shown that to Chelsea, she'd stared wide-eyed, then said, "If this were the seventeenth century, you'd be burned at the stake."

Sarah came into the kitchen, yawning, wearing pink pajamas, her feet bare. She winced at the noise of the coffee grinder. When it whirred to a stop, she said, "Hi, Aunt Harper."

"Good morning. Chelsea and I were about to discuss our plans for the day. We might go hiking. Do you want to come along?"

"No, thanks. I have plans of my own."

Harper wanted to ask her what they were. She thought she probably should ask, but she didn't want to seem to be prying. So many things about Sarah left her unsure. Harper definitely didn't want to alienate her. She didn't want to assume the role of parent. She preferred the role of friend.

"Anything fun?" she asked, dumping the ground coffee into the filter.

"Just hanging out."

Harper nodded, as if she had gotten an answer. "Well, I'm glad you've made some friends here," she added. "Are you sure you don't want to come with us? We enjoy your company. We'd like you to come."

"No, that's okay. Thanks, though." Sarah poured some shredded wheat and milk into a bowl and sat down to eat it while Harper waited for the coffee.

Since their return from Mendocino, Harper and Chelsea had spent every day together, sometimes alone, sometimes with Sarah. The three of them had gone to San Francisco, doing the usual tourist things. Sarah had seemed like a fourteen-year-old again that day, all agog at the Golden Gate Bridge, Fisherman's Wharf and Coit Tower, which they ascended for a magnificent view of the city skyline. They had spent a day in Santa Cruz as well, playing pinball at the boardwalk, riding a roller coaster, eating fish and chips on a pier with pelicans gliding low beside them. While they were there, Harper had taken them to the UCSC campus for a quick look at her alma mater.

"I wish I could go to school here," Sarah had said.

"Where are you going to college?" Harper asked her.

"I may not be going."

Harper, stunned, said, "Why not?"

"It's so expensive, you know. Mom and Dad will let me go to Wheaton if I live at home. I don't know how I can afford it on my own, though."

"So what's wrong with Wheaton," asked Chelsea.

"Nothing's wrong with the school," Sarah explained. "It's the living at home part that's the problem. It's been bad enough while I'm in high school. It would be impossible. I'd have to be home by ten o'clock every night. I'd just die. I wish I could do what Aunt Harper did. Just go thousands of miles away where Mom and Dad wouldn't have anything to say about it."

"You can get pretty homesick," Harper pointed out.

"I'd be willing to take that chance."

As they left the campus, Harper had made a mental note to discuss this situation with Neil and Kathy. Given Sarah's intelligence and enthusiasm for learning, she had to go to college. Harper didn't see any choice in this matter and hoped that her parents were like-minded.

Throughout all of these activities, Sarah remained agreeable, enthusiastic and apparently happy. The raging tyrant that Neil and Kathy had come to know and dread was nowhere to be seen. Harper knew that it was just a matter of time, however. Sarah was relishing her freedom. She was on her best behavior because she and Harper didn't know each other well and because they hadn't yet tried to test one another's limits. Harper bought her a bus pass and let her come and go as she pleased, including making frequent visits to Mary's house. She always returned with ideas swimming in her head. One day she even returned with a painting of herself. Mary had painted her sitting in a huge chair, reading a book, in front of library shelves filled floor to ceiling. The chair's size was exaggerated, making her look like a child of ten, as if she had lofty aspirations to read all of those books. It was a charming painting.

Sarah opened herself up, absorbing everything she could from Mary, from Chelsea, from Harper. Chelsea spent an evening with her going over the lines of her song, refining her word choices. Then Harper wrote down the music, and the three of them put it all together. They all lamented the fact that Sarah wouldn't have time to learn to read music herself. She promised Harper that she would take lessons, that she would learn to play the piano as soon as she got home. Now, of course, she wanted to be a musician, a pop singer. *Nothing wrong with that*, thought Harper, *as a dream*.

Remarkably, this inspiration wasn't a one-way street. Because of Sarah, Harper was recording the soundtrack for her new documentary herself. Roxie had agreed to help, and when Harper returned from the Cape, she planned to put together a small group of musicians to record some additional tracks.

"You know," Chelsea pointed out when she heard about this, "you're only a step away now from writing your own compositions."

That idea had seemed far-fetched to Harper, but it was working on her subconscious, occasionally peering out at her enticingly.

Harper took the coffee back to her bedroom where Chelsea

had put on a shirt and was propped up in bed with pillows. Harper sat beside her, handing her a cup.

"So, what about today?" Harper asked. "What are we doing?"

"Let's go down the river. I can borrow a kayak from a friend. It's going to be blistering hot. A good day to be on the water."

"Okay. I'll make sandwiches."

Chelsea sipped her coffee, then said, "I think that Sarah could be a real handful if you got on her wrong side."

"I know. I'm just holding my breath, hoping that I don't set her off. So far, it's been great. We're still friends."

"Yes, she really looks up to you. I still can't get over how she ended up at Mary's house like that. And that Mary let her stay! How bizarre is that?"

"I think Mary's lonely. I think she misses you."

"Yes, well," Chelsea said, embarrassed, "she doesn't have to be alone if she doesn't want to. She has options."

Harper remembered the young woman she had seen with Mary at the symphony. Is that what Chelsea meant by "options"? Chelsea didn't like talking about it, so Harper knew almost nothing about what had happened between them, about why they had broken up. She assumed it was the same as before—Mary was unfaithful and Chelsea was disillusioned. It was inevitable. There was no way that the awestruck girl from eight years ago could have survived. Nobody could live up to the image she'd had of Mary. Harper knew, though, that Chelsea had no such illusions about her. Chelsea had seen her flaws from the beginning, pointing them out on occasion, gently, as observations, not as demands for change.

Chelsea had matured so much over the past eight years that Harper often felt she was the younger of them. Chelsea's rate of maturation had been accelerated, perhaps, by her close association with a mentor so much older and more experienced than herself. Harper liked that about Chelsea, appreciated her sound judgment, her caution, her realistic viewpoint. When it was required, Chelsea was extremely steady and reliable, but she

218

still was also optimistic, trusting and playful.

It was as though she had taken the best possible lessons away from her association with Mary. She had not become jaded or pessimistic from the blows she had received. Harper knew that the gifts Mary had given her were considerable. It was hard to imagine that Chelsea wouldn't feel gratitude for that for the rest of her life. That was a kind of love. It was a bond the two of them would always have. Harper was certain that bond would draw them together again someday. She just hoped it would be under vastly different circumstances, as friends instead of lovers.

Between the joy of having Chelsea back in her life and the joy of mentoring Sarah, Harper was quite simply overjoyed. This summer, full of unexpected twists, was turning out to be such a happy surprise. She tried not to think about what would come next. In the past, the end of summer had always signaled a huge shift in her life. For that reason she was purposely not thinking too much about the fuzzy cloud beyond August and trying to root herself in the present. If this time with Chelsea was destined to be just another summer romance, she wanted it to be the best that it could possibly be, even if that meant clinging resolutely to the belief in a never-ending summer.

They ended up on the river by noon, gliding on a mostly gentle current downstream. The occasional stretch of whitewater snatched them, adding a bit of a thrill to their drifting pace.

"Duck!" yelled Chelsea, tucking her own head down between her knees as the kayak rushed over a small waterfall and into a thicket of tree branches. Harper ducked too, feeling the branches scrape her shoulder and tear a hole in her shirt. She dug her paddle hard down to the streambed and pushed away from the shore. They glided into a gentler section of the river then and relaxed. Chelsea steered with her paddle, straightening the kayak so that it pointed downstream again.

"Well, that was exciting," she said. "At least we didn't capsize."

Harper fingered the hole in her shirt and the tiny scrape on her skin underneath it.

"Look," Chelsea called, pointing ahead to the right-hand bank.

"What?" Harper saw nothing but a dense green bramble under scrawny oak trees.

"Blackberries!" Chelsea said. "Let's stop."

They steered toward a clearing along the bank and pulled the kayak onto dry grass. The mass of tangled blackberry vines made a solid wall along the shore for about forty feet. They walked around the back of the bushes and found the branches dripping with clusters of black, red and green berries.

"I've never picked wild blackberries before," Harper said.

"Be careful."

Harper, peering into the dense tangle, saw that the vines were covered with a menacing coat of hard thorns.

"Take the ones that fall off with just a slight tug," Chelsea said, demonstrating by pulling a berry loose. She put it to Harper's lips, and Harper took it in her mouth, tasting the sweet juice.

"That's so good," Harper said.

Chelsea ate one too. "Reminds me of being a kid," she said. "We used to pick them in the cow pastures around our house. We'd pick buckets full and eat big bowls of them with milk. Grandma would make pies. Nothing like a wild blackberry."

Harper, despite being aware of the danger, got pricked by a thorn more than once and smashed several berries between her fingers while trying to pull them loose, staining her fingers purple.

They picked an overflowing handful each and then returned to the kayak and poured some water from their water bottle over them to wash off the dust. Then, sitting facing one another on the grass behind the blackberry hedge, shaded by an oak tree, they fed each other berries as floaters and kayakers passed by out of sight.

"This flavor means summer to me," Chelsea said, putting a berry between Harper's lips. "What means summer to you?"

"You do," Harper said.

Chelsea leaned forward and kissed her. A moment later they

were lying in the grass, wrapped in one another's arms, kissing in earnest. Within hearing of the people floating by on the river, Harper and Chelsea lay together in a heated tangle, the smell of ripe berries wafting over them.

"I love you," Chelsea said, running a hand over Harper's shoulder, sticking her pinkie into the newly torn hole in her shirtsleeve.

"Why?" Harper asked.

"Why? Seriously?"

Harper nodded.

"Because you're beautiful." Chelsea grinned and then became more serious. "Because you don't struggle against life. You live your life as if it's a gift. You embrace it and flow with it. Because I can see wonder in your eyes and that makes me happy. Because you're joyful." Chelsea kissed her. "And because you're a terrific kisser."

"I love you too," Harper said.

"Why?"

"Oh, I can't put it into words like you do. I just feel it."

"Try."

"Okay. You're sincere and articulate. You're funny. You make me laugh. I just feel good whenever I'm with you. And you're a terrific kisser."

They kissed deeply. Harper closed her eyes, smelling hot grass, listening to the buzz of insects, losing herself in the sensation of Chelsea's mouth on hers. When she opened her eyes, she saw Chelsea looking intently at something to Harper's right. She turned to see a reddish brown steer standing only fifteen feet away, watching them placidly with watery brown eyes, steadily chewing.

Harper jerked herself to her side, startling the steer, which leapt back a few inches. He then stood calmly watching them again.

Chelsea started snickering. "You're not afraid of him, are you?" she asked.

Harper shook her head. The steer reached his long, thick

221

tongue up over his nose to chase away a fly, then, bored with them, moved off slowly, biting off grass as he went.

They lay in one another's arms, unmoving. After awhile, Harper asked, "Are you happy?"

Chelsea lay her head on Harper's shoulder and said, "Deliriously."

"Me too."

This summer felt to Harper nearly identical to that other summer, the first one with Chelsea. The only difference, really, was the knowledge of how that had ended, of how her happiness and sense of awe had abruptly given way to sorrow and confusion. The knowledge that something this good could end was forever on her mind. Perhaps, she thought, that made it even more intense. This must be treasured and savored, she thought, every moment of it. It should be absorbed like sunlight through all the pores of the skin. She turned onto her side and drew Chelsea close, kissing her berry-stained mouth, feeling grateful and pushing away her fears.

Chapter 27

JULY 18

"Professor Plum in the library with the rope," said Sarah, moving the purple piece across the Clue board to the library.

It was obvious to Harper that this contest, just like the last one, was between Sarah and Chelsea. For some reason, she had never been good at this game. Chelsea, shielding her cards from Harper, showed something to Sarah, whereupon Sarah nodded knowingly and made a clandestine notation on her score sheet. Although Harper was destined to lose, she was enjoying the camaraderie and the music, provided this afternoon by the classical program on the local NPR radio station. At the moment, Professor Plum's antics were being accompanied by a Vivaldi bassoon concerto.

Chelsea, a sly smile on her face, said, "I'll stay where I am and I'm going to say Mr. Green in the kitchen with the rope."

Sarah and Chelsea looked at each other with some secret

understanding. They obviously knew something, by which Harper knew that the game was nearing its end.

"Nothing," Harper said, after examining her cards.

"Me neither," Sarah added.

Chelsea narrowed her eyes and looked from one to the other of them. "Your turn, Harper," she said.

The Vivaldi concerto had ended and a mini news segment was on. Harper's attention was suddenly drawn to it when she heard a familiar name.

"Sophie Janssen," the announcer said, "the celebrated sculptor, died last night at her home in Marin County. She was diagnosed in March with pancreatic cancer."

"Your turn, Aunt Harper," Sarah said.

"Just a minute," Harper said, listening more intently to the radio.

"Since that diagnosis," the announcer continued, "Janssen has donated all of her major works to local communities and museums. She is best known for her oversized metal art, such as the giant steel butterfly now installed on San Francisco's Embarcadero near Pier thirty-nine. Janssen also worked with hammered copper and aluminum. Most of her pieces are characterized by curved rather than angular lines. She was the recipient of the two thousand and two Wolf Prize."

"That's your sculptor," Chelsea said. "The pear in Oak Park."

Harper nodded. "Yes. I didn't even know she was ill. She was such a huge talent. And only in her fifties."

"That's really a shame," Chelsea said.

"Aunt Harper," Sarah asked, "is that one of your documentaries?"

"Yes. I haven't shown you that film, but Sophie Janssen was my fourth. She was only just beginning to get the recognition she deserved."

"I'd like to see the film," Sarah said.

"Me too," Chelsea added.

As she went to get the DVD, Harper recalled her two meetings with Sophie Janssen, once at Oak Park where her

224

sculpture was unveiled and once at her home where Harper had filmed the interviews for the documentary. Long divorced from her husband by then and childless, she lived there alone. The house had been large and impressive, yet another aspect of the sculptor's life that emphasized her small size. Sophie had been what Harper's mother would have described as "scrawny." She stood about five-two and weighed around a hundred pounds. She was sinewy and scrappy and moved with sudden, jerky bursts of energy.

When Harper had asked her if her small stature had anything to do with the massive scale of her sculptures, she had looked thoughtful and said, simply, "Hmmm," as though this had never occurred to her before. Standing next to one of them, the pear, for instance, she looked even more diminutive, since the pear was fifteen feet tall even without its stem.

Harper had been a little intimidated by Sophie's intensity, but she was otherwise easy to talk to. Her life was interesting, a story that told itself without much interference from Harper. Sophie had been born in Norway. She married an American, then moved to northern California where she got a degree in mathematics. Her particular specialty was geometry, an interest that translated directly to her art. Arcs, spheres and cylinders showed up everywhere in her works.

Harper recalled how uneasy she'd been during her interviews with Sophie because of her personal math phobia. She remembered almost nothing about geometry, except that the shortest distance between two points was a straight line.

Her trouble with geometry, actually, had always been her tendency to see every problem as a metaphor for life. She couldn't approach it as math. She might as well have been in a literature or philosophy class, for her mind would wander into musings like, "Is the shortest distance between two points really a straight line?" The way a human life unfolds nobody really travels in a straight line, and who would want to go from birth to death anyway along the shortest distance? She was surprised she ever managed to pull a "B" out of that class.

As the documentary played, Harper and Chelsea sat on the sofa, their legs threaded together, while Sarah sat in the armchair in the lotus position. The three of them watched silently, listening to Mozart play behind scenes of a half dozen outdoor sculptures and their unimposing creator, occasionally pictured with welding equipment and headgear.

Harper's voice could occasionally be heard on the film. "How has your background in geometry influenced your art?"

"Geometry is all about symmetry," Sophie replied, a subtle accent still detectable in her speech. "This goes all the way back to the beginning, to Euclid. Geometry was invented to describe the symmetry found in nature. Patterns of nature are so often two-sided, mirror images, you know, like the two sides of your face, and the more symmetrical they are, the more perfectly beautiful. At least, that is the classical ideal of beauty. Early sculpture was modeled on that ideal, going so far as to create geometric symmetry where it didn't actually exist. My approach is the opposite, to destroy that ideal by creating asymmetrical forms by subtle distortion. In nature, asymmetry is often considered inferior, but it adds interest because there's something just not quite right about it, do you see?"

"Well, this object here certainly looks like a circle," Harper's voice said as the camera lingered on one of three bronze oranges hanging from a bronze tree. The tree was a work in progress and was destined to be located in an orange grove between real orange trees, which was just the sort of thing Sophie Janssen liked to do with her art. It reflected her sense of humor and irony.

"It looks like a circle, yes," she said, "but it isn't. If you measure it, you can determine that. Every orange on this piece is off kilter a bit, and every leaf is bisected just slightly off center."

The camera zoomed in to show the veins of a single leaf, offset from one another and off center as Sophie described. "It's not mathematically coherent," she continued. "But all of these variables are small, small enough to allow your brain to compensate and render the entire piece perfectly in tune with nature. In that respect, my sculptures are all illusions. Or, if you want, impressionistic."

Harper noted that Chelsea was nodding appreciatively. The idea of an impressionistic sculpture that was nearly mathematically identical to the original object was a curiosity that had struck Harper as fascinating at the time, and apparently it was having the same impact on Chelsea.

"If the variation is so slight that we can't see it," she heard herself ask on the video, "then why make it at all?"

"Because on some level, perhaps subconsciously, your brain detects the imperfection. Like everything in nature, your brain also strives toward symmetry. So when it senses a small enough wobble, it can correct it. Nevertheless, it has detected it, and that creates tension. It creates interest, gets the emotions stirred up."

"Like in music," Harper said. "Tension is created by dissonance."

"Exactly," Sophie replied. "It's the same in all art forms. Writing as well. That uneasy juxtaposition creates tension. Without tension, a work of art is flat. It doesn't engage you."

Harper remembered that during the interview she had been struck with how thoroughly the two disciplines, math and sculpture, had been fused together in Sophie's work. It reminded her of comments her father had made while talking of quantum mechanics or higher math where comparisons with ballet, for instance, or music would have been entirely appropriate. Listening to Sophie, it was clear that her art was founded on math and that math was founded on nature and that it all tied together in some mysterious relationship that Harper's father would have called the Theory of Everything. The Theory of Everything, Harper knew, was a physicist's pie in the sky.

Another thing Harper had learned from her father was that the laws of physics, as determined by science, were approximations, not the precisions generally assumed by the layperson. The more complex the problem being investigated, the more one had to allow for a wiggle factor. She had always liked the idea that these "laws" and "theories" had problems. They were flawed. Sophie's sculptures were flawed as well, intentionally, representing the idea that although nature strives toward symmetry, it doesn't always succeed.

Sophie's work also highlighted the companion idea that the human psyche, when it detects a flaw, if the flaw is not too obvious, converts it to perfection. That was a scary idea. It meant your brain was capable of "seeing" something that wasn't there or removing something that was there. Visual input, filtered through the mind, was potentially as far removed from reality as something that was simply imagined. This made Harper think of Wilona's blind grandson and his mind images, about how they might be just as valid as her own images based on sight.

Hilda Perry had once reminded Harper that art was artifice, a trick played on the mind. It was a representation of reality, but it wasn't reality. Sophie Janssen couldn't have demonstrated that any clearer. Her intention was to play an eye-mind game with the viewer.

So what is the point of art, Harper asked herself, *if it is unable to represent reality?*

Truth couldn't be found in art, Harper concluded. Or religion. Or even science. Truth could only be found in nature. And Harper, who had always trusted her heart more than her mind anyway, felt somewhat justified in that.

She gazed at Chelsea, who was watching the television. *I love this woman*, she thought. *I love her absolutely with the truth of nature, and I don't know what art or science or even language can tell me about that.*

"The point of my art," Sophie Janssen was saying on the monitor, "is to reflect reality as in a distorted mirror, in a way that encourages us to look back from the reflection to the real thing with a renewed sense of curiosity and a keener vision."

The video ended. Harper couldn't remember if she had asked Sophie that question, what was the point of art, but thought she probably had. It was a question she had always asked, at least in her mind.

"Wow," Sarah said. "Who knew there was so much to say about a giant pear? Maybe I should be a sculptor."

Chelsea laughed. "Last week you wanted Mary to teach you to paint."

"And before that," Harper said, "you wanted me to teach you to play the piano."

"So what's wrong with being good at everything?" Sarah said smugly. "Oh, that reminds me, I have to go." Sarah leapt out of her chair and headed toward her room. "I'm going to wear that new dress you bought me, Aunt Harper. Mary's taking me to a gallery tonight. We're going to a Joan Miró exhibit. He was one of our preeminent surrealists, you know."

Sarah said this with exaggerated aplomb. Harper assumed she was quoting Mary.

"I wonder what she will end up doing," Chelsea said when Sarah was gone from the room.

"I don't know. Something she feels a real passion for, I hope."

Chelsea took hold of Harper's foot and massaged her toes. "That film was gorgeous," she said. "As usual, so beautifully constructed."

"Thank you. I think she was happy with the way it turned out."

As Harper laid her head back against the arm of the couch, enjoying the foot massage, the phone rang. She was about to reluctantly pull her foot away from Chelsea to answer when Sarah streaked into the room wearing only a towel and snatched it up. After saying hello, she frowned and then handed the phone to Harper, saying, "It's for you."

Harper wondered who Sarah had been expecting as she disappeared into the bathroom.

"Hello?" she said into the receiver, offering up her other foot to Chelsea.

A youthful-sounding man introduced himself as Tom Janssen, the nephew of Sophie Janssen. As soon as Harper heard this, she extricated her foot from Chelsea and sat up.

"I've been contacted by a producer at PBS," Tom said, "about a retrospective of my aunt's life and work. Your documentary is one of the few video interviews that we're aware of. And it's fairly current. I was hoping you might want to collaborate on this project and let them use your footage."

"Oh, uh," Harper said, "I'd be honored to do it."

"That would be great. They're sort of in a hurry, as you can imagine. They're going to want to get this on air within the week. I can give the guy your name and number. He's in San Francisco. You can work out the details with him."

After hanging up, Harper explained the project to Chelsea, who said, "You're going to be on PBS! Fantastic."

"If they like the material," Harper said cautiously.

"What's not to like?" Chelsea jumped off the sofa. "I have a feeling, Harper. Once they see this video, they're going to want to see all of them. Maybe this series you've been putting together is destined for PBS, after all. It always did seem like the right place to me."

"Oh, come on," Harper said dismissively.

"No, no, seriously. This is your opportunity knocking, Harper!"

Chelsea took Harper's hand and twirled her around as Sarah emerged in a sleeveless navy blue dress and stockings, looking mature and sophisticated.

"What's up?" she asked.

"We're celebrating," Chelsea said. "The film we just watched, or at least parts of it, are going to be in a PBS special."

"Oh, wow, that's wicked awesome! Congratulations." Sarah hugged her, then headed for the door. "I'm going to wait for Mary outside. See you guys later."

When Harper turned to look back at Chelsea, she saw that there was a grin on her face.

"We're alone," Chelsea said in a whisper.

"So how are we going to finish our game of Clue? We've lost our third player."

"No problem. I can tell you who dunnit."

"Really?"

Chelsea nodded, looking pleased with herself. "It was Chelsea in the bedroom with a silk scarf."

Chapter 28

SUMMER, SEVEN YEARS AGO

Eliot reached down to take Harper's hand and heave her up to the next granite boulder. Her legs were getting tired. A rigorous climb like this would have been a challenge even in her twenties, so she was satisfied with her progress. They were going to make it to the top of Mt. Dana, there was no doubt, and it was going to be exhilarating.

"Only a little further," Eliot said, consulting his GPS receiver. He sounded breathless. At this elevation, the air was thin. They had always been lowlanders, so they were both struggling. Eliot, tall, lean, a little gaunt, led the way, his boots carefully picking footholds. Harper followed, wiping perspiration from her forehead, admiring the view, which was getting better and better the higher they climbed. Here above the tree line there was still patchy snow in July. The higher they went, the colder it got. If she hadn't been working so hard, she would definitely have needed a jacket.

They were both silent for the remainder of the hike, moving steadily in single file up to the high point of the mountain. When they arrived, they sloughed off their daypacks and surveyed the staggering view of Yosemite stretching out to the west with its smooth granite shoulders and deep-forested crevices.

"This has to be one of the most beautiful places in the world," Eliot remarked, running a hand through his floppy mop of brown hair.

They were alone at the peak and had passed only one other group on the way up, one of the advantages of hiking here mid-week.

"How about lunch?" Harper asked.

They sat on a flat slab of light gray stone with a view of the world stretching out before them and ate their sandwiches. A chilly but welcome wind slowly dried the perspiration on Harper's neck. *This is magnificent*, she thought, feeling happy and peaceful. When she had finished eating, she stretched out prone, resting her chin on her arms, gazing out across the landscape to the east, down to Highway 395 and Mono Lake, a round splotch of turquoise on a bare volcanic landscape. The only sound was the faint whistle of the wind between boulders. In between gusts of wind, the sun's heat intensified on the bare skin of her arms and legs, hovering on the edge of burning.

This was their second day at Yosemite. The weather had been perfect for hiking, warm, but not too hot.

Eliot lay nearby on his side, supporting his head with his hand. "There's an opening in the science department at Chabot College in Hayward," he said. "I'm thinking of applying."

Harper, startled, said, "Why? I mean, that would be a step backward, wouldn't it? From a state university to a city college?"

"Well, obviously, Harper, the point would be to move here, to be with you full time." He rolled over on his stomach so he could look at her directly. "I think it's time we built a life together. We should get married."

232

"Married?" Harper replied, astonished. "Since when do you want to get married? And why? What's wrong with things the way they are?"

He frowned. "This is no kind of relationship. It was okay for a while, but we're not kids anymore. Didn't you always figure that we'd get married someday?"

"No, I didn't. That's so conventional. You're getting old, apparently, Eliot. This is a great thing we have. It's our thing. It's what we do. We're free spirits."

"Yeah, but you can't be a free spirit all your life."

"Why not?"

"A person gets tired. And sentimental and nostalgic. A person wants to put down roots, have some solid footing. Maybe a person wants kids."

"Kids!" She leapt to her feet. "Eliot, we are definitely not on the same wavelength here. What the hell has happened to you?"

"Conventionality isn't inherently bad," he said. "If you think about everybody we were in college with, they're all married and have kids now. And some of them are actually happy."

"I can't believe this," Harper said.

"I don't know why you're surprised. We've talked about this before."

"Yes, in theory. But you're not talking theory now. You're talking about moving."

He sat up, looking disappointed. "So you don't want me to move?"

To have him always around, to have him there all year long, have to arrange her life around him...The idea horrified her. She wanted her freedom. That was the reason this arrangement had worked for so long. And now he wanted to mess it up. Get married and have kids! She couldn't believe what she was hearing.

"Can we talk about this later?" she asked him, annoyed that he had marred her perfect day.

He shrugged. "Okay, but I have to decide within the next couple of days whether or not to apply for the position."

Harper wasn't sure why she had reacted so negatively to the

idea of marrying Eliot. It wasn't like there was someone else. There had never been anyone else who mattered. Everyone who knew them, friends and family members, assumed they would marry someday, most likely when they managed to get closer together, geographically. That's what Eliot assumed, obviously. Harper wasn't so sure. She had tried, on occasion, to imagine life married to him, but she just couldn't see it as something that could be labeled "family." Even when they had lived together in college, they had lived like roommates, buddies in a way. Or maybe "friends with benefits."

It wasn't Eliot's fault. She knew full well what a traditional family consisted of, its mommy and daddy, couple of kids and their pets, but she had always known that there was something about that picture that didn't suit her. She wasn't sure why, and she didn't know how to define a version that did suit her. She glanced over to where Eliot lay on his rock, looking dejected. Whenever she made a mental list of his attributes, his qualifications as a husband, he came out looking pretty good. He was a decent-looking man, kind and compassionate. He was smart and easy-going. And he loved her.

It was the way she felt about him that was the problem. There must be something wrong with her. Why couldn't she fall in love with Eliot? Or somebody? She was thirty-one years old and had never felt the pain or joy of passionate desire for another person.

Looking at Eliot, his chin resting on his hands, Harper felt sorry for him and a little guilty. She reached into a pocket of her backpack and took out a package of miniature doughnuts, the kind with powdered sugar on them. Waving them in front of his face, she was rewarded with a little boy smile of delight. He sat up and took the doughnuts from her, happily unwrapping them.

Nothing came of the job in Hayward. Eliot never brought the subject up again. Harper decided that he had just been feeling her out and, after getting no encouragement, had let it drop. She was relieved. He had apparently just had a momentary attack of sentimentality.

234

Chapter 29

JULY 24

The special on Sophie Janssen was scheduled to air at eight o'clock on KQED. Harper had turned all of her material over to the San Francisco PBS station, then spent two days helping its film editors weave it into a cohesive production. She had been allowed into this process mainly as a courtesy, but it had enabled her to observe and learn. She did her best not to be a nuisance. The people she had dealt with were polite and respectful, and she had made a couple of good contacts. She had yet to view the final product, though. Like the rest of the Bay Area, she would see that for the first time this evening.

Deciding to prepare for her trip east with Sarah later in the week, she went into the guest room to get her suitcase from the closet. She discovered first that her suitcase was missing and then that Sarah's clothes were gone. All of Sarah's things were gone, she saw, inspecting the room more carefully. Sarah had left the house after breakfast, announcing that she was going to the public library. Nothing had seemed out of the ordinary at the time.

Harper checked the time and, seeing that class was over for the day, called Chelsea at school. "What am I going to do?" she asked. "We're supposed to be on a plane on our way to the Cape in two days."

"Did she leave a note?" Chelsea asked.

"No."

"Why do you suppose she's done this?"

"The only reason I can think of is that she doesn't want to go home."

"I'll come over as soon as I leave here. I've got some copying to get done before tomorrow, but it should just be a few more minutes."

While waiting, Harper logged into her e-mail to see what Sarah had sent from her account. There were some short notes and photos sent to her sister and parents. Nothing to anyone else. If she was in contact with anyone, it was not through Harper's e-mail account, which wasn't much of a surprise.

By the time Chelsea arrived, Harper was distraught.

"Why didn't I ask more questions?" she said. "I should have asked for names and addresses. I have no idea who these friends of hers are. Neil is going to kill me."

"You were trying to give her some freedom," Chelsea said gently.

"Obviously, I gave her too much."

Chelsea pressed her lips together in an expression that indicated she agreed. "So we have nothing? No ideas at all?"

"I have only one idea. Maybe she went to Mary."

"You could call her."

"I think I should just go and check. If I call and she's there, she'll be alerted and might take off. I can't afford to have her bolt on me."

"You'll have to do this on your own, Harper," Chelsea said.

Harper nodded. She drove to Mary's house and approached the door with apprehension. Since her last visit here, a lot had happened. She knew that Sarah had kept Mary informed to some extent. She certainly had to know that Chelsea was back in her life. She didn't know what Mary's attitude toward her was anymore, but she didn't see how it could be friendly.

A full minute after she rang the bell, the door opened. Mary stood in the doorway wearing a smock covered with paint smears and a scarf tied around her head, a short streak of lime green on her left cheek. Her expression was sour. "What is it now, Harper?" she asked, obviously irritated. She brushed the shock of silver hair from her forehead.

"I'm sorry to bother you, Mary, but I'm looking for Sarah."

"She isn't here." Harper must have looked skeptical because Mary said, "Really, I haven't seen her for a couple of days."

"I think she's run away."

Mary raised one eyebrow. "From you, you mean?"

Harper nodded.

"Well, isn't that a hoot! What'd you do to cause that?"

"I think she doesn't want to go back home. Look, do you have any idea where she might have gone or with whom?"

Mary studied her for a moment, probably trying to decide whether or not to help. Then she sighed. "There's a boy. Jake Starling. If she isn't with him, he will know where she is. I've dropped her off there before. I can give you the address."

"Oh, Mary, thank you so much."

"Wait here. I'll get it."

Harper felt slightly frustrated that Mary knew about this boy and she didn't. Was it because Sarah trusted Mary more? Was it because she viewed Mary as even less of a parent figure?

When Mary returned with a piece of paper and handed it to Harper, she said, "I understand you and Chelsea are back together."

"Yes," Harper said, avoiding Mary's eyes as she took the paper.

"Well, enjoy yourself, Harper," she said, with that curious smiling frown of hers, "while you can."

She shut the door then, leaving Harper on the porch with

her mouth open. *What did she mean by that?* Harper wondered. She left feeling a bit shaken. This situation had taken on mythic proportions for her long ago, filled as it was with associations with Orpheus and Eurydice. Now it seemed that Medea had entered the story. Medea, the bitter, spurned wife of Jason, who destroyed his new bride with a poisoned dress in a most gruesome murder. Medea, powerful and ruthless, who made sure Jason paid dearly for leaving her. Harper could still see the frightening illustration of her from her childhood book.

Mary terrified her, Harper realized. Pure and simple, she was afraid of her and had been ever since Chelsea had returned to her two years ago. At the time, she had pictured Mary as some sort of enchantress who had a supernatural power over Chelsea. That was silly and Harper knew it. Mary was no witch, and Harper wasn't afraid of a supernatural power. She was afraid of something entirely natural—the loyalty of a young woman whose first serious love wouldn't release her.

An involuntary shiver ran through her, fluttering the paper in her hand and reminding her of a more immediate crisis. Returning to her car, she made her way to the address that Mary had given her. It was a two-story house in one of the newer subdivisions, and it looked much like all the other houses on the street, all pinkish stucco with rounded edges. Sarah and a boy her age were sitting on the front step kissing. Harper parked at the curb and had walked up the path to within six feet of them before her footsteps registered and they broke apart. Sarah, recognizing Harper, looked alarmed. The boy, Jake, she presumed, stood and faced her, assuming an air of authority.

"You looking for somebody?" he asked.

"Uh, that's my aunt," Sarah said. "Hi, Harper." She stood, looking uncomfortable. "You should become a detective. You're getting really good at finding people."

Harper noticed that Sarah had dropped the "Aunt" from her greeting. Too childlike in front of her boyfriend, she guessed.

"Sarah," she said without amusement, "please get your stuff and let's go."

"I'm going to stay here, if you don't mind," she said formally. Jake slipped an arm around her waist protectively.

"I do mind. I'm taking you home with me now."

"You have no right to do that," Sarah said, defiantly. "You're not my mother. You're not even my guardian."

Jake grinned at Harper with a self-satisfied expression. A dozen retorts flitted through her head. None of them seemed likely to help, however.

"Can we talk privately for a moment?"

Sarah nodded at Jake, who kissed her briefly, then went into the house. Harper sat on the step, patting the spot beside her. Sarah sat next to her.

"Why did you do this?" Harper asked.

"Why do you think?" Sarah's voice was no longer defiant.

"Don't want to go home, I guess."

"Right."

"It can't be that bad."

Sarah said nothing, just wrapped her arms around her knees.

"Is it because of him?" Harper asked.

"Jake? Oh, maybe a little. Well, not really. He's just a guy."

"What is it then?"

Sarah frowned, staring down at the step. "They don't want me to grow up. They don't trust me. Everybody else my age has a car. I haven't even got my license yet."

"I don't think it's that they don't trust you. They're just afraid. They think they're still supposed to direct everything you do, to make sure you don't make a mistake. They don't know how to let you make a few mistakes."

"Whatever," Sarah said dismissively, but she was listening.

"It's natural, don't you think, for them to clamp down harder the more you disobey?"

"If I didn't disobey, I'd never get to leave the house. I've had so much fun here. I knew I would. I knew you wouldn't treat me like a kid, like they do. You let me go wherever I want and do whatever I want. And here I am, still alive, not a drug addict and not even pregnant."

Harper smiled. "Still, I think I've been a little lax. I was afraid to put my foot down because I didn't want you to see me as the bad guy. I didn't want you to dislike me like you do them."

Sarah turned suddenly, looking alarmed. "I don't dislike them."

"No?"

"No, of course not."

"Lots of resentment, though. That's what I've been hearing."

"Yeah, I guess."

"I can talk to them. Maybe we can all have an adult conversation about why you feel so oppressed. I think they would listen, maybe make some changes."

Sarah rested her chin in both of her hands and sighed, clearly resigned. "It's been amazing, though."

"Yes," Harper agreed, "it's been *totally* amazing." She stood. "Come on. Let's go home."

Sarah retrieved her backpack and the suitcase she had "borrowed," saying a quick goodbye to Jake in the process, and they drove home to find Chelsea grilling hamburgers on the deck. They ate outside on paper plates.

"I hope I get my phone back," Sarah said, her mind now on her return home. "It's like being an alien or something with no phone. How am I supposed to talk to people?"

"There's the phone in the house," Chelsea said.

"No, I mean, not talk talk. Like text. Jake says, 'text me,' and I'm like, dude, how am I gonna do that?" Sarah shook her head, exasperated. "Okay, okay, I'm going to go call him on the land line."

After Sarah went into the house, Chelsea said, "I'm looking forward to her being back where she belongs." She stacked their plates and grabbed the bottles of ketchup and mustard.

"You are?" said Harper, startled.

Chelsea nodded. "Sure. Then I can have you all to myself." Chelsea kissed Harper briefly before carrying the things into the house.

Harper followed her, finding Chelsea shoving paper plates into the trash can. "But we've been having a lot of fun with her."

"Yes, but she's practically driven her parents insane. If she stayed here any length of time, she'd probably do the same to you."

"Maybe." Harper felt ambivalent.

Chelsea scowled. "Like today, running away like that. Whenever something isn't the way she wants it, she runs away. How irresponsible is that? Did she even apologize to you for the worry she caused?"

Harper shook her head. "Well, teenagers are difficult. I think she's basically good. She just wants to spread her wings and fly."

Chelsea wiped her hands on a dishtowel and stepped up to Harper. "And so she shall. She'll fly all over New England and, if her parents walk that fine line between discipline and indulgence, her wings won't melt."

Chelsea put her arms around Harper and kissed her mouth tenderly and then more ardently. Desire washed over Harper like a warm surf. As their mouths came together again, she was startled to hear the water running. She opened her eyes to see Sarah rinsing out her soda glass in the sink.

"Oh, Sarah," Harper said, stepping abruptly away from Chelsea, "I didn't hear you come in."

"It's okay. Just here for a second. Resume." Sarah waved her hand at them like the queen granting permission, then left the room.

Chelsea looked embarrassed. "Like I said, it will be good to have you to myself."

Harper gave Chelsea another quick kiss. "Hold that thought. In the meantime...it's time for the show. Come on."

The hour-long documentary that celebrated Sophie Janssen's life and work included ten minutes of interview footage from Harper's video, as well as interviews with Janssen's friends, colleagues and her nephew Tom. There were lots of images of her sculptures, of course. Harper smiled when she saw the completed bronze orange tree, now on location in a Southern

241

California grove.

At the end of the show, Sarah jumped up to point to Harper's name among the credits. "Look, look!" she exclaimed. "Aunt Harper, this is so exciting. Can I get a copy to take home with me? I want to show everybody."

"Sure. My official copy hasn't arrived from the studio yet, but when it does, I'll make you one." Harper felt a little sad, as she always did about transitions. This film marked the end of an impressive career, after all. Chelsea moved closer and put her arm around Harper's shoulders.

"Are you happy with how they used your material?" she asked.

Harper nodded. "It was seamless. Really professional."

"They even left the music. That was nice."

Sarah grabbed the remote control and shut the TV off. "Maybe I'll be a filmmaker," she announced emphatically.

Chelsea and Harper looked at one another with simultaneous smiles.

Chapter 30

SUMMER, TWO YEARS AGO (AUGUST)

As soon as she came back from the Cape that first week in August, moments after dumping her suitcase on her bedroom floor, Harper called Chelsea, aching to see her again. Their romance was just two months old, boiling over with passion.

"Oh, Harper," Chelsea said, obviously excited, "I'll be right over. It seems like months."

"Take your time," Harper said, "I've only just arrived anyway. Well, on second thought, don't take too long. I can't wait to see you."

"Should I bring something for dinner? You're tired and hungry, probably, right?" Chelsea sounded breathless.

"'What care I for figs and flagons,'" Harper quoted in her best bedroom voice. "'Nor roasted meats nor honey-wine. I have my lover's lips to sup, her eyes to drink. Her body is my repast. I'll eat and drink my fill, then sleep, intoxicated by her liquor.'"

243

"Oh, my God!" Chelsea cried. "Okay, I'm leaving now!"

Their relationship continued to take place mostly in bed, as it had before her trip back East. They did go out, to eat, to listen to music, to hike, or to play on the beach, but always with the understanding that they would make love once they returned to the privacy of Harper's house or Chelsea's apartment. Their time together revolved around sex, and it was incredible sex, the intensity of which Harper had never known. Just the touch of Chelsea's hand caressing her shoulder could send her body into a hot torrent of desire.

Harper knew that time would temper their physical desire for one another, which wasn't a bad thing because at some point she would need to go to work, do laundry, read a book or a hundred other things that she was now finding no time for. She envisioned a future where she and Chelsea would occupy the same house companionably, content simply with one another's presence. For the first time in her life, she was thinking seriously about spending the rest of her days with one person, and these thoughts filled her with wonder. She had never thought of herself as suited for that kind of life. But now she couldn't imagine ever tiring of Chelsea's sweet face.

Harper kept these thoughts to herself. It was all too new and overwhelming to talk about. She was waiting for it to feel less like a dream. It was too early, obviously, to say the things that reverberated in her mind—*I love you, I want to marry you, I want to give you everything, every day for the rest of my life. I don't want anything at all but you. You're all I need to be happy.*

Likewise, if Chelsea was thinking anything similar, she was not voicing it. The closest she came was one morning, saying goodbye as she left the house, when she said, "It's so hard to leave, even for a few hours. I want to spend every moment with you. You make me so happy."

For the time being, that was more than enough to lead Harper to believe that the two of them were in concert with their feelings.

And then, without any warning, one day in late August, all

of this joy and all of Harper's hopes about the future came to an abrupt and devastating end.

"I'm going back to Mary," Chelsea announced.

Harper was stunned, uncomprehending. "Why?" she asked.

"She wants me back," said Chelsea, her expression sorrowful. "She asked me to come back."

"You don't have to go," Harper objected, still not grasping what had happened. Chelsea was obviously not happy about the idea. She looked like she was about to march off to the guillotine.

"Yes, I do," Chelsea said, tears forming in her eyes. "She needs me."

"Needs you? What the hell does that mean? I need you too."

"I'm so sorry, Harper." Chelsea began to cry freely. "You've no idea how hard this is for me. I hate doing this to you." Chelsea's shoulders shook as she attempted to hold back sobs.

Harper, beginning to understand that she was about to lose her darling, took Chelsea in her arms and kissed her deeply, transporting them both into the familiar territory of arousal. She felt Chelsea respond to her, moving closer, kissing more insistently, pressing her fingertips into Harper's back until Harper pulled away, breathless, and asked, "Do you want to give this up?"

"No, of course not," Chelsea said. "I don't want to. I adore being with you. But I have a history with Mary. We had something real. I have to give it another chance."

"Aren't we real?" Harper asked.

"I'm sorry," Chelsea repeated. "You and I, we're really good together, but it's been less than three months. We don't know each other that well. We're still in the initial hot physical stage. It's so good partly just because you're new at this. You love being with a woman. I don't know if you love me. I don't even know if you know me."

Harper didn't know that either. She knew how powerful her physical attraction to Chelsea was, but only time could prove an enduring emotional attachment.

"It feels like love," Harper said, helplessly.

Chelsea touched her cheek tenderly. "Yes, it does to me too. You can't tell the difference between lust and love in the beginning of a relationship."

Chelsea thought it was just about sex, Harper realized. Whatever her version of love was, this apparently didn't qualify. And Chelsea, like Harper, certainly knew that if it was just about sex, it would burn itself out and leave nothing of substance behind.

Harper, in a desperate maneuver, proposed that they could still see one another, on occasion. If all they had was sex, then why not? Mary apparently didn't require or value sexual fidelity.

"I can't do that," Chelsea told her. "It doesn't matter if Mary wouldn't mind. I'd mind. I'm not made that way. Besides, that's part of the deal. She's promised me there will be no one else."

"Please don't do this to us," Harper pleaded. "Make her wait. Give us a chance to find out if we really dislike each other under all of this incredibly good sex."

Chelsea smiled, but it was a sad smile. There were no arguments that could dissuade her. She seemed to think she had no choice. She behaved as if she had no ability to defy Mary's will. Within a couple of days, she was simply gone, swallowed back up into the sphere of Mary's dominion, like Persephone returning to the underworld.

Harper and the world above ground grew cold and rotated into autumn.

Chapter 31

JULY 27

"So Chelsea is back in the picture, huh?" Danny asked, cracking sunflower seeds with his teeth.

Harper sat with her brother on the porch in back of their childhood home, looking out over the pines behind the house. *The Greek Myths*, which Sarah had returned to her, lay open in her lap.

"Yes. It nearly killed me to come here this year. I didn't want to leave her."

"It's going well, then?" Danny shoved another handful of seeds into his mouth.

"Extremely. The better I get to know her, the more I can't see myself ever being with anyone else."

"Is it mutual?"

"I think so. There's that nagging idea in my mind all the time, though, because of what happened before."

"Have you asked her about that? Have you asked her what she would do if Mary wanted her back?"

"No. I'm afraid to. Things are so good. I don't want to spoil it. And I'm not sure she would be able to answer me anyway. She might not know until it happens."

"I hope it doesn't happen, then."

"Thanks."

Danny uncrossed his legs, stretching. "So, I guess the sex is as good as before?" he asked, grinning.

Harper looked askance at him. "Don't get me thinking about that or I'll have to go lock myself in the bathroom like you used to do when you were a teenager."

He laughed. "She couldn't come along this trip and meet the wacky family?"

"No, she's teaching. They have year-round school and the summer break is over."

"Too bad, since it's your birthday tomorrow. She'll miss that. The big three-nine, right? Wow, nearly forty! How does that feel?"

"Not as bad as you make it sound."

"You're still young at heart, though."

"Yes, even though I'm not young in body, apparently."

"Didn't really mean it that way. But, as usual when you're here on your birthday, you're sharing your party with a real youngster."

"Yes, Sarah is about to turn seventeen, a scary prospect, I'm sure, for her parents."

"Wow," Danny exclaimed, "what did you think when she showed up at your house?"

"I was shocked, of course."

"Yes. Everybody here was so relieved, though. Before you called, we were imagining all kinds of horrible things. Poor Neil was out of his mind."

"I guess that was sort of a dangerous thing she did."

"We're lucky she made it safely." Danny adopted a pseudo-Asian accent and said, "There is much evil in the world,

248

Grasshopper."

Harper smiled. "Well, all's well that ends well. They seem to be happily reunited."

Danny nodded. "Was she a pretty big handful, then?"

"No, not really. She was actually a lot of fun. She's really smart. She's got the motivation, you know, to do something with her life."

"What does she want to do?"

"I don't think she knows. She seems to have suffered from a lack of role models. Her head is bursting with undirected ideas and passions. Before I leave, I want to talk to Neil and Kathy about their plans for college."

"So you feel like you have a stake in that, do you?"

"Well, she is my niece. She's got potential. No point wasting it."

"No, you're right. We should do what we can for her. Do you see yourself as a role model for Sarah, then?"

"Well, not really. I see her too rarely because of the distance. I'm hoping she'll get a couple of really inspirational professors."

The book in her lap lay open to the story of Icarus. The accompanying illustration showed him falling out of the sky, his wings dripping molten wax. Harper stood. "I think I'll go talk to them about it now, while it's on my mind."

She stepped into the house and immediately heard yelling from the kitchen. She arrived to see Sarah in tears, confronting her father whose face was a deep and alarming shade of red.

"Did you think you could just run off like that," he said, "and worry us all to death and then waltz back here without any repercussions?"

"I can't believe you're doing this!" Sarah screamed. "This is such bullshit! I wish I'd never come back! I wish I was dead!"

Neil and Sarah both noticed Harper simultaneously. Sarah ran past her out the back door. Neil took a deep breath, frowning.

"So?" asked Harper, leaning against the counter.

"Apparently she's surprised that she's being punished for all of the trouble she caused us, and you, by running off to

249

California."

"What's the punishment?"

"I've grounded her for three months, and that includes pushing back her driver's license."

"Yikes," Harper said. "That's got to hurt."

"Yes, well, that's what punishment is about. They have to be punished."

"I suppose."

Neil, gradually calming himself, sat down at the kitchen table.

"Unfortunately," she said, sitting in the chair beside him, "that punishment is the same thing that drove her away in the first place. Are you sure you aren't just trying to prevent her from growing up?"

"What are you trying to say? Do you have some special insight, now that you've been in charge of her for, what, one whole month?"

Harper realized that Neil was angry at Sarah and that it was spilling out onto her. She didn't resent it. "No," she said. "I really can't imagine what frustration you must feel."

He drew a hand through his sandy hair and looked dejected. "Sorry. I know you're just trying to help. And we appreciate the time you spent with her the last few weeks. She couldn't stop talking yesterday about everything she did while she was there."

"We had a good time. This may not be the best time to discuss it, but I was wondering what your plan is for her higher education."

"Oh, Harper, I don't know. I don't think we're even going to survive high school. We were hoping to send her to Wheaton and let her live at home. At this point, I don't think any of us would go for that. Kathy and I have discussed other possibilities, like sending her to the university and letting her live in the dorm. The money isn't really a problem. We've prepared for that, but I just wonder what we could expect from her if we gave her that much freedom. I'm afraid she'd just go wild."

"Sarah isn't into drugs or anything like that, is she?"

"Not that I know of. She's just defiant. Up until recently, she was the most well-behaved girl you ever saw. We were patting ourselves on the back for what a good job we did raising her. No sex, no drugs, no crime, not even cigarettes. And then all of the sudden, bang, she turned into Ms. Hyde."

"It would be a real shame if she didn't get a degree."

"Yes, it would. She's a bright girl. The offer is still on the table, but I don't think she's going to take it. She can't wait to get away from us. If she thinks she can do it all on her own, she's going to be in for a shock. Maybe one semester, maybe two if she's determined. When you first start supporting yourself, money is tight and, suddenly, you just don't see the point of pouring it all into school when the whole world is lying at your feet, or so you think."

"I did it," Harper pointed out.

"Yes, you did. You were exceptional. Sarah reminds me of you. That little scene just now, in fact, reminded me of the day you told Mom that you were going to California no matter what. You said you would rather die than stay here."

"I don't think it's unusual for teenage girls to rather die than do what their parents want them to."

He laughed shortly. "I guess that's true. Maybe Sarah will run off to California too and make a fine life for herself. She definitely seems to think it's the land of enchantment."

After giving Neil a reassuring hug, Harper left the kitchen and went looking for Sarah. She found her, eventually, sitting at the end of the dock with her legs dangling over the water, just where the two of them had sat two years earlier talking about epic poetry.

Harper sat next to her, noting the solemn look on her face.

"Hey," she said, knocking against Sarah's shoulder with her own.

"Hey," Sarah replied half-heartedly.

"This is a beautiful place, don't you think?"

"Yeah. I've always liked visiting Grandma and Grandpa."

"I really missed this place when I left."

251

"You like California, though, right?"

"Oh, sure. I love it. That's why I'm still there. But a lot of people do go back home, later, after they're over being impulsive, angry or whatever it is that drove them away in the first place."

"What drove you away?" Sarah asked.

"That was something I couldn't have answered for most of my life. At the time, I thought I was just playing follow the leader, the leader being my best friend Peggy. She was going to California, so I wanted to go too."

"But?"

"I think it was fear of failure. Your grandfather is a brilliant man, which you may not see so much when you're sitting in a fishing boat watching him sleeping under his hat. He always put a lot of pressure on us to accomplish something. There was never any question about all three of us being college graduates. It was so thoroughly understood that I don't think any of us ever imagined not doing it. I know I didn't. Your father did excel, as expected. He was a science whiz, just like your grandfather. I looked up to him all through my childhood as the model of what Dad wanted from us. He was about to graduate from college when I was graduating from high school and I just couldn't imagine doing as well as he did. I always thought of myself as average. That wasn't tolerated in our family."

"Average?" Sarah looked shocked. "You? No way."

Harper nodded, amused by the disbelief. "So I left. Nobody could watch me from way over here. Nobody would know if I screwed up."

"And that's why you left?"

"Well, that and a little bit of the other too. I think I was sort of in love with Peggy, but I didn't know it."

Sarah smiled. "I guess it worked out okay."

"It usually does. Sometimes we think everything hinges on some decision that we make at some crossroad, as if one choice will lead us to success and happiness and the other to utter destruction, but I don't really think most decisions in life are that critical. I think it usually ends up okay, whichever way we go."

Sarah, her face tinted pink from the setting sun, looked Harper in the eye and said, "Are you trying to tell me something?"

"No. Just making conversation."

Harper had been chewing on an idea for a while, something she'd kept to herself because it was unformed and she was unsure. But it seemed to be taking a concrete shape now in her mind, so she decided to explore it further. "Do you have any particular college that you feel compelled to go to?"

"Not really. Wheaton is the default, of course. Mom went there. It seems okay."

"What about Berkeley?"

"Berkeley? You mean, your Berkeley?"

Harper nodded. "What if you applied to Berkeley this coming year, and maybe San Francisco as a backup? If you work hard and really want it, you can turn yourself into a desirable commodity. If you didn't get accepted right away, you could start at one of the California state colleges and then transfer as a resident after a year or two."

"A resident? Aunt Harper, what are you talking about?"

"I'm inviting you to come live with me while you go to college." There, she'd said it. Sarah didn't go running off screaming to her mother like she had two years ago when Harper had invited her to visit. She sat calmly where she was and gazed thoughtfully at her aunt.

"Why would you do that?" she finally asked.

"Oh, you know. Education is important. It will make a big difference in your life. I want to see you fulfill your dreams."

Sarah looked away, looked out across the lake, her eyes moist. "Wow," she said quietly.

"It's an option," Harper said. "Think about it."

As Harper moved to stand, Sarah turned to her and threw her arms around Harper's neck, hugging her tightly.

It was only on her way back to the house that Harper thought about the ramifications of her plan. She called Chelsea and told her what she had just done.

"Are you serious?" Chelsea asked. "You'd have to be her

mother, you know. You couldn't let her run amok like you did for the last month. It would be a big responsibility, an investment of time and money and peace of mind."

"No, I know that. I'm sure there would be problems. But I think it would be worth it."

"It's an incredible gift you're offering her. Do you think she'll accept?"

"I don't know. She might."

"That's a very generous thing to do."

"Well, her parents do have a college fund for her. It would come with her, I'm pretty sure."

"No, that's not what I meant. I meant it's generous in terms of sharing your life."

"I suppose," Harper said. "What about you? How do you feel about it?"

"Uh, I don't know," Chelsea said. "If you want to do it, that's great. I think it's cool that you feel this strongly about her future. Unexpected, but cool."

Harper didn't ask again because she didn't know how to say what she was really trying to ask. She was reminded that Chelsea had been anxious to see Sarah leave after only a month. She wanted to know if she and Chelsea could have a life together if they opened their home to a college student, this particular college student. To ask such a question, though, meant asking so many other questions by implication. She would have to talk about the future and she didn't know how to do that. Sarah wouldn't start college for another year. Perhaps Chelsea didn't see this as her issue. Perhaps she didn't see herself in Harper's life a year from now.

"Love you," Chelsea said as they prepared to hang up.

"Love you too," Harper said, a wave of sadness washing over her. "Talk to you tomorrow."

Chapter 32

JULY 30

After lunch, Neil and family piled into their car. Sarah stuck her head out the back window, saying her goodbyes. She had promised Harper to work hard on grades and extracurricular activities and to apply to Berkeley and a couple of state colleges and even Morrison, if her parents thought they could afford it. Neil and Kathy had been skeptical of the plan at first, but after they discussed it for a while and Harper had made certain concessions regarding rules, they had agreed that it might be the only way Sarah would ever get her degree. Sarah herself had gotten quite excited about the idea overnight. Harper had too, thinking about teaching Sarah how to play the piano and sharing her favorite books with her. Harper didn't know if it would actually happen, but she hoped it would. The more she considered the plan, the more she wanted to be the one to guide Sarah through college. She had so much potential, but she was unfocused and needed nurturing. Harper thought she could do that, that Sarah would continue to listen to her and learn from her.

After they were gone, the house became hushed, even more so than before Neil and Kathy's arrival. Harper's parents appeared to be worn out. Both of them lapsed into partial hibernation, her father reading a magazine, her mother watching television and hemming a skirt. Harper decided to make dinner and give her mother a break and was surprised that her mother so easily surrendered the task. "Thank you, dear," she said without protest.

After dinner, Harper did the dishes, struggling with one stubborn pot that wouldn't come clean. She searched the kitchen drawers and cupboards for a scouring pad but couldn't find anything useful. Looking for her mother, she went to the family room where Danny lay on the sofa, dressed only in cutoff jeans, his eyes on the television.

"What are you watching?" Harper asked.

"Reruns of *Golden Girls*. They're having a marathon. This is the one where the girls are mistaken for prostitutes and hauled off to jail. Hilarious."

"Are you sure you're not gay?"

"I was planning on it, but there's only one allowed per family, and since you're older, you've got dibs." He grinned. "Wanna watch?"

"Maybe later. I'm not done in the kitchen."

"Oh. I guess I should have offered to help you tonight, huh?"

"No, no, dear brother." She patted his head. "Tomorrow is your turn, and I wouldn't dream of interfering then."

He frowned. "By the way, Sis, excellent meal. We don't get California cuisine here often."

"Yankee pot roast?" She slapped at him playfully. "That's what Mom had thawed out. Tomorrow I'm going to the store. Mom and Dad should be eating more fish and green vegetables. I don't know why they don't have a vegetable garden here anymore. Where's Mom anyway?"

"I think she's in the rumpus room." Danny launched himself

256

to the arm of the couch, facing her. "If it's my turn to cook tomorrow, we're going to have an old-fashioned clambake on the beach. I'll bring the guitar and you can serenade us."

"Peachy-keen, bro," she said. "Let's get up early and dig those clams. Man, I dig those clams, man." Harper, dancing in place, took her brother's hand as he pushed off the couch. He twirled her, both of them singing, "Man, I dig those clams, man, I dig those clams, man."

"It's been great having you here, sis," he said, letting go of her hand. "Even when I can keep Mom and Dad awake past eight o'clock, they still aren't very lively. Although they will consent to an occasional bout of Scrabble."

Harper kissed Danny's cheek. "I love you too, my beamish boy."

She danced out of the room, singing, "Man, I dig those clams, man."

Opening the door to the rumpus room, Harper saw her mother seated at a long table on the other side of the exercise bicycle. Alice looked up as Harper entered the room. She wore a pair of glasses with a magnifying lens attached to the left side. Her hair was held captive by four mismatched clips, keeping it securely out of her face. In her hand was a thin paintbrush. A porcelain thimble stood on a small platform connected to a movable metal arm. Alice removed her glasses and looked up inquiringly.

"Sorry to bother you, Mom," Harper said, approaching. "I was looking for a scouring pad for one of the pots. Do we have any?"

"Yes. I think there are some in the right-hand drawer on the back porch. Check there, dear."

"Thanks. Do you mind if I look at your collection?"

"No, of course not. Most of these are new. Next month we'll be selling them at the bazaar."

On a shelf near the window were scattered a dozen thimbles. Harper approached the shelf with curiosity. She had seen these before or their predecessors anyway.

"Keep working," she instructed her mother. "I'll leave you alone in just a minute."

Alice put her glasses back on while Harper examined the tiny paintings. She saw that many of them contained elaborate scenes. Some were Biblical, some scenes from nature, some floral patterns. One was an intricate seascape, so carefully detailed that Harper recognized a sea star and conch in the sand of the beach.

Harper held a thimble with an intricate design of several shades of green on white. After peering at the design for a moment, she determined that it was an ivy vine, originating from one side at the base and branching out over the top and all sides of the thimble. On the side where the branches were small and thickest, a pair of brown eyes peered from behind them, perfect brown eyes with flecks of gold, partially hidden by branches. *How intriguing*, Harper thought.

These little bits of paint and glass were magnificent, she decided. She turned, filled with enthusiasm, to tell her mother. Alice sat concentrating on the fine touches of the paintbrush, her movements so slow and so minute that she seemed almost motionless. Her mouth was shut tightly, her left hand pressed against the table to moor her body against the destructive twitch.

Harper watched with wonder. Not until the brush lifted from the thimble to be daubed onto the palette did she dare to speak.

"Mother," she said, breathless, "these are so beautiful. It must be very difficult."

Alice put down her brush and removed her glasses. "It is. It takes a long time to do one. If I was younger, it would be easier. I can't see as well as I used to, and my hand isn't as steady as it should be. I move very slowly."

"They're masterpieces. Each one is a masterpiece."

"Oh, Harper, for heaven's sake, don't be so melodramatic."

"But it's true. Oh, Mom, can I please have one?"

"Well, sure. Take whichever one you want."

"Could you pick one out for me? It would be more special

that way."

"I suppose so." Alice got up and approached the shelf. After a moment of scrutiny, she picked up a thimble and handed it over. "How about this one?"

Harper examined it. There was a girl dressed in blue, standing in air, playing a lyre of gold with silver strings. The music emanating from it took the form of an undulating river of silver and gold that circled the thimble several times. At the end of the river, on the top of the thimble, was a perfect blue sphere outlined in the gold and silver of the river. "I call this one Harmony," Alice explained. "Do you like it?"

Harper threw her arms around her mother and said, "I love it."

Alice returned to her chair and resumed her work. Harper peered at her thimble, absorbing its details. This was not a simple hobby, she thought. Her mother was an artist after all! How could she have dismissed her mother's art? Sitting with her brush in hand, these glorious scenes in her head, she let the life force that was in her come out in a tiny stream of paint on porcelain. The creative spark burned within her and flourished.

Harper, struck with an idea, ran from the room. Danny still lounged on the sofa, now eating little cheese-flavored fish.

"Danny," she said, startling him. One of the fish fell on the floor. "Where's your video camera?"

"In my room," he answered, tossing a fish into the air and catching it in his mouth. "On the dresser. Why?"

"Can I borrow it?"

"I guess so."

She found the camera and returned to the rumpus room where her mother greeted her with slight irritation.

"Mom," she explained, "I want to shoot you working. And then I'd like to interview you about your art. It's a thing I do. Biographical videos of women artists."

"I'm not somebody like that, Harper. Nobody's heard of me. They're just thimbles."

"Please, Mom, I really want to do this."

After a few minutes of arguing, Harper prevailed. She filmed her mother busy at her work, filmed her self-conscious discussion about how she got interested in thimble painting, how many she had done, what happened to them, where the ideas came from and, once Alice got involved in the interview and relaxed, a couple of anecdotes about particular thimbles. Harper managed to keep her talking for a good half hour, which wasn't easy because it was obvious that Alice hadn't ever discussed this with anyone before and didn't have much insight into the why or the how of her art. She was accustomed to just saying "Thank you so much" when someone praised an individual thimble and that was it.

The next day, after digging clams, Harper went into town and coaxed Father Thomas and two church women into being interviewed, videotaping their praises of Alice's thimble art.

"Alice's thimbles are legendary around here," Father Thomas said. "And we always sell out."

All three of the interviewees had purchased one of the thimbles themselves, which they displayed for the camera, each one an incredibly vibrant testimonial to the creative force. Harper burned all of these interviews onto a CD to take home with her. Already she was hearing music in her head that would accompany the footage.

This wouldn't be for her documentary series, obviously. It was for herself. She had discovered something new about her mother. This discovery made her think that she might not know her mother as well as she had thought. The fact that Alice Caitlin Harper Sheridan didn't talk much about her dreams and flights of fancy didn't mean that she didn't have any. For some reason, she had always accepted her mother at face value only. She did that a lot, she realized. She had always had a problem seeing below the surface of people and situations or, rather, imagining below the surface. She didn't much question things, just accepted them. This characteristic had led her down many interesting paths, some productive, some not. Perhaps it was time, she thought, to push herself past this limitation, to cultivate a more critical approach to life.

Chapter 33

AUGUST 6

"Harper!" cried Peggy over the phone. "Is it really you? Your mother told me you would be coming to visit this summer."

"I come every summer. I'm just around the corner," Harper said. "I was wondering if I could come over and say hi."

"Sure! It's been a long time. You won't recognize me. I can't wait to see you."

The enthusiasm of Peggy's response quelled any fears Harper had about lingering grudges. As soon as she hung up the phone, she changed into her sneakers and set out for Peggy's house, just as she had done hundreds of times as a teenager.

The woman who opened the door was short and petite with a kind expression and ruddy cheeks. "Hi," she said, smiling warmly. "I'm Chris."

Harper shook her hand and came inside.

"Peg's mentioned you many times over the years," Chris said, "so it's good to finally meet you."

Chris called Peggy, who came in from the kitchen, a fuller-figured version of her teenage self. Harper recognized her immediately, however. Her eyes, mouth and facial expression were quintessentially Peggy. Her auburn hair was now cut quite short, which gave her an impish look. When she saw Harper, her eyes lit up and she reached out for her, hugging her tightly. Then they both stood grinning at one another.

"I'll let you two talk," Chris said. "I'll check in on Kate. She's probably wondering where her dinner is."

Peggy led Harper to the family room, where they sat on the sofa. "Wow," Peggy said, "you don't look much different. Other than being older, of course."

"I just turned thirty-nine," Harper said, as if she couldn't believe it herself.

"I know how old you are, silly. We're the same age."

"Yes, of course we are! So tell me everything you've done since college."

Their conversation was lighthearted and lively as they recounted the intervening years since they had last seen one another. Peggy had settled in San Jose and had left a successful career to return to the Cape to care for her mother.

Chris brought them each a crab salad and turned on some lights, as it was now getting dark out. "Thanks, honey," Peggy said, her gaze washing fondly over Chris.

She's happy, Harper thought, feeling grateful and relieved. This was not something she had to feel guilty about any longer.

"To think that we've been just a few miles from one another all of these years," Peggy marveled, sampling her salad. "We should have kept in touch."

"It's not too late. We can make a point of getting together during my summer visits."

"Yes, we can. And while you're here this year, let's plan something. Chris, me, you and Danny. The four of us can go to a concert or up to Baker Point for the day or something."

"That would be fun. This crab is delicious."

"I caught it myself," Chris said, proudly. "I'm learning how to be a New Englander." She twirled around once on her toes like a ballerina, then returned to the kitchen.

"She seems really nice," Harper said.

"She's wonderful. We've been together nearly ten years."

"Congratulations. Is she okay with living here, then?"

"Oh, sure. She wasn't sure at first that she'd like it here, but she's adjusting. I promised her we could go back to California if we want to in a few years. Depending on Mom, you know. We could take her with us too. It's just harder for an older person to uproot."

"Peggy," Harper asked, "why did you want to go to California in the first place? I know you said you wanted to get as far from your family as possible, but I never understood that. I always thought you got along okay with your parents."

"Well, I did, and I wanted to keep it that way. My mother was nothing like yours, Harper. She couldn't have stomached it, the humiliation, the guilt, the despair even. As it was, I barely left in time. People were already talking. I couldn't have lived here. It would have destroyed my parents. Mother, anyway."

"You mean you went to California because you were gay?"

"Right. You hadn't figured that out yet?"

"I didn't know you knew it before college. You had boyfriends."

Peggy laughed. "Well, sure. That's just what a girl does in high school, while figuring things out. After all, you have to have somebody to take you to the prom. By the time I left home, I knew it absolutely, though. I thought you knew it too, on some level."

"I was pretty dense."

"Maybe it was something you didn't want to know. After all, we were such good friends before Nate's party."

"I was really sorry for hurting your feelings," Harper said. "I was afraid you might still be hurt and wouldn't want to see me, even now."

Peggy tossed her head. "No, no," she said, "it wasn't your

fault. I never blamed you for being straight. My God, how could I? And I really didn't pine over it that much, Harper. Once you and Eliot got together, I just moved on. You were the one who avoided me, if you remember. I don't blame you for being uncomfortable, though. But, when it comes right down to it, it wasn't that big a deal. Right?"

Harper nodded. "Right," she said. "Seemed like it at the time, though."

"To me too. I was devastated. But that's the way it is with nineteen-year-olds. By the way, what ever happened to Eliot?"

"Ah, well," Harper said, "we lived together for a while during graduate school, and then we both got jobs, me in California, he in Washington."

"So you broke up, then, after college?"

"We didn't quite break up. We kept up a sort of part-time relationship. We saw each other in summers. Occasionally we got together other times of the year, but mainly in summer."

"Oh, really. For how long did you try to keep that up?"

"Until two years ago, actually."

Peggy stared in disbelief. "What! You and Eliot were together until two years ago?"

Harper nodded. "We both saw other people during the school year. It seemed to work for us for quite a while."

"Wow, how absolutely Seventies chic. Then what made it stop working after all that time?"

Chris returned with a bottle of wine and glasses on a tray.

Harper opened her cell phone case and pulled out Chelsea's picture. She handed it to Peggy, who looked thoughtfully at it. Then Peggy looked up and sighed. She shook her head and handed the photo to Chris.

"Who's this?" Chris asked.

"Harper's girlfriend," Peggy said matter-of-factly.

Chris, surprised, turned her gaze to Harper. "I thought you said she was straight."

"She thought she was," Peggy explained.

Chris handed the photo back to Harper.

264

"You never were what we would call a quick study," Peggy joked. "I guess you're like the tortoise. You do get there eventually."

"And, like the tortoise," Chris added, "it looks like you won the trophy. That girl is hot."

"Yes, she is," Harper agreed.

Chris put three glasses on the coffee table. "Would you like some wine?"

"Sure."

Chris filled the glasses, then sat on the floor next to Peggy, draping her arm over Peggy's knees.

"Did you keep in touch with Nate?" Harper asked.

"Yes, I did, actually. I've seen him from time to time. Sweet guy. He's gay too."

"No!"

Peggy nodded, then turned to Chris and said, "Is this reminiscing boring you, honey?"

"No, no. It's always interesting to meet your lover's first *objet d'amour*." Chris raised her glass to Harper.

"But you," Peggy said, placing a hand on Chris's shoulder, "are my last."

They looked natural together, a compatible and comfortable couple.

"To prove it," Chris said, "we're getting married this fall."

"Yes!" Peggy said. "Too bad you won't be here then, Harper. You could come."

"I could make a special trip," Harper suggested. "Send me an invitation. I'll do my best to come."

"Tell us all about your girlfriend," Peggy said. "And don't leave out anything."

When the wine was gone and Harper was more or less caught up to the present, she asked to see Peggy's mother. Kate was sitting in an armchair in her bedroom, watching television. She didn't remember who Harper was, but she was friendly. She seemed pleased to have a visitor. She had grown smaller and pale, and her eyes didn't focus very well. Harper chatted with her for several minutes before taking hold of her hand and saying, "I'll be going now. It was nice to see you again, Kate."

"Thank you for coming," she said to Harper, and then, looking around the room, said, "Where's Chris? She was going to bring me some milk."

"I'll remind her," Harper said before leaving. It was interesting, she thought, that Chris had become the most important person in Kate's life. She wasn't a relative and at one time she had been entirely objectionable, but now she was indispensable and possibly the last person Kate would be able to recognize.

Harper walked back home in the dark to her parents' house, remembering with a certain wistfulness how comfortably Peggy and Chris had moved together in the same space, their unity apparent in every look, every word, every touch. No one could be in the same room with them and doubt that they were in love. Harper felt hopeful and anxious to get home. More than anything else, she decided, that was what she now wanted for herself with Chelsea.

Chapter 34

AUGUST 9

When she found out the morning of August 9 that her August 10 flight had been canceled, Harper scrambled to switch to an earlier flight. She managed to get one that would arrive that evening. Her departure from Cape Cod had to be rushed, but that was her choice, to leave earlier than anticipated rather than later. While Danny drove her to the airport, she called Chelsea's apartment, leaving a message explaining about the earlier flight. Chelsea must have left for work already. Harper called her cell and left another message.

Once the plane was on its way west, she retrieved her thimble from her carry-on. *What a little masterpiece*, she thought again, examining it. She had no doubt that her mother had been thinking of her when she painted that girl with the lyre. She had called it "Harmony," and it did appear to represent at least two dimensions of that concept—musical accord and harmony with the world. The musician appeared to be playing among the clouds, above the earth. Her music encircled the planet like a protective shell.

The image of the musician as protector left Harper thoughtful. To her, the minstrel had always been a solitary figure, a freethinking, unencumbered seeker of truth, channeling wisdom from the seers to the common air through song—channeling, but not necessarily absorbing or even understanding.

And yet this little lyre player seemed to be accepting responsibility for uniting the whole world. She was not a passive conduit. There was no one else in the scene, not another person— a composer, for instance—or even God, which she might have expected from her mother. The little musician was holding the world together all by herself.

Harper knew that her mother had not been thinking these things while painting the scene. Alice produced thimble scenes out of the wordless part of herself. While she studied the details of the thimble, Harper noticed that there was a minuscule object hanging from the belt of the lyre player. She squinted, trying to see what it was. At last she was able to make out a heart-shaped fob on a chain, a locket that was partially open to reveal an image of a girl or a long-haired boy. Smaller details were not possible on this scale. It was astonishing enough that anything at all could be conveyed on this scale.

So the lyre player wasn't alone, after all, she realized. She had a beloved, the inspiration for the song. Alice was a romantic! This thimble was like a passionate epic poem, telling a story about a minstrel enveloping the planet in a song of peace, protecting and watching over it because she loved someone who lived there. And that, thought Harper, was the story of humanity, of parents and children, of lovers, of heroes and their charges.

Wow, Harper thought. *My mother created all of that!* Harper would have liked to have called her mother and discussed these ideas, but she knew that wasn't possible. All of this resided in her mother's subconscious. Alice created her scenes in the same way that Harper played music, with emotion, not thought.

The point of art, Harper thought, was to communicate that emotion with another human being. That had to be the point, ultimately. It was true of poetry and painting and music. The artist produced an object that represented her soul. In that respect, art really did express the artist's authentic self. Harper realized that she had come full circle, but she thought she had arrived at some conclusion this time. Art might not be nature, but it was as close as humans could get to understanding one another on a natural, gut level. The thimble that Harper held in her hand told her more about her mother than any conversation they had ever had. She recalled something a guest soloist with the symphony once said during a pre-performance interview: "I'd have no means of expressing truth without music." The most interesting thing about that was that the "truth" was unique for every artist, which ran counter to the usual assumptions people made about the truth.

Harper pictured her mother maneuvering her tiny paintbrush and noticed that she was hearing music in her head again. But the music wasn't familiar to her. It was something new. It was composing itself in her mind. She took a notebook out of her bag and started writing down notes. This was the music that was playing behind the scenes of her mother's art. *Ironic*, Harper thought, rapidly transcribing the music in her head onto paper. *My mother has become my muse after all.*

Arriving without incident several hours later, Harper checked her phone. There were no messages. She called Chelsea's cell phone while waiting at the baggage carousel. Still no answer. "I'm home!" she exclaimed into the phone. "I mean, I'm at the airport. I'll be home in half an hour." Excitement, barely under control, twitched in her muscles as she anticipated being reunited with her lover. When she got to her house, she checked her voice mail. Nothing of interest there. It was five o'clock. Chelsea should have been off work at least an hour by now.

Harper showered and changed her clothes. Having still gotten no call from Chelsea, she called her cell phone again and left another message telling her that she would wait for her at her apartment. Then she left the house.

Harper had known for quite awhile that she wanted to spend the rest of her life with Chelsea. She planned to tell her that soon, perhaps even tonight. She let herself into Chelsea's apartment with her key. She wasn't home. The light on the answering machine was blinking, indicating a new message. When Harper played it, she heard her own message telling Chelsea that she was coming home early. The machine then reported in its mechanical voice that there was one old message, which began to play. Harper was about to press Skip when she recognized the voice of Mary Tillotson.

"Chelsea, are you home from work?" said the voice. "Oh, dear one, please pick up if you're there."

The pain that hit Harper in her chest was so keen that it felt as if her heart had stopped beating.

Mary's voice was pleading and whiny like a child's. "I'm so sorry for everything. You know I didn't mean it. You know how I am. Please come back. Please forgive me. I'm languishing here all alone."

It was all too easy to picture her on the other end of the line, lying on her sofa in a melodramatic pose. Harper, seething, wanted to smash the answering machine to bits.

"Darling child, you mean the world to me. I know you won't let me suffer like this. You're too good, too kind."

Mary's voice turned more formal, more metered as she proceeded to quote poetry.

"'Come lie on my bed of roses and speak of love as you did once. No, not once, but many times. In our youth, you lay your sweet body across mine and put violets in my hair and kisses on my face. Come let me remind you of the mirth our hearts often shared in those days.'"

After a click, there was silence. Harper stood, frozen, for a minute or more, then moved slowly toward the machine, circling it, as if it were an animal that she intended to pounce upon and kill.

She didn't want to hear the message again—God, how she

270

didn't want to—but she had to find out when it had been left. She replayed it, listening for the date and time. Mary's message was three days old. Chelsea had listened to it three days ago! And then what? She'd said nothing about this to Harper in any of their phone conversations. She had kept it to herself.

Three days, thought Harper, thinking back on the last few phone calls she had made to Chelsea. There had been nothing odd, nothing at all to alert her that something had happened. It was now almost six thirty. Chelsea wasn't home and she still wasn't answering her cell phone.

Where is she? Harper wondered, fearing she knew the answer. Her head began to spin. Why had she ever let herself believe that this could be more than a summer fling? That's all there ever was for her. Summer was nearly over now, and Mary had come to reclaim her beloved. It was Hades and Persephone all over again. She had only let Harper borrow her for the summer, as before.

Harper's knees buckled, and she sank to the floor, feeling her heart breaking. She knew how deeply rooted Chelsea's sense of loyalty to Mary was. She also knew—all too well—that Chelsea would sacrifice herself and her own happiness if she felt that it was the right thing to do. Mary had appealed to that weakness, with her talk of languishing and suffering. How could Chelsea resist? The poor girl had probably flown to her, unable to deny that powerful, autocratic will. They were probably together right now discussing how Chelsea would break up with her when she returned tomorrow.

Harper sat on the floor for a few minutes, her mind blank, until suddenly she felt like fleeing, like she had to escape this unbearable situation. She left the apartment and started driving toward home, then changed her mind and headed for Roxie's house. She wanted to hide. She wanted sympathy.

Kevin, Roxie's twelve-year-old, answered the door. "Mom," he yelled into the house. "It's Harper."

"Harper," called Roxie from somewhere in the distance, "come on into the kitchen."

Kevin ran off. Harper shut the door and made her way to the

271

kitchen where Roxie was loading dishes into the dishwasher. One look at Harper made her stop what she was doing and cross the room, putting her arms around Harper tenderly.

"What happened?" she asked.

Harper cried freely now, letting her tears fall on Roxie's shoulder. "I've lost her," she managed to say.

Roxie maneuvered her into a chair at the kitchen table, gave her a box of Kleenex and a glass of water and waited for the sobbing to subside. "Tell me what happened."

Harper told her about the phone call from Mary. "I've lost her," she repeated.

"It doesn't seem like that's the inevitable conclusion here," Roxie said. "Don't you think you're being a little irrational? Despite some of the things I've said about Chelsea in the past, I can't deny that she seems to really love you."

Harper said nothing. She felt defeated.

"Don't you think you should at least talk to her?" Roxie asked.

Harper shrugged. "I just don't want to hear it again, the excuses, the explanation about why she has to go back. I'd rather she just goes and doesn't say anything."

"Aren't you even going to put up a fight?"

She hadn't even considered that, Harper realized. It didn't seem possible to counter Mary's hold on Chelsea. All of her dreams had been pinned on the hope that Mary no longer wanted Chelsea, that she wouldn't ask for her back.

"Put up a fight?" she asked weakly.

"Well, yes, if you want her. God, Harper, from what you've said, you don't even know if there's any reason to be upset. There are lots of possible explanations. You can't just give up."

Earlier in the summer Sarah had advised her to fly to Chelsea and drag her back from the hounds of hell. Was it possible to do that a second time? she wondered.

"You're right." Harper took a deep breath. "This is too important to forfeit. I'm going to go get her back." She stood, filled with a sudden sense of purpose.

"I didn't mean right this minute. Don't you think you should wait until you calm down before you do anything else? You know how you are when you're upset. Impulsive and reckless. How about something to eat? I've got some spaghetti left from dinner."

Harper shook her head. "No, I have to go. I have to do this now."

She had no plan and no idea what would happen next as she drove to Mary's house, but that was familiar territory for her. She knew that she would do whatever felt right, that no premeditated plan, no matter how sensible, had much of a chance with her.

Her biggest regret, she realized, was that she had not communicated to Chelsea more clearly her feelings about the future, about their potential future together. Why hadn't she told Chelsea that she wanted to be with her forever? Why hadn't she told her that she wanted them to live together, to be a devoted couple in every possible old-fashioned sense?

Because she did want that. She believed in that kind of commitment in a way she never had before. Even if Mary was willing to share Chelsea, Harper was not.

Mary's house looked peaceful and deceptively benign from the front. The doors of the three-car garage were shut. If Chelsea's car was here, it was out of view inside. Harper walked up to the front door and rang the bell. Impatiently, she rang it again a few seconds later. There was no response. She then banged on the door, imagining Chelsea and Mary inside ignoring her.

Hearing faint sounds of laughter from the side yard, she went around to the unlocked gate and let herself in. In the still evening air, the pool lay tranquil before her, the surface of the water glassy. She stood listening but heard nothing more.

She moved deeper into the yard, walking through the long evening shadows of elm trees toward a wrought-iron gazebo partially covered with a wisteria vine. She heard the scrape of metal against concrete from within the gazebo and thought she could see movement between its bars. Fearing what she would see, but knowing she had no choice but to see it, she moved stealthily to the middle of the yard. What she saw inside the structure left her numb.

Mary was lying back in a chaise lounge, wearing a long white robe, secured at the waist, partially open at the chest to reveal one vulnerable-looking breast, pale and fragile. From beneath the robe, the lower torso and legs of a shapely girl protruded. A girl wearing tan shorts and pink flip-flops. A girl who was not Chelsea. Mary's head was thrown back, eyes closed, mouth open. Her hand gripped the chair's frame above her head. Harper stood paralyzed on the spot, watching with fascination as Mary's body moved in a regular rhythm to the tune of her veiled lover's touch.

Gradually, Harper's thoughts began to emerge from the tempest of emotion that had propelled her into this absurd position. She needed to find a way to leave before she was discovered. She could make a run for it and depart the way she had come. Or she could sneak into the house and look for Chelsea while Mary was preoccupied outside.

Before she could act, she heard Mary shriek, a blood-curdling yell that yanked Harper's attention violently back to the gazebo. Mary was sitting upright now, clutching her robe to her chest, and the girl who had been lying between her legs was now on the ground beside the chair. Both of them were staring at Harper.

The girl was not as young as Harper had imagined, but a woman in her thirties with dark hair, cut short, and narrow eyes that were, at the moment, trained on Harper with an expression of intense hostility. "Who the hell are you?" she asked, rising to her feet.

Mary rose too, facing Harper with grim indignation. "This is my gadfly!" she shouted in answer to her lover's question, gesturing dramatically with her arms as she exited the gazebo. "Have you no shame, Harper? Have you come merely for titillation? Or did you think I was giving lessons this evening?"

Harper knew she should probably apologize, but she was still focused on the reason she was there. "I've come for Chelsea," she

274

said firmly.

Mary stared, looking confused, then approached her in her bare feet. "Harper," she said, "let's go inside and have a chat. Diana doesn't need to be a part of this discussion." She looked at the woman in the gazebo, who had taken a seat on the chaise lounge and was now coolly watching them. "I'll be back momentarily. Don't forget where we were."

Mary extended a hand, inviting Harper to go into the house. When they reached the sunroom, she dropped gracefully into a white wicker chair.

"So where is she?" Harper said.

"You're extremely demanding tonight," Mary said. "And extremely rude. Sit down and calm down. Can I get you a drink?"

Harper shook her head. She tried to maintain her anger, but something about Mary's demeanor, which was solicitous and inoffensive, was sapping it from her. She took the seat Mary indicated and the fight drained out of her. She felt as she always had, that Mary was invincible, a force that couldn't be opposed. She had no more defense against her than Chelsea did.

A small, contented smile appeared on Mary's face as she realized that she had gained the upper hand. The breeze from the overhead fan played capriciously with the silver shock of hair on her forehead. From a decanter on the table between them, she poured herself a glass of golden brown liquor.

"You know, Harper," she said, "these impromptu visits of yours are getting on my nerves. I believe that I'm going to have to insist that you wait for an invitation before coming to visit." She tasted her drink, then turned a calm gaze toward Harper. "So, why are you here? What's gotten you all riled up?"

"I want Chelsea," Harper said.

"Yes, so you said, but what does that have to do with me?"

"Isn't she here?"

Mary shook her head matter-of-factly. "Why would she be here?"

"I heard your message on her phone, begging her to come

back to you."

"Begging?" objected Mary. "Oh, please, that just isn't the right word at all. Cajoling, perhaps."

"I don't care what you call it!" Harper was exasperated and on the verge of losing control.

"Please, Harper," Mary said softly. Despite the circumstances, her voice had a mysterious soothing effect on Harper. "Okay, so you heard one of my messages on her phone. So what?"

"*One* of your messages?"

Mary shrugged. "There have been a few. There are times, when I'm here alone, that I feel like having friendly company. It's a weakness of mine. I can't stand being alone."

Oh, God! thought Harper. *This has been going on all along. She's been playing with poor Chelsea whenever she feels like it, on a whim, just to prove that she can.* She lowered her head in defeat, thinking, *I can't be a part of this.*

"You don't trust her, do you?" Mary said, standing in front of her, both hands around her glass.

Harper looked up, confused.

"You have no faith," Mary persisted.

"I don't understand."

"Just because I've called her doesn't mean she's come." Mary's expression was one of compassion.

"You mean...?" Harper asked.

"As much as it irks me to admit it, Chelsea belongs to you, Harper. She's committed to you. Oh, my God, dare I say it—she's in love with you. She's been inconsolably in love with you for the last two years." Mary raised her glass to Harper, as in a toast, and took a swallow. "Not that you deserve it, for here you are, suspecting her of betrayal."

"Really?" Harper felt the heaviness in her heart lifting.

"Really. She hasn't been a barrel of laughs for the last couple of years. I've wondered why, sometimes, she ever bothered to come back to me. Well, I guess I know why. She's serious about her commitments. She wanted to honor her vows to me."

"You mean, you haven't seen her at all? She hasn't responded?"

276

"Oh, she *has* responded. She called me two days ago and told me to quit leaving such ludicrous messages on her answering machine. I was offended. I thought my messages were rather entertaining. Chelsea used to swoon when I quoted poetry. But I'm afraid she doesn't find me as amusing as she once did. She's grown up and her sense of humor has been tempered a bit by life."

Harper felt suddenly buoyant. "So she really doesn't love you anymore?"

"You needn't look quite so overjoyed. And I wouldn't go that far. That girl will always love me. But she isn't *in* love with me anymore. She's in love with you. And although she will always have a prominent place in my heart, little birds gotta fly." Mary waved one of her hands in imitation of a bird's wing.

Harper sat silently for a moment. She realized she still didn't know Mary's position.

"And you?" she asked. "Do you love her?"

"Of course I do. Chelsea's very special to me. She always will be. I hope she'll get over being hurt, eventually, and we can have some sort of association again." Mary cast a conciliatory glance at Harper. "Okay, a platonic one if necessary."

She sat down again and looked at Harper with an uncharacteristically serious expression. "I'm afraid I just couldn't be what she wanted me to be. I tried. I've never tried for anyone else. She wanted to change me. How hopeless is that?"

She looked resigned. "You know, Harper, I'm a child of the Sixties. My generation ushered in the sexual revolution and the feminist movement before you were even born. To be a lesbian back then was a radical position. It was a political stance, not just a personal one. We rejected everything that represented the establishment, and that included their whole concept of love, the whole 'one man, one woman' image of sexuality. My lifestyle has always reflected that unconventionality. I never wanted to be tied down to one person or to have kids or live inside four walls. I wanted to be the free, independent woman that my generation fought to make space for in this society. You've read all the literature. Even if you didn't live it, you know what I'm talking about."

"Yes, I know," Harper said slowly, realizing that Mary was describing the lifestyle that she had always admired and sought for herself.

"I never wanted a *relationship*," Mary said, emphasizing the word with distaste. "I'm not that kind of person. Chelsea somehow got through my defenses. She's an exceptional girl." Mary smiled to herself. "But what she wanted wasn't something I had in me."

So that was it, thought Harper. Chelsea loved in the most traditional way there was. That was how she loved Harper too, and for that realization, Harper was ecstatic. She leapt to her feet.

"Harper," Mary warned, her voice suddenly stern, "she deserves someone who will never falter. Do you know what I mean?"

Harper nodded. "Yes, I understand." What she understood at that moment was a great deal more than she could say.

As Harper turned to leave, her phone rang. It was Chelsea's cell. She answered immediately. Mary sat back in her chair and sipped her drink, looking composed and satisfied.

"Where are you?" Chelsea asked. "I got your message that you were home, but I've been there and now I'm at my place, but you're not here either. I'm wondering if we're passing each other on the street, you know. That damned faculty meeting ran long or I'd already be lying naked in your arms with a smile on my face."

"I'll be there in a couple of minutes," Harper said breathlessly. "I've missed you so much."

Mary rolled her eyes.

"Me too," Chelsea said.

Harper pushed her phone into her pocket. "I'm sorry," she said to Mary. "Sorry for intruding and for being such an idiot."

"Well," said Mary nonchalantly, "you can't really help that, can you, dear?"

278

Harper laughed and noted with gratitude that Mary's smile contained genuine affection.

"By the way, Harper," Mary said, "did you ever get that lovely niece of yours back to her parents?"

"Oh, yes, I did. I've just returned, in fact. But I don't believe you've seen the last of her. I think she's going to be back next year to go to college."

"Really? That will be interesting. I'll definitely look forward to that."

"I'll let myself out," Harper said.

"Yes, you do that, and I shall return to my entertainment. And please, Harper, don't drop in on me again, okay? Not without calling first."

Chapter 35

WINTER

The stairs creaked under Harper's feet as she climbed to the second floor of another unique old house encircled by stately oaks, a scrubby lawn and a narrow, shady street in the neighborhood surrounding the university. The banister was polished wood, worn dull in places by many grasping hands. Below her lay the front room with its hardwood floors, refurbished fireplace and large unadorned windows letting in refracted heat and plenty of light. The real estate agent was downstairs turning on lights and opening blinds, dispelling any hint of gloom. Although it had warmed up considerably outside, the chill of morning still lingered in the vacant rooms.

This was the third house that they had seen today, but already Harper felt differently about it. From the moment she stepped up to the front porch with its weathered railings and overgrown wisteria vine, she could easily imagine sitting there contentedly on a summer evening. It reminded her of the porch behind her parents' home. As she reached the second-floor landing, Chelsea poked her head out of a room along the hallway, grinning, and said, "Check out the master bedroom."

Harper followed her into a spacious room with windows overlooking the backyard. She admired the wainscoting and the light fixture, a gaudy old thing that looked like it might be original. The master bath had been remodeled and modernized, but someone had taken care to preserve the antique details so it didn't look out of place in this turn-of-the-century house.

"I've just got a feeling about this one," Harper said.

"A feeling?" Chelsea laughed. "Of course you do."

"Don't you like it?"

"Yes, I do. But, let's be practical for a second. It needs some work, which means money. If we could talk the price down a bit, that would help. We ought to be able to get some reduction just for the dry rot."

"Dry rot?" Harper asked, perplexed.

"Around the downstairs windows. They must be leaking. Probably should be replaced. You didn't notice the dry rot, did you?"

Harper shook her head.

Chelsea smiled her crooked smile and said, "Or the rain gutters, rusted through in several places. Or the fact that a couple of the doors are warped and won't actually shut."

"It's a mess," Harper said, suddenly disheartened.

"No more than the others we've looked at. It's an old house. There are going to be things like that. It just needs some attention." Chelsea hooked her hair behind her ear as she looked critically along the ceiling. "However, on the positive side, there are plenty of rooms to spread out in, and that sunny room in the back is just right for your music room. An ideal workspace for an aspiring composer, don't you think?"

Harper just smiled. She had written only one piece of original music so far, the background for the film about her mother, which Chelsea, with her limited musical knowledge and slight

281

prejudice, had pronounced a "magnum opus." Harper herself thought it wasn't half bad. If Chelsea's aspirations for her musical career were any indication of the future, there might be more such compositions on the horizon. And that would be fine with Harper. She was also considering teaching music. Her mind kept returning to Wilona's grandson, Andrew, and the possibility that there were ways that she could share her musical gifts that would really make a difference in people's lives. Now that the semester was in full swing, though, she hadn't had much time to devote to music, other than the symphony. Still, she thought, with a space as inviting as that delightful music room, she might be able to make the time. It would even be possible to teach out of her home, something that was out of the question in her current house, especially now that Chelsea had moved in.

"And a big, mostly finished basement," Chelsea added. "That really adds living space. The perfect place, in fact, for a college student to live. By next fall, we could have that fixed up so cute. She'll love it."

Harper faced her. "You're really okay with that?"

"Oh, sure. It'll be fun. But it would definitely be better to have a house like this where she lives on an entire subterranean floor of her own."

"Agreed. I'm sure she would prefer it too."

They made their way to the end of the hall and a square, empty room with a slanted ceiling and one tiny, cloudy window looking out into the maze of oak branches behind the house.

"Storeroom," Chelsea announced. "Must be. It's a funny place for a storeroom, though."

"This house has character," Harper said. "I can see us living here."

"There's room for a dog. You're okay with a dog, right?"

Harper nodded.

Chelsea wanted a home of the most conventional sort, occupied by two thoroughly committed people who cherished the peace in their house, in their hearts and in their minds. Harper wanted the same thing. That had not always been true, but it was true now. The need didn't exist independent of Chelsea, however. She had taken a convoluted path to get here, traveling at the pace of the proverbial tortoise, but she felt that she had finally reached the end of her journey.

Chelsea tugged open the old-fashioned latch on the window casement, then pushed on the frame. It didn't budge.

"It would be fun to spend holidays here, don't you think?" Harper asked. "With the fireplace ablaze and the smell of turkey filling that big old kitchen?"

Chelsea cast a glance over her shoulder. "Is that your Christmas tradition? Turkey?"

"It's what we always had when I was a kid. Turkey for both Thanksgiving and Christmas. I haven't done a traditional Christmas that much as an adult, but sometimes I've gone back East for it. Then, yes, it's always turkey. Everyone would throw a fit if it wasn't. What about you?"

"Sometimes turkey," Chelsea said, examining the frame around the window. "My mom isn't stuck on tradition. She likes to mix it up. Once we had a goose. And Yorkshire pudding and mincemeat pies made with actual meat. A strange and extremely fatty meal. She does stuff like that. You'll see for yourself. She wants to have us over this Christmas."

"Sounds like an adventure."

Harper realized she knew nothing about Chelsea's winter traditions. Just as Persephone disappeared into the underworld for six months of the year, Chelsea had been completely absent from Harper's world in non-summer months. But not anymore.

"What are you smiling at?" Chelsea asked.

"I was thinking about Persephone."

"Oh, yes, your whole mythology analogy. You know, I still have to laugh when I think about Mary as Medea. Or, even worse, Hades. God, Harper, you cast her in such a harsh light."

"At the time, yes," Harper admitted. "But not now. I mean, it was just insecurity. I'm over all that."

"Good. As you should be."

Chelsea gave the window another shove and it broke free, opening with a small shower of paint chips and dust. "Ah! Damn thing was painted shut."

Harper approached the window and looked out at the patchy lawn below. "I saw Mary at school the other day. She came into the library. She was very friendly and chatty. Nothing Medea-like about her. She's going to Morocco for the holidays."

"Really? She'll enjoy that. Just her sort of thing. No roast turkey for her."

"Do you think you might want to see her soon?"

Chelsea looked pointedly at Harper. "Yes, I might. I haven't even spoken to her since August."

"I think you should."

Chelsea looked momentarily thoughtful, then nodded. She turned back to the window and pulled it shut, struggling with the latch until she had it locked in place. "I like this house," she said with sudden resolve. "It feels so comfortable. Just right, you know?"

"Now *you've* got a feeling!"

Chelsea raised one eyebrow with a look of mild skepticism, but didn't deny it.

"Do you want to make an offer?" Harper asked.

As Chelsea turned in a hazy shaft of light, a look of affection spread across her face. She nodded, ducking under the eaves of the storeroom, and took Harper's hand. "I love you," she said quietly, "despite the fact that you don't see dry rot."

Harper slipped her arms around Chelsea's waist. "I love you too, despite the fact that you do." She kissed Chelsea briefly.

"What made you think about Persephone?"

"I was thinking that I now know what it was like before Hades abducted her, when she was living in the world all year round."

Chelsea, comprehending, gave her a look of gratitude. "Perpetual summer, you mean?"

"Something like that, yes."

"Frankly, I've been looking forward to winter. It's cozier."

For the first time in a long time, Harper was looking forward to winter too. Not just this winter, but all of the winters—and springs and summers and falls—yet to come. She didn't need perpetual summer to feel warm and alive, not anymore, not now that she had Chelsea. She kissed her again, longer this time, until Chelsea broke away with a carefree laugh.

"Let's go tell that guy downstairs the good news." Chelsea grabbed her by the hand and pulled her toward the doorway.

Harper stopped on the landing, turning Chelsea around to face her. "So this is it? We're really taking it?"

Her eyes shining with happiness, Chelsea nodded and said, "Welcome home, Harper."